BRING ME CHILDREN

Finish this business with the graveyard and coffin first, Lyon tells himself, getting his fingers under the edge of the lid and lifting slowly, holding his face back, excited and curious and scared all at the same time, his heart bass-drumming as he opens the lid enough to shine some light in.

"Claire! Do you see this? *Claire!*" he shouts.

Still holding the coffin lid open with one hand, Lyon is looking up when a brilliant light fills the grave, blinding him. He thinks Claire has found another flashlight somewhere—but why is she shining it right in his eyes?

"Claire?"

And why doesn't she answer him?

"CLAIRE!"

Then somethinnd grabs Lyon by

———

"Grisly tableaux— ̄ the kind of poetic sensitivity that makes them even more shocking—unerringly reflect psychosocial horrors beneath: there's nothing gratuitous in Martin's baroque encounter with evil. . . ."   —*Kirkus Reviews*

"*BRING ME CHILDREN*, David Martin's new book . . . would undoubtedly do Hannibal Lecter proud."   —*New York Newsday*

Books by David Martin

Bring Me Children
Lie to Me

Published by POCKET BOOKS

Bring Me Children

DAVID MARTIN

POCKET **STAR** BOOKS

New York   London   Toronto   Sydney   Tokyo   Singapore

This book is a work of fiction. Names, characters, places and incidents are products of the author's imagination or are used fictitiously. Any resemblance to actual events or locales or persons, living or dead, is entirely coincidental.

A Pocket Star Book published by
POCKET BOOKS, a division of Simon & Schuster Inc.
1230 Avenue of the Americas, New York, NY 10020

Copyright © 1992 by David Martin

Published by arrangement with Random House, Inc.

ISBN: 0-671-88611-8

First Pocket Books printing June 1994

10 9 8 7 6 5 4 3 2 1

POCKET STAR BOOKS and colophon are registered trademarks of Simon & Schuster Inc.

Cover art by Gerber Studio

Printed in the U.S.A

ARABEL, ALL WAYS

. . . that great sea, whose ebb and flow
At once is deaf and loud, and on the shore
Vomits its wrecks, and still howls on for more.
—*SHELLEY*

Bring Me Children

1

AFTER WALKING THREE HUNDRED FEET INTO THE earth, three hundred feet along a descending stone passageway—naturally formed but resembling a miniature subway tunnel—he stops in total darkness to unbutton his overcoat. The cave's year-round temperature of 54 degrees feels warm relative to the March weather outside. He waits until his breathing regulates and he has stopped sweating, then continues on with confidence because although this man carries no light—and this underground blackness is absolute— he knows his cave by heart, knows exactly where he's going, how to get there, and what he'll do when he arrives. He reviews it all in his mind, *sees* the route clearly, keeping his left hand on the corridor's wall, cradling in his right arm a well-bundled infant, moving easily through the dark. He's done this before.

Five years ago he spent an entire month living alone in this cave, mapping its inches with his hands, its passageways with the careful shuffling of his feet, memorizing each boulder and every rock overhang, contemptuous of cavers with their fetish for light. They never enter a serious cave without three independent sources of illumination: carbide lamp, flashlight with batteries fresh from the package, and candles to be lighted with waterproof matches. But to travel a cave like this, *blind,* that's a challenge he considers worthy—to see it in your mind, to know, as he knows right at this moment, that the chamber is exactly one hundred and forty-three steps away. This will be the fifth child he's delivered to that chamber in the past five years.

"Not too much farther," he tells the infant, who at the sound of the man's voice stirs within her blankets.

Five acts of absolute faith, each requiring certain ritual, tremendous risk, meticulous planning—and resulting in enormous profit.

When the baby cries, the man places the bundle up on his shoulder, patting her back and speaking in a soothing voice. "Almost there." He continues walking as he speaks, the fingers of his left hand trailing along the cool damp limestone wall. Fifty-two more steps. He's able to count them off even as he talks to the infant, even as he thinks of other things.

After she becomes quiet again, the man continues more quickly along this familiar route, hurrying through a maze of stone and darkness, no longer needing to touch the corridor walls, ducking at precisely the right moment to miss a low-hanging shelf of rock, slowing only when he finally enters a large cavern that is cathedral-like in its immensity and its quiet: the chamber.

In the center of this cavern is a crevice twenty feet wide, twice that long, a hundred feet deep. The man has dropped rocks down that crevice and knows what's at the bottom—an underground lake, perpetually cold and home perhaps to blind, white fish.

"There, that wasn't such a bad trip, was it?" he asks the infant as he probes with a finger to find her warm face within the folds of the blankets.

Feeling that finger on her cheek, the baby turns a hungry mouth.

Chuckling, he allows the infant to suckle his fingertip. Then he asks in a gently teasing voice, "What're you getting from that finger, hmm? *What?* Nothing, right? Absolutely nothing."

The man slides one foot in front of the other until he finds the crevice's very edge. He moves along that irregular edge, counting steps consciously now, touching boulders he uses as guideposts, finally locating a pathway that leads across the crevice, a natural rock bridge that varies in width from five feet down to less than two. He steps onto that narrow path.

Here's the tricky part. If his feet slip off either side of this limestone bridge, if he allows himself to imagine too vividly his precarious position, on a thin ribbon a hundred feet above a perpetually cold lake . . .

But the man's powers of concentration are considerable. He slides his feet forward, moving out into the very heart of that rocky yawn before carefully lifting one foot to tap around with the toe of his shoe, searching until he finds a small domed boulder—roughly the size of a footstool—in the middle of the bridge. Holding the child firmly in his right arm, he kneels and moves his left hand over the boulder's rounded top. "Nothing!" he shouts, his voice a mixture of triumph and anger.

The sudden loudness of his voice startles the child into crying.

One hand supporting the infant's head, the other at her bottom, the man places her gently upon the footstool rock. She's crying harder, working her arms free of the blankets.

He waits a moment and then stands, backing up now, slowly making his way off the bridge.

Because the baby is hungry and because the hard, round top of the rock is uncomfortable, her crying quickly elevates to an angry shrieking. She is trying to roll over on her stomach, the bundle of blankets slipping as she squirms.

Having stepped off the bridge, standing well back from the crevice's edge, the man cannot see the infant in the blackness of this cave, but he knows precisely where he left her, knows how many inches she has to maneuver.

The louder she shrieks, the angrier he becomes. His hands have tightened into fists. Rage is causing him to tremble.

Then from his right fist he sticks out a stiff thumb and jabs it into the dark above his head—as if trying to thumb someone in the eye. "Well?" he asks.

Then shouts it. *"Well?"*

He's waiting for an answer as the baby continues screaming from the top of that rounded boulder in the center of that narrow path in the middle of that deep crevice.

But the only answer he gets is the one he supplies himself.

"Nothing!" the man shrieks. He repeats it again and again—"Nothing! NOTHING!"—with his head thrown back, both fisted hands in the air, his outraged howling competing for volume with the baby's crying

until the two of them are joined in a single awful, echoing crescendo.

He's muttering all during the return trip, pausing only when he's near enough to the cave's entrance to feel the outside weather, pausing to listen. He can still hear her. She's lasted much longer than any of the others. He continues on to the entrance and stops there, waiting. Then her crying abruptly ends and the cave reasumes its silence, the man confirming her fate in a low and acid voice— *"Nothing"*—as he steps out into a March that is bitter with cold.

2

No LONGER RECOGNIZING THE TRUTH WHEN HE HEARS it, John Lyon sees little point in joining the debate played out in front of him, a producer and an editor arguing about the wording for a twenty-second piece on the national debt.

"Three minutes to air!"

The producer and editor come to an agreement, certain words struck, phrases changed—rearranging grains of sand on the beach, Lyon thinks.

Sliding the pages toward him, the producer asks, "Okay with you, John?"

"Sure," he replies without having read either the original version or this newly edited one.

The producer and editor exchange looks: *His Lordship can't be bothered.* They think Lyon is haughty because he's overly enamored of his background, coming as he does from Old Money and private schools. But Lyon's aloofness is in fact his protection.

His family was like the huge, many-turreted house in which he grew up: pristinely white and forbidding on the outside but crumbling and wormed-through at its very center.

As the producer and editor wait for Lyon to say *something,* he refuses to look at either of them and they eventually move off, the editor saying, just loudly enough for Lyon to hear, "No wonder he doesn't have anything going for him here at the network."

What John Lyon does have going for him at age fifty—eight years writing for newspapers, eleven years with local stations, ten years at the network—is a reliability that approaches the absolute. Able to take over any assignment no matter how late he's brought in, no matter how little preparation he is given, on camera Lyon is un-rattle-able, a rock.

He's been called in to read the news this particular Sunday afternoon because an ambitious young field correspondent who was supposed to fill in for the vacationing anchor suffered an attack of appendicitis just thirty minutes before the broadcast was to begin. By the time Lyon was contacted and limo-rushed to the studio, there were only eight minutes to air—but here he sits behind the anchor's desk, his makeup being applied, sipping coffee, waiting for the final clean copy to be printed out, and looking for all the world as if this is just another day of the office.

"Do you know who you remind me of?"

He's never worked with this makeup person before but Lyon knows what she's going to say. William Holden. People have always commented on the resemblance but more so in the past five years. Lyon usually expresses surprise, claiming he doesn't see it himself. He is, however, secretly pleased, not because

Holden was considered handsome, but because Lyon admired the innate dignity which that actor brought to the roles he played.

"Bill Holden," the woman says.

"Really?"

"Yeah. My mother did makeup in Hollywood and I met him once when I was a little girl. Tragic the way he ended up though, wasn't it? Fell down drunk, hit his head, they found him with his pants around his ankles. Or was that Errol Flynn?"

"Two minutes to air!"

When the clean copy is handed to him, Lyon reads it over and then stares into camera one, barely seven feet from his face. But something about one of the stories bothers him. Lyon flips back through the pages and then calls a producer, Nancy Greene, over to the desk.

"Are these figures right?" Lyon asks, pointing at the copy.

Hell of a time to be asking, Greene thinks as she leans near Lyon's shoulder to read. "Yeah, unfortunately they are. More than a thousand children killed each year in *reported* child abuse cases, with another thousand—three each day—estimated killed in cases that go unreported."

Lyon is still troubled.

"In the unreported cases," Greene explains, "cause of death is usually listed as accident or illness. You die under unusual circumstances as an adult, you get an autopsy. But a lot of states, especially in the South, order an autopsy in only one out of three children's deaths."

"One minute!"

Seeing that Lyon is still frowning, the producer asks, "Okay?"

"No," he replies sarcastically, "it's *not* okay that two thousand children a year are murdered in this country."

She flushes red. "I know *that's* not okay, John, what I meant was—"

Still looking down at the copy, he holds up a hand, dismissing her.

Gritting her teeth and growling under her breath, Greene heads for the control room where she finds the pace running at its usual level of hysteria, one feed from San Francisco—slated for use in the second half of the newscast—not even in yet. Greene walks over to stand behind the senior producer, a perpetually worried man who glances at the monitor showing Lyon's placid face and wonders if anything at any point in Lyon's life has ever given him the nervous sweats. This afternoon, however, the senior producer is particularly grateful for Lyon's icy demeanor.

Lyon pulls his suitcoat down and tightens his tie. He can't stop thinking about the story on murdered children. Jesus, such filth out there. Six children a day murdered by their parents or their parents' friends or by relatives or baby-sitters—and half of those deaths not even reported as murders? A horror show. Lyon doesn't have any children of his own, never married. A week after he turned fifty, just three months ago, his best friend, Tommy Door, died and now . . .

Lyon shakes his head. Why the hell am I thinking about all this when I'm going on camera in a few seconds? He looks at the people running around on the set, all of them so damn frenetic, so self-important, overly ambitious, and . . . But Lyon also forces that thought to drift away unfinished. He has noticed lately a tendency in himself toward bitterness, which he finds unattractive and makes a conscious effort to curb.

"Thirty seconds!"

Lyon repeats the straightening of his suitcoat, the tightening of his tie—and then once more stares into camera one. But his famous face is no longer placid.

In the control room, producer Nancy Greene is staring at a monitor showing that face, Lyon's expression causing her stomach to tighten. She stands there with the fingers of one hand nervously tapping her lips.

Two years ago Greene had a six-week affair with Lyon. She instigated it and she ended it, no closer to understanding Lyon at the end of those six weeks than she was at the beginning. Most of the men she's slept with eventually revealed to her a personality distinctive from the one they used out in the world. A hard-charging cynic in the office turns out to be surprisingly sentimental and timid with his lover. Or just the opposite, a shy man in public becomes aggressive or even violent in bed. John Lyon, however, never yielded any secrets. He made love the way he reads the news: proficiently but without ever putting his heart into it. Greene never did see behind his facade, concluding finally that there was no facade: Lyon is icy through and through.

Why then does his face look so strange right now, almost anguished? Or is it her imagination? She grabs a nearby shirtsleeve and indicates the monitor. "Does he look all right to you?"

"Like the iron man he is," comes the technician's distracted reply.

Like he's about to cry, Greene thinks. She's tempted to open Lyon's Interruptible Feedback and ask him if he's okay, but if this causes a disruption right here at the beginning of the broadcast and Lyon turns out to be all right, Greene will spend the rest of her career working on public service programming.

Her stomach tightens all the harder and her fingers tap all the faster when Lyon is given the cue, camera one's red light coming on, the newscast launching—Nancy Greene listening carefully for a catch in Lyon's voice but hearing only the modulated tones of a consummate professional.

As he continues reading the news she continues watching his eyes. Am I going crazy, Greene wonders, or are they really filling with tears? *Something* is catching the studio lights and causing those blue eyes to glisten. Why hasn't anyone else noticed? Too busy doing their jobs. Nothing I can do about it now, Greene decides.

Two minutes and thirty-three seconds into this Sunday June 24 afternoon newscast, toward the end of that item about the national debt, John Lyon becomes consciously aware of it himself: he's going to cry. This sudden realization astonishes him into silence. Lyon pauses and looks dead into camera one, his normally viewer-comfortable face put out of kilter by the queerest of expressions.

The silence causes people on the set and in the control booth to stop what they're doing, most of them thinking at first that there must be a problem with the sound system. But then they look at Lyon or at monitors showing Lyon's face and see that the reason they don't hear anything is that Lyon isn't speaking.

In the control booth, the senior producer screams the question that's on everyone's mind: "What the hell's wrong with him!"

Nancy Greene is the only one with an answer. "He's

going to cry." Now everyone is looking at *her* with fierce expressions, as if it's all Greene's fault. She shrugs.

Then Lyon ends that strange six-second pause, shakes off the queer expression, and finishes the item about the national debt. On the set and in the control booth a collective breath is released.

Lyon himself, however, remains horribly aware that the urge to cry has not left him. It is, in fact, growing stronger and, with a sense of on-the-air panic that is new to him, Lyon realizes that very shortly it's going to happen, really happen—he is going to bust out crying right here, on camera, on live network television. Lyon doesn't know what to do about it except soldier on and hope against the inevitable.

Exactly two minutes and forty-four seconds into his newscast, Lyon begins reading the piece about the number of children under the age of nine who, experts say, are murdered each year but whose deaths are officially listed as caused by accidents or illnesses—an average of three each day.

Nine seconds into this item, John Lyon sobs.

His immediate reaction is embarrassed surprise, as if he had just belched. Lyon closes his mouth and forcibly presses his lips together, which only increase the pressure of what has come alive inside of him, clawing to get out, unavoidable, irresistible, and finally escaping, rendering Lyon quite helpless as he sits behind the news desk and sobs a second time, those wet eyes now overflowing with tears, his face gripped by what seems to millions of television viewers a sadness altogether soul-deep, wretched, inconsolable.

But then, incredibly, Lyon steels himself against this emotional firestorm and stumbles through a few more sentences about the murder of children before the director finally manages—mercifully—to cut away to a commercial.

Members of the crew rush to Lyon's side.

"John!"

"What's wrong?"

He is doubled up as if in pain, still sobbing.

"John! Is it your heart?"

Having rushed to the set from the control booth, Nancy Greene is kneeling beside him with her hands on his left arm. "Let me help you up, John. Come on, we have to move you someplace where you can lie down." Actually her assignment is to get Lyon the hell off the set before the commercial ends. She signals to a sound technician to grab Lyon's other arm. But they can't get him to stand. Greene steps back and calls for more help.

Lyon's removal from the set turns out to be an effort requiring four producers and crew members who finally half-carry, half-drag him away. Not that he is resisting them. It's just that John Lyon is crying so hard he can't hold himself upright.

3

A FEW MILES FROM THE STUDIO, A SIXTY-TWO-YEAR-OLD black woman sits staring at her television screen. Claire Cept is astonished that the sign she's been waiting for has been delivered with such clarity. The heartbreaking anguish that John Lyon suffered when he started to tell that story about murdered children is an undeniable message from eighteen babies lying in their graves in West Virginia. It was those babies who made John Lyon break down and sob—so that Claire Cept won't forget them, won't ever give up.

For the longest time she just sits there staring at the television even though nothing has registered with her since Lyon's distressed face left that screen. The way he cried! You hardly ever see a man cry like that, at least not on television. Not for real.

As Claire Cept thinks about the pain Mr. Lyon must have been suffering, large tears well in the corners of her eyes and run down her cheeks. He feels the same way I do! She *must* talk to him.

But Claire Cept has had considerable experience in the difficulty of trying to meet people in power, people who are famous. She knows what will happen if she shows up at the studio and asks to see John Lyon. The receptionist will listen impatiently for a few seconds and then dismiss her. If Claire Cept doesn't leave, security will be called. There are government and newspaper offices in New York City where Claire Cept is so notoriously well-known she can't even get past the front door.

But her experience in these matters has also led her to certain directories and other underground sources of information about famous people—where they live, for example.

Claire Cept struggles up from her easy chair and walks into the tiny kitchen where she puts a pan on the stove and places in it two blocks of paraffin. While the paraffin is melting she gathers together her papers and places them in a nine-by-twelve envelope. Then she begins writing notes and instructions.

Later that evening she searches the back of a closet until she finds a small wooden box that cost her a hundred and fifty dollars. It is six inches long, three inches wide, two inches deep, painted white. The box has been fashioned from wood stolen from the coffin of a man who killed his twelve-year-old niece with a hammer and was himself shot in both eyes by his own brother, the girl's father.

Into that powerful box Claire Cept places a paraffin figure adorned with feathers, wrapped with colored string and human hair, and covered all over with the letter *Q*, which she has cut out of newspapers and magazines. She shakes dirt from a quart jar, sprinkling it on the figure, the dirt collected from the graves of those eighteen children down in West Virginia. Claire Cept has a dozen jars of this dirt in her closet.

She uses string to secure the top on the white wooden box, wrapping the string longways and sideways, tying elaborate knots.

When she finishes writing the last of her notes and instructions, she places them in the envelope along with the other papers. Before sealing this envelope, Claire Cept sprinkles in a handful of salt.

All the rest of that night she prays.

Claire Cept was reared in the Pentecostal church, converted to Catholicism in her forties, and has practiced hoodoo since the age of thirteen. *Covering all the bases,* she used to joke to friends back when she could still joke about these things, back before she began losing her mind—before she found out about the eighteen children.

After completing her seventh Rosary, Claire Cept opens a shoebox containing her most powerful grisgris. Reaching in, she selects a bone from the ring finger of a man who died on the gallows the year she was born. He was innocent.

If she can't get past the security desk at John Lyon's apartment, she'll wait for him out on the sidewalk.

4

NOT UNTIL THREE DAYS LATER—JUNE 27, A WEDNES-
day—does John Lyon's mortification recede enough
that he is able to face another human being, in this
case his agent.

If Lyon's reliability was his singular asset to the
network, then obviously the on-camera breakdown
has made him a profoundly useless employee. But
what hurts Lyon even more is his *personal* humiliation.

Ever since leaving newspapers for television some
twenty years ago he has maintained a keen sense of
personal dignity, priding himself on never sucking up
to management, panting after celebrity, or maneuvering for promotions and choice assignments. He knows
that this superior attitude has kept him off the fast
track and, yes, he also knows that his attitude has
earned him a nickname—*His Lordship*. But Lyon
can't change this image he has of himself—private,
reserved, dignified. It's been with him too long.

It's the way he acted when he was fourteen years old and had a friend over for dinner. They were both home from boarding school and the dinner was formal, always a formal dinner whenever father was in residence. Lyon's mother came into the dining room perfectly coiffed, tastefully made up, a single strand of pearls, a brocaded blouse that belonged to her grandmother, and wearing absolutely nothing from the waist down. Lyon's classmate gave out with a nervous laugh and then caught himself, turning bright red, unable to take his eyes off the fifty-year-old woman's copse. Lyon's father didn't miss a beat, telling his daughter, "Millicent, take your mother up to her room." Lyon's mother, meanwhile, reacted with surprise, as if it were her husband who was being irrational. "But, Ronald, I haven't eaten yet." Lyon's father refused to acknowledge her. *"Millicent."* And then when Millie returned to the table, the four of them completed dinner in a silence that weighed tons.

When leaving the Lyon household that evening, the classmate wanted to say something. An expression of sympathy, perhaps, or questions to satisfy his curiosity. But Lyon would entertain no comments or inquiries. He simply shook his friend's hand and bid him goodbye, quickly closing the door, ending their friendship. Even at fourteen, John Lyon was using an image of himself—private, reserved, dignified—as protection.

Sunday afternoon he lost that self-image in the worst possible way.

"At least you haven't been fired," his agent, James Tapp, is telling him during their evening meeting at Lyon's apartment. "In fact, you have a strong sympathy factor going for you."

"Pity, you mean." In the past three days Lyon has

received a stack of faxes and an hour's worth of messages on his answering machine. "My colleagues are always thrilled when a potential competitor is gelded."

Tapp does not say what he is thinking, that viewers consider Lyon aloof, management thinks he's pompous, and Lyon lost his status as a potential competitor years ago. Instead, Tapp tries to put the best possible spin on the matter. "The network will come across as heartless if they fire a guy whose only sin is crying over murdered children," he tells Lyon. "Did you see the editorial in *The Atlanta Constitution?* Says that after so many years of watching newscasters deliver the worst possible news in a manner devoid of any emotion it was almost 'refreshing' to see one of them finally put a human face on tragedy. And *People* has called twice now—"

"I am *not* going to be interviewed by *People* magazine. I am *not* going to be among that weekly lineup of people taking their grief and personal problems and addictions public. Pitiful."

"Odd attitude for a newsman."

"I'm not a newsman, James. I haven't been a newsman since I left the *Trib.* It's the producers and correspondents and camera crews who assemble and report the news. I just read it."

Tapp is nodding but not agreeing. He's heard this rap from Lyon before and finds it tiresome.

In his twenties Lyon was a reporter for the *Chicago Tribune* where he wrote a series of articles about unsafe nursing homes, winning a Pulitzer, and he can't let go of this attitude that his newspaper work was superior to anything he's done in television. Tapp knows, however, that the truth lies in the opposite direction entirely: it is newspaper people who are inferior in power and prestige to their counterparts on television, and this assertion is easy enough to measure—you just count it out in dollars.

In his early thirties, thin and high-strung, a shark at making deals, Tapp walks around the living room repeatedly sitting and standing as he talks to his client. "The right kind of article in *People* could be the first step in saving your career," Tapp insists. "The network will not fire you, I'm pretty sure of that. But unfortunately your contract is up August first, five weeks from now, and I don't think they're going to renew. Probably offer a severance package with extended medical coverage."

Lyon translates "extended medical coverage" as psychiatric care. Does this mean network management thinks he's gone insane? Lyon doesn't *feel* insane, no voices or delusions or night sweats. Except for the breakdown itself and then the quite understandable embarrassment he's suffered these past three days, Lyon considers himself perfectly normal. He has no idea why his emotions slipped out of control Sunday afternoon, but he's certainly not insane. Then again, if you're insane, do you know it?

"I did get a call from a publisher," Tapp is saying, "who wanted to know if you had any special interest in children as murder victims, for a book project."

Just like Tapp, Lyon thinks, to call a book a book *project.* Lyon shakes his head.

"Does that mean no? We're talking a hundred thousand dollar advance."

Lyon mutters something about the gruesome bastards in publishing, recognizing again the bitterness that's become so intimate a part of his outlook lately.

"There *is* one possible solution to this entire mess," Tapp says, pacing the room. "Now please don't interrupt until you've heard me out. First you talk to *People* and tell them you've been a hard-assed journalist all your professional life, forced to take on a tough veneer as protection against all the shit you've seen, winning a Pulitzer for exposing the rat-infested firetraps that old people were forced to live in back in Chicago. But when you came to that story about murdered children Sunday afternoon, your cold, cold exterior finally melted. But now you don't care. Sure, crying on the air is going to hurt you professionally, but for godssakes you're a human being with *feelings*. Then you give *People* this exclusive: you're accepting a book contract to expose the horror of children as murder victims, donating the entire advance to some appropriate charity. If there isn't one for murdered children, we'll start it up ourselves.

"After the article comes out, I put you on the talk show circuit. You appear with experts, show photographs, put a human face on the cold statistics. Here it is, John, here's why the plan works—*the entire focus of what happened Sunday afternoon gets changed,* away from you and directed to this issue of little kids getting knocked off, their murders falsified as accidents or illnesses. You're protected because any criticism of you comes off as cold-heartedness toward little murdered children.

"Then I go to the network and say, hey, let's not waste all this publicity, how about John doing a special on children as murder victims? If they won't do it, one of the other networks will. You win a couple awards, bingo, you're back on network salary, all is forgiven, happy ending, fade-out."

Lyon sits there absorbing everything he's heard. When he finally speaks he does so in the measured tones he uses to deliver the gravest of news to the viewing audience. "I don't think I want to work with you anymore, James."

"What?"

"The strategy you just outlined is reprehensible, it's dishonest and—"

"Okay, then what do you suggest I go to the network with? Please put John back on the air and he'll try real hard not to bust out crying again?"

"You're not going to the network with anything, not on my behalf. You're fired."

Tapp's eyes grow large. "Fired?" Then he smiles. "John, you don't understand. You're at the end of your career. You blubbered and sobbed on national television and had to be dragged off a set. If you don't do something dramatic to change the current perception of you, you'll never work in television again— not network, not local, not even PBS. The fact that I didn't immediately drop you as a client is testimony to my loyalty, my generosity. And now you think you're firing *me?* You got it all wrong, John. You got it backwards. You fire your agent when you're at the *top* of your career, when you no longer want to be associated with someone who knew you from the old days. At the bottom of your career is when your agent fires *you.*"

Lyon stands and walks to the door of his apartment, opening it for Tapp. "Let's consider this a mutual firing then, shall we?"

Tapp steps into the hallway before turning for his parting shot. "My plan would have put you back on television, but I didn't mention that it had one requirement—that you go see a psychiatrist. I wasn't about to put *my* credibility on the line by trying to resurrect the career of someone who really has lost his marbles. And that's still my advice, John. Go see a shrink. Immediately."

Lyon closes the door.

It's a little after ten that evening when he sits down with a Scotch whiskey and his regrets. Firing Tapp was morally satisfying but stupid. What Lyon really wanted Tapp to do was ask the network if he could come back on board as a producer—real reporting again, off-air, off-camera—but now Lyon has no one who can speak to the network on his behalf.

Got to take a walk. Been holed up and hiding in this apartment for three days now, Lyon thinks, and if I don't get some air, I *will* go crazy.

As the elevator glides downward, Lyon tries to convince himself that all is not necessarily lost. Go to the network brass in person . . . no, go to a psychiatrist first, get the doctor to write an opinion that Sunday's episode was caused by overwork or underwork or whatever it was caused by, but in any case it was an isolated incidence and will never, ever be repeated. *Then* go to the network brass, show them the psychiatrist's opinion, offer to take some off-camera duties at a salary cut . . . no, don't propose a salary cut, they'll smell that like blood in the water. He wishes he had discussed this with Tapp. Okay, offer to work at the same salary but without a contract until my emotional stability is reestablished . . .

The elevator stops on the ground floor and Lyon steps out thinking maybe this is exactly what he needs at age fifty, something to fire up his competitive spirit and burn away the nagging self-pity he's been prone to recently. Hell, back when he worked for newspapers and during his first decade and a half in television,

Lyon was a hotshot. Maybe his entire problem is that he's been in a rut lately, and then a few months ago he turned fifty and his best friend Tommy Door died . . .

When Lyon reaches the apartment building's front door he is glad to see the rain, which should keep pedestrians distracted enough not to recognize him. Walking through the rain will clear his head, Lyon is convinced of it.

The doorman greets him in the usual obsequious manner, asking Lyon if he wants an umbrella.

"Thanks, Jonathan, but it's not raining that hard." Then Lyon hurries out, not giving the doorman a chance to say anything about Sunday's program.

As soon as Lyon reaches the sidewalk, a woman approaches him. She looks to be in her sixties, dressed in a ratty, torn raincoat, carrying a small cardboard box under one arm, her face very black—African black. As she reaches her free hand toward Lyon, he tries to sidestep her but the woman manages to latch that gnarled hand onto Lyon's arm.

He goes into a pocket and brings out a dollar, but when Lyon tries to give it to the woman she looks at the bill as if she has no idea what it is. In fact she allows the dollar to flutter to the sidewalk and then begins tugging on Lyon's arm to make him look at her.

He pulls his arm free.

"Those children need to be avenged," she says, her face puffy, eyes opened alarmingly wide.

"Hey you!" the doorman hollers, rushing out into the light rain and interposing himself between the woman and Lyon. "Go on get out of here or I'll call the cops on ya!" Then he turns his head toward Lyon. "She's been hanging around since Monday morning, wanting to come up and see you. I've run her off half a dozen times myself."

Lyon nods and backs away. "Thank you, Jonathan." He walks quickly, turning once to see Jonathan herding the woman down the sidewalk in the opposite direction.

Lyon sets a brisk pace, shoulders hunched, the collar of his Barbour jacket up, protecting himself more from being recognized than from the warm rain. He starts thinking about what he'll do if his contract isn't renewed in August, running through a quick tabulation of the money he's saved over the years, the property he's bought, the money and property he's inherited. I'll survive this just fine, he decides. At least I won't be like those other men whose positions were eliminated in all the cutbacks of the past few years, men with children in private schools, with wives who defined themselves through shopping, with three or four mortgages and a dozen different credit card bills. Thank God I don't have obligations. Those men were suicidal when they got the axe, but all I have to do is support myself, I don't have anyone burdening me, I don't have anyone . . .

He starts sobbing.

This attack, hitting with all the severity of the one Sunday afternoon, comes upon Lyon even more unexpectedly. One moment he is walking, the next moment he is doubled over crying so hard he can barely breathe.

Lyon moves in a crouch to the closest building, his hand against the brickwork for support, *sobbing*. When he glances up and sees a pedestrian heading for him, the man about to speak, Lyon angrily waves him off. Goddamn tourist.

The weeping eventually ebbs away, leaving Lyon with a stuffed nose, wet eyes, and small whimpering aftershocks of inexplicable sadness. Just like Sunday afternoon, except for one addition: a headache, a real blinder.

As he crouches there next to the building, not able to straighten up quite yet, Lyon realizes that he now faces an entirely different situation. The Sunday afternoon outburst obviously was *not* a once-only phenomenon. Something *is* wrong with him. If it's happened a second time, it could happen again, without warning, at any time. He can't go to the network brass and ask for a reassignment because he might start crying right there in the meeting.

Maybe it's something organic. A brain tumor—and maybe that's why he has this headache. Should he catch a cab and go to the hospital? No, never get a cab in this rain, go back to his apartment first. Circle around and slip in the side entrance so he won't have to face the doorman.

Patting a pocket to make sure he has his keys, Lyon begins walking home, the migraine causing his eyes to wander in and out of focus, Lyon striding faster and faster until he is running the last ten yards to his building's residents-only side entrance.

As he stands at the door fumbling his keys, the black woman steps from the shadows and rushes Lyon, so startling him that he yelps in surprise and drops the keyring. She still holds that small cardboard box, which is falling apart in the rain, and with her free hand she once again latches onto Lyon's arm.

The two of them dance circles—Lyon trying to escape and the woman holding him in a powerful grip—away from the door and across the sidewalk.

"Let go, damn it, I don't need this shit!" He jerks his arm violently but can't get loose. Although the woman's fingers are twisted with arthritis, she holds to him like a pit bull, staring wildly into Lyon's eyes.

"Goddamn it, let go of me you . . . stupid *nigger!*"

So shocked is he by what he has just said that Lyon instantly stops struggling, allowing the woman to pull close to him. Lyon has the liberal's usual horror of that word, having never spoken it in his life except to quote someone else, to prove that the person being quoted is a Neanderthal.

"I'm sorry," he tells her.

But she's shaking her head, concerned about something more serious than a word. "They need your help. You're the one, I know you are, I knew it as soon as I saw you on the TV. You're the one to bring Mason Quinndell to justice."

"Who?"

"The monster."

"Here let me give you a twenty, okay? Get yourself a good meal."

"I have all the information you'll need, right here." She tentatively releases her grip on Lyon's arm, pausing to see if he's going to try to run. Then she puts the soggy cardboard box on the sidewalk and takes from it a nine-by-twelve manila envelope. The woman slowly pulls down the zipper of Lyon's Barbour jacket and places the envelope inside where it will be protected from the rain. She zips him up and pats the jacket gently, like a mother about to send her son out into the weather. "Mason Quinndell is powerful, you'll have to be careful. Never see him alone or unarmed."

Unarmed? "I'm sorry," Lyon tells the woman, "but I don't know who you're talking about."

"Quinndell operates by discrediting his enemies."

Lyon stands there looking down at her face. "I'm afraid I've already discredited myself."

"No, no," she insists, smiling now for the first time. "Sunday when I saw you crying over those children

27

. . . did you know they're the ones who made you cry? They did that to lead me to you."

"Here, let me give you some money, please."

"I used to be a good nurse, until Quinndell ruined me. Everyone knew what he was doing, behind his back they called him Doctor Death, but when I came forward to file charges against him, that's when he discredited me. And since then, others have tried to bring him to justice, but the children never talked to those men, not the way they've talked to you."

"I'm afraid I still don't understand." Lyon glances behind him, gauging the distance to the door.

"There's only one way to do it," she tells him earnestly. "You'll have to dig up their graves and see for yourself what he did to those eighteen babies."

"Jesus."

"You read what's in that envelope, you'll understand." She's smiling again, the weary and relieved smile of someone who has just completed an onerous duty, happy to be done with it but too tired to feel elated. "Just be careful. Quinndell is a monster. That's not a figure of speech, Mr. Lyon—he's a *monster.*"

Lyon realizes now that in spite of the woman's appearance and the way she's accosted him, she is not in fact a raving street person. The woman has been educated and is totally earnest about what she's telling Lyon.

"I wouldn't send you after Quinndell without some protection." She bends down to the ruined cardboard box at her feet and takes out a small white wooden box which she hands to Lyon.

He tries to give it back to her. "I really don't think I should—"

"As long as you keep this in your possession

Quinndell won't be able to hurt you. And someone will watch over you, I promise."

Lyon decides that the easiest way to get rid of her is to let her finish whatever she's come here to say, then he can throw away this stuff she's given him and—

"In fact," the woman is saying, "I'll be there watching over you myself."

"Okay." He is smiling falsely as the woman backs away from him and moves toward the street.

"I swear you won't be alone, Mr. Lyon."

"Okay," he says again, smiling and nodding.

The rain turns suddenly heavy, soaking Lyon and the woman, pounding into mush what's left of the cardboard box. Remembering something, the woman returns to the box and folds back the soggy lid until she finds the object she's looking for, Lyon doesn't see what. Then she steps off the curb.

The traffic is running fast in spite of the rain, Lyon pulling his collar tight to his neck, not knowing what to do with the wooden box in his hand, telling the woman, "Hey, be careful."

She turns her head in his direction, a beatific smile showing through the rain. "I wouldn't send you after Quinndell alone, I wouldn't do that to you, Mr. Lyon!" she says, shouting to be heard above what has become a drenching downpour.

Lyon wants to get out of the rain but notices a cab approaching fast in the curb lane. He realizes what the woman is going to do at the precise moment she does it: turning her head toward the cab, gauging its approach, and then taking two quick steps directly into its path.

The right side of the cab's high bumper hits the woman with such a violent impact that her arms go into a brief, wild windmill motion (Lyon imagining the woman waving him goodbye) before she is slammed to the pavement and seemingly sucked under the cab, its right front tire traveling over her body, directly over her face, the right rear tire following the same path.

Lyon *sees* the impact in such fine detail that it seems he is watching it on film, frame by frame, but in fact the woman is hit, run over, and dead in the time it takes Lyon to exchange a single lungful of air.

The cab doesn't manage to get stopped until near the end of the block, Lyon rushing into the street and kneeling at the woman's body, the driving rain washing away the blood as it pours from her crushed face.

The cabbie comes running, both arms in the air, shouting to Lyon, "Hey, she stepped out right in front of me!"

Lyon feels suddenly guilty, a predator caught at his bloody prey. He stands, backing away. "I didn't see it," he says, speaking too softly for the approaching cabbie to hear. Lyon hurries to the sidewalk.

"Hey buddy, I need a witness!"

"'I didn't see it!" Lyon hollers, turning and rushing for the door to his apartment building.

"Hey *asshole!*" the cabbie screams, bypassing the woman's body to pursue Lyon.

Picking up the keyring he had dropped earlier, getting the door unlocked, opening it, Lyon pauses only long enough to shout at the cabdriver one last time. "I didn't see it!" Then he slips into the building, letting the heavy glass door slam behind him, entering the elevator as the cabbie reaches the locked door, which he beats on in frustration and anger.

It's not until Lyon is in his apartment that he realizes he's still holding the little wooden box, which he immediately tosses into the trash. Drenched from the rain, still wearing his wet Barbour, Lyon stands in his kitchen shakily pouring a glass of Scotch. Lifting the drink he sees bloodstains on the glass. *Jesus.* How'd he get her blood on his hands? Lyon doesn't even remember touching her. And the way the rain was washing everything away . . .

After furiously cleaning his hands in the sink and getting another glass, Lyon pours a fresh drink. Sipping from it, he unzips his jacket, the manila envelope falling out and landing at his feet.

5

DEEP INTO THE FOLLOWING SATURDAY NIGHT, JUNE 30, Mary Aurora is rudely awakened by the buzzer located on the wall above her bed. Putting both pillows over her head doesn't help because she can still hear the buzzer and she knows too that he'll keep his finger on the button until she makes an appearance. Throwing off the pillows, Mary hollers, "I'm coming, asshole!"—immediately regretting it because if Dr. Quinndell heard her . . .

Worried now, she quickly gets out of bed, flips up the light switch, pulls on a pair of jeans and a teeshirt, and glances at her image while walking past a mirror. Forty-three years old but clinging to the illusion she can pass for thirty-five, Mary wonders why none of it shows—everything she's *done* this past year, you'd think she'd be scarred by it somehow. The buzzer is still squawking. Two more weeks, she tells herself, and I won't have to listen to that goddamn buzzer ever again. Two more weeks and I get out of hell.

Mary Aurora has lived in a self-imposed hell for exactly fifteen days short of a year—the length of time she's been working for Dr. Mason Quinndell here in Hameln, West Virginia. And in just fifteen days, on the one-year anniversary of the deal she made with the Devil, Mary will be given two envelopes, one of them containing a cashier's check for $250,000. In the second envelope will be an address and twelve photographs.

To obtain the contents of these two envelopes, Mary has performed acts of such degradation that had someone described them to her beforehand, she would have denied even being *capable* of such acts, much less doing them voluntarily, doing them routinely.

The buzzer is incessant.

Mary hurries downstairs and stops at the double doors leading to Dr. Quinndell's office. She takes a breath, trying to compose herself and trying *not* to speculate on what the doctor wants her for this time. She raps hesitantly on one of the doors.

"Enter."

The office is of course completely dark, Mary expected that, but where's he hiding this time? Is he going to jump out from behind one of the doors and grab—

"Mary?"

She finally lets out that breath. He's at his desk near the back of the office, Mary safe from his touch at least for the moment. "Yes, doctor?"

"I want you to drive me someplace."

She wonders if that's all he wants.

"Are you wearing your uniform?" the doctor asks in that soft and cultured voice he's so proud of.

"No."

"Would you mind terribly putting it on?"

"Of course not." Why's he being so nice to me? Mary doesn't see the point of wearing her uniform, but if wearing a uniform is all the doctor requires from her tonight, Mary's grateful. "I'll go put it on right now."

"Thank you."

She turns toward the double doors.

"By the way, Mary."

She freezes. "Yes?"

"Were you having sexual intercourse when I buzzed you?"

"What? *No,* of course not."

"I was just wondering."

When he says nothing more, Mary continues toward the doors.

"Because I distinctly heard you shout something."

She freezes again, her palms becoming instantly wet.

"Upon achieving sexual climax—either an authentic climax or a faked one, if indeed you can any longer distinguish between the two—don't you usually proclaim that you are 'coming'?" He waits for an answer. "Mary?"

"Yes."

"Yes what?"

"Yes, I say that."

"You say that you're 'coming.'"

"Yes."

He pauses a moment before continuing. "Which is why I assumed you had a lover upstairs—because I heard your fishwife voice screeching out that you were 'coming.' In fact, you said, 'I'm coming, *asshole.'* Didn't you?"

She knows better than trying to lie to him. "Yes."

"You see why I'm confused. If you were announcing a climax, you were also referring to your lover by the rather odd endearment of 'asshole.' But now you're claiming you *weren't* having sex. Pray tell, to whom were you addressing that statement—*I'm coming, asshole,* hmm?"

In contrast to her wet palms, Mary's mouth is so dry she can't swallow.

"Mary?"

"I was . . . it was, uhm, it was sort of an automatic reaction to being suddenly awakened by the buzzer."

"You mean that statement was addressed to *me*. You were calling *me* an asshole."

Although the doctor loves toying with her like this, Mary knows that the consequences of these games—if she makes the wrong move, utters something to set him off—can be horrifying. "I was still half-asleep, I didn't know what I was saying."

"Which wounds me all the more deeply, Mary. Your low opinion of me is apparently so ingrained that even when you're not fully conscious you immediately brand me with that coarse and most common epithet—is my assessment correct?"

If he's in the mood for it, this kind of argumentative pedantry can go on for an hour, maneuvering Mary into untenable positions, making her feel increasingly stupid. She tries to cut it short this time by mumbling a simple "I'm sorry."

And the doctor surprises her by accepting the apology. "Thank you. Now run along and dress, I'll be waiting for you in the car."

On her way upstairs, Mary keeps telling herself, two more weeks, just two more weeks and I can go back to being human.

* * *

As the car travels the empty and unlighted streets of Hameln, Dr. Quinndell shows off by instructing Mary where to turn at each intersection they come to—instead of simply telling her their destination and letting her find it on her own.

"To punish you for cursing me," the doctor says once they've passed through the gateway to Cemetery Road, "I brought along a rubber glove."

Her heart squeezes painfully in her chest. Two more weeks, two more weeks.

"But now I realize I don't need to punish you because I'm already in a good mood, in the best possible mood. You *know* why I'm happy, don't you?"

"No, sir."

He makes a contemptuous sound. "You sleepwalk through life, Mary, you really do. You must not fear death because how could it possibly differ from the way you live your life?"

She doesn't reply.

"I'm happy because *she* is in her grave."

"Oh." Mary knows who he's talking about. Her funeral was today.

"And we're going to visit that grave. Do you think you can find it?"

"Yes, sir."

"Excellent."

Mary drives slowly down the cemetery's graveled lanes, and on the second turn the car's headlights find the freshly turned dirt of a new grave. Mary stops, gets out, opens the doctor's door, and leads him there.

He asks if the headstone is in place, and Mary tells him it is.

"What's the inscription?" he asks.

Mary shines her flashlight on the stone. "Just her name and the dates of her birth and death."

"How wonderfully minimalist," he says, chuckling. "Show me."

Mary directs him to the stone, Dr. Quinndell leaning down to run his hand over the chiseled letters and numbers. "Get my case from the car."

When Mary returns carrying a small black zippered case, she finds Quinndell standing on the fresh dirt directly in front of the headstone.

"I'm here."

"Yes, I know, I can smell you," the doctor says, removing his suitcoat and handing it to Mary before turning up the sleeve of his shirt.

Mary opens the case, prepares the hypodermic, and injects Quinndell. He pulls his lips back and hisses through clenched teeth. Mary turns away.

When she hears him unzipping his fly, she flashes the light on his face and sees that he is smiling. "You want me to do it *here?*" she asks, incredulous.

Dr. Quinndell is momentarily confused but then laughs genuinely, pounding his palms together, just the bottoms of his palms hitting so that the applause makes no sound. "Oh my dear, you are so absolutely Pavlovian, it's beyond belief, it really is."

After a short silence Mary hears a stream of liquid splashing on the tombstone, finally understanding why the doctor got her out of bed to drive him to the cemetery at this time of night.

"You see," he says, talking without interrupting the stream of urine, "Claire and I were alike in that we both *believed*. Doing this would be pointless unless we both were believers."

Mary is surprised that after a year with Dr. Quinndell she still has the capacity to be shocked.

"I assume you have a flashlight."

"Yes," she replies softly.

"Good, you won't want to miss this next part." He's undoing his belt. "Lefthand pocket of my jacket please."

She reaches into that pocket and finds a nearly depleted roll of toilet paper.

The doctor is holding out his hand.

"Scented," he says, putting the small roll to his nose. "Interesting concept, don't you think—*scented* toilet tissue. I mean, what's the *thinking* behind it?"

When he drops his trousers, Mary asks, "May I wait in the car?"

"Mary Aurora *squeamish?*" He laughs—and then turns quickly angry. "Go on, get out of here, this is between Claire and me. It has to do with the power of symbol, which you're *incapable* of appreciating. Go on!"

Returning to the car, Mary hears Quinndell humming show tunes. She never sees the figure in white step from behind a large tombstone to watch the doctor defiling Claire Cept's grave.

6

On Sunday evening, July 1, one week after crying on national television and four days after witnessing the woman kill herself, John Lyon arrives at a cabin he has rented eighteen miles into the mountains outside the town of Hameln, West Virginia. He has driven thirteen hours straight through to get here and what Lyon wants most from life right now is a hot shower and cold drink.

Before getting out of the rental car, however, he checks his face in the rearview mirror. It's habit more than vanity, Lyon's appearance being one of the commodities he has on sale to the public. He assesses his face, therefore, in a coldly analytical manner, usually satisfied with what he sees, with the ways the years have tugged and creased and settled his face to create a look of placid strength that plays well on a medium as cool as television. It's a good face, square and strong-jawed, looking exactly its age, fifty years, no more, no less. But Lyon's professional eye now recognizes a weariness in his face that has been caused by something more than thirteen hours of driving—a haunted quality that wasn't there a week ago.

He sits a while longer in the car. Lyon feels thick and bloated, like a dog that's been castrated in its advancing years and has forgone the chasing of small mammals in favor of sitting by the fire. How long has he been like this, without direction, mentally sitting by the fire? *Years.*

Although stiff and sore from all those hours of driving, he is still reluctant to get out of the car. Lyon doubts the wisdom of being here. But what was the alternative?

The morning after the woman killed herself, Lyon went out for the papers to search for news of her death. In the rain and confusion of the previous evening, the cabbie had not recognized him but Lyon didn't know this as he sat in his kitchen flipping through pages of newsprint, his fingers inky and the newspapers lying in heaps and tents on the floor all around him. He expected at any moment to come across his name and photograph.

'Crying' Newscaster Flees Scene of Fatal Accident

There was something pathetically funny about being holed up in his apartment furiously checking through the newspapers for word of the "crime," like some character from a Hitchcock movie, the normal man caught in a web of abnormal circumstances. Lyon began laughing.

He reached down and gathered up an armful of newspapers and threw them wildly into the air, laughing harder and harder until the laughter slipped out from under his control, escalating into something close to hysteria, Lyon standing there in his kitchen laughing until he was heaving for breath, tears wetting his face.

Then he started crying. The strength of the emotion invested in the laughter did not diminish, it was simply somehow transferred instantly and totally into weeping until he collapsed at his kitchen table and—just like Sunday afternoon, just like Wednesday evening in the rain—sobbed.

Then the migraine arrived with crippling effect, Lyon walking bent over to his bedroom where he lay down with a wet cloth across his eyes. His friend Tommy Door used to have an occasional migraine. Lyon appreciated now how Tommy must have suffered.

As he lay there in pain Lyon wondered whom he might call. No name came to mind. Maybe an old girlfriend, a colleague from the network. What would he say, how exactly would he open the conversation? "Hello, this is John. John *Lyon.*" And he could just imagine how this person would react to such a call, face twisted into an expression of mockery, an index finger making circular motions by the ear—then later telling people about the call and agreeing with them that, yeah, we always suspected John Lyon was a little too tightly wound for his own good.

He finally gets out of the rental car and stretches, looking up at the surrounding hills. The rectangular log cabin he has rented is in a valley clearing of less than an acre, a heavily forested ridgeline completely encircling the valley or, as they call it here in West Virginia, the "holler." And Lyon does indeed feel as if he is standing in the hollow of a large hand, protected.

Waving away wasps that seem to be lazily lost in the final hour of this day's heat and light, Lyon goes around to the trunk and takes out a box of supplies which he carries toward the cabin.

Her name was Claire Cept. She was sixty-two, born in New Orleans but lived the majority of her years in West Virginia, working as a registered nurse. The envelope she had so carefully placed in Lyon's jacket contained copies of official documents (transcripts from hearings, depositions from witnesses), various theories and speculations (some typewritten, some in her own hand), and one master list of the names and dates of birth—and death—for eighteen children under the age of one who died in a ten-year period while under the care of Dr. Mason Quinndell of Hameln, West Virginia.

Lyon places the box of supplies on the cabin's porch and returns to the car for his suitcases. He feels a vague need to hurry—to get settled in the cabin before the light is gone from this valley.

Reading through Claire Cept's material several times, Lyon eventually pieced together her story:

While working at a county hospital near Hameln, she became suspicious when Dr. Quinndell twice refused to allow mothers to see the bodies of their infants who had died after being brought to the hospital with high fevers. In the second incident, Claire went looking for the infant's body herself but was told it had already been moved to a funeral home. Claire called there and was informed that no body had been picked up from the hospital that evening. By the following day, however, everyone's story had changed, the director of the funeral home insisting that the infant's body had indeed been picked up the previous evening and then telling Nurse Cept that she most certainly could *not* come over and view the body.

Checking hospital records, Claire discovered that in the previous year five infants had died just hours after being admitted to the hospital by Dr. Quinndell. Two of those five babies were from indigent families, the other three the infants of unwed teenage girls.

Although the rural county hospital was a closed society, reluctant to acknowledge grisly accusations against one of its prominent physicians, Claire was so insistent that a hearing was finally held. Charges and countercharges were exchanged between Nurse Cept and Dr. Quinndell, the upshot being that the doctor was exonerated and the nurse was fired.

She continued investigating on her own, eventually coming up with that list of eighteen infants she accuses Quinndell of murdering over a decade that began fifteen years ago and apparently came to an end five years ago when Claire Cept went public with her accusations. The woman spent those past five years, the last five years of her life, in a crusade to bring Quinndell to justice.

One of the most remarkable items in Claire's envelope was a typewritten account of a telephone call that Claire claimed Quinndell made to her just last year, a call during which Quinndell admitted that he had indeed killed those babies, had in fact butchered them. According to Claire's notes, she asked Quinndell why he was confessing this to her and Quinndell replied, "Because you have to stop me before I do it again." At the bottom of the account of this telephone call, Claire wrote a note to John Lyon: "Now it's up to you to stop him. You have to open those graves, Mr. Lyon. The babies are lying there in the ground waiting to indict Quinndell."

Lifting his two suitcases out of the trunk, Lyon sees the little white box Claire Cept gave him right before she killed herself. He brought it along with him at the last minute, after his suitcases had been packed. He doesn't believe the box has any power, of course, but he couldn't see any harm in having it with him.

After digging it out of his trashbasket late that night, he found the box contained a carelessly molded wax figure. The arms and legs were only short stumps, and the face was coarsely outlined, two thumbprints for the eyes. The figure was identified with cutout letters, the *Q*s obviously referring to this Dr. Quinndell.

Spooky shit. When Lyon first opened the envelope containing Claire's notes and files, for example, some white crystals fell out onto his lap. The stuff looked like common table salt but Lyon wasn't about to taste it to find out. He has to keep all this to himself because if he starts talking about voodoo, the network really would be convinced he's gone off his nut.

He takes the two suitcases to the porch and then returns for the white box. On one level Lyon is able to step back and see how untenable his position is, but on another level—deeper or more basic, more primitive—everything that has happened to him this past week seems now to be loaded with great seriousness, with a portent that he finds intriguing but also terrifying.

Standing on the porch he searches through his pockets for the cabin's keys, which he was given—along with a packet of information—when he signed the rental form at a Hameln hardware store. Lyon had arranged for the rental by telephone, using information contained in Claire Cept's envelope. Another of her handwritten notes to Lyon urged him to stay at this cabin and not in the town of Hameln itself because "Quinndell owns nearly everything and everyone in the entire town." Lyon noticed that nowhere in Claire's notes did she refer to Quinndell as *doctor*.

He pauses after unlocking the cabin's door, thinking he might actually be able to pull it off. If Claire's accusations against Quinndell are true, if the doctor really is a baby killer, if Lyon is the one to break the story. The *possibilities* making him smile.

He loses that smile, however, when he realizes how this goddamn business has made him a ghoul. If people at the network hear a plane has crashed at Kennedy, they're excited, happy, *pumped*. Then when the second report comes in, saying that the plane simply skidded off the end of a runway, no loss of life, they're visibly disappointed. And now here I am speculating on how I might use baby murders to revive my career. Hell, I fired my agent for suggesting something like this.

Lyon steps into the cabin and finds the light switch but when he flips it up, nothing happens. With the box of supplies under one arm, he makes an immediate left through a doorway and into the living room. The lights there don't work either. On the other side of the living room is the cabin's single, small bedroom and even tinier bathroom—none of the lights in those rooms work either.

The cabin's interior—clean, the furniture cheap but cheerful—is already too dark for reading so Lyon carries the box of supplies back out to the porch where he goes through his packet of information and finds a note saying that the electricity will be turned on before noon Monday, July 2. Tomorrow.

Further reading reveals that the cabin's water is supplied by an electric pump and heated by an electric heater, meaning no shower tonight. No ice for his drink. Lyon stands on the porch feeling the frustration tangle knots in his stomach.

The box of supplies still under one arm, Lyon manages to pick up both suitcases before he goes back inside, turning right this time to enter the darkened kitchen, immediately stumbling over something, barking both shins, cursing, nearly falling on his face.

Lyon drops everything and bends down to rub his shins. A big crate has been left right in the middle of the goddamn kitchen, Lyon angry enough that he could kick it.

He finds an oil lamp on one of the counters and lights it, seeing that the crate is six feet long, three feet wide, two feet deep, painted white, and wrapped both lengthways and around its width with colored string tied in elaborate knots.

He rushes out to the porch, finds the little box that Claire gave him, and brings it into the kitchen.

"Jesus."

Lyon stands there for the longest time.

"Jesus."

If Claire Cept somehow arranged for this big crate to be delivered here, what has she placed inside for Lyon to find? Documents? A life-size paraffin doll? He isn't sure he wants to find out.

And the longer he stares at the crate, the more afraid he becomes, afraid in ways he knows are irrational—afraid because the kerosene lamp's yellow light lends an eeriness to the kitchen, afraid because he is a city dweller totally isolated out here in these mountains, afraid because it is nighttime and he has no one to turn to. There's no phone in the cabin but if there was, who would he call? Tommy Door is dead. So are Lyon's parents. He hasn't seen his sister in nearly seven years and wouldn't recognize his niece and two nephews if he met them on the street. People at the network are his colleagues, not his friends. There's no woman in his life, hasn't been for over a year. He fired his agent. *Who* then?

The thing to do is leave.

But go where? Back to Manhattan? Make an appointment with a psychiatrist? Call the police?

And yet a portion of Lyon's mind is urging him to get down on the floor, unwrap that string, and open the crate. Go on, you know you're going to do it, do it now.

He's sweating, excited, afraid, *pumped.*

Lyon drops to his knees, placing the kerosene lamp on the floor next to the crate. He tugs on one of the knots, finding that it pulls loose easily. Then another one. Then another. He freezes, feeling like someone in a movie audience, watching a horror film, except *he* is the one up on the screen, and he's shouting warnings at himself, *Don't do it, Don't do it,* but of course it's too late for warnings; Lyon is opening the box.

He holds the lamp high in one hand, his other hand opening the lid slowly, half expecting something to jump out at him, then finally seeing by the flame's yellow glow that the crate contains a woman's body.

7

BACK FROM THE CEMETERY, DR. QUINNDELL HAS BEEN sitting at his desk for more than an hour, tapping his long fingers, feeling oddly at a loss now that his enemy is dead, her grave defiled. The doctor is in the mood for . . . something. He could of course summon Mary from bed again and harass her, but Quinndell has grown weary of those games. He has one final torment in store for Mary, all in due time.

Quinndell picks up the telephone and punches in the number for the county jail. Carl, the deputy, is on duty.

"Hey, Doc, what can I do you for?"

"Mr. Gigli is lonely for a new friend, Carl."

The deputy chuckles. "Good old Mr. Gigli."

"I seem to remember that you mentioned you might have a likely candidate."

"Sure do, Doc. Henry Robarts, forty-three, white male, no fixed address, no family that he admits to. I been holding him for you."

"Interesting."

"I didn't run a sheet on him so nobody knows we got him, but he's a yardbird all right, right down to the jailhouse tattoos."

"But the question is, is he *disposable?*"

"Say what?"

"Is he wanted by any law enforcement agency, is an ex-wife after him for child support, does he have an elderly mother who's waiting for her precious Henry to visit?"

"Not that I know of. Got him talking just like you always said, Doc, and he didn't mention any family or friends. Far as I can tell he's drifter, shit bum, white trash—through and through."

"A *perfect* friend for Mr. Gigli."

"Yeah."

"Tell me again how Henry came to your attention."

"Caught him stealing tools from Martin's barn out there by the highway. Says he's looking for work, they all say that, but you know how it is, he was just passing through, stealing stuff small enough to fit in his pockets, then he sells it at some filling station down the road, gets enough money for a meal. Strictly small-time."

"Does he wear glasses?"

"Nope."

"Well then by all means do bring Henry over for a visit. You know the routine, Deputy."

"Sure do, Doc."

Forty-five minutes later Henry Robarts is on an examining table in a small windowless room in the back of Dr. Quinndell's house. Henry's wrists and ankles are strapped to the table; a rope is around his neck and knotted under the table to keep his head down. Henry allowed the deputy to secure him in this fashion because the deputy told him there'd be forty bucks in it for him: forty dollars to allow some local doctor to examine him.

Henry figures the doctor is queer. He's had shit like this happen to him before. In prison of course, but also in his travels. He'll be hitching a ride and some cheap-suited businessman will pick him up and they'll get talking and the guy will give him a look, embarrassment and lust all mixed up together, and the guy will mention how he's going to be stopping for the night soon and maybe Henry—you said your name was Henry, right?—would like a bed for the night too. Then in exchange for a room and a meal and maybe twenty bucks or whatever Henry can hit him up for, the guy gets to suck Henry's dick. That's the weird part. It's not like prison. On the outside, they want to suck *your* dick—and pay you for it too.

So what Henry figures is, the deputy brings men to this queer doctor who also has a kink about tying you to his examining table. A good deal for Henry on two counts: first, he gets forty dollars and, second, after all this they ain't going to charge him with anything and take the chance of Henry saying something to a judge about being delivered to a local doctor for some dick sucking.

Henry lies on the examining table wishing the doctor would hurry up and get here. The deputy left fifteen, twenty minutes ago and Henry is dying for a cigarette and though he wouldn't want to admit it to anyone, he's getting kind of horny for what this doctor is going to do to him too.

Then finally the door to the examining room opens

and in steps this nicely dressed man, suit and tie and a shirt that is very white.

"Hello," the doctor says in a deep voice like what you might expect to hear on one of them classical stations on the radio.

"Hiya," Henry replies, raising his head slightly, straining his neck against the rope to get a better look at the guy. Handsome.

"I understand your name is Henry Robarts. I'm Doctor Mason Quinndell."

"Nice meeting you, Doc." Henry wonders why the doctor gave his name, they usually don't do that.

"Do you notice anything unusual about me, Henry?"

Henry keeps watching him as he crosses the room and leans against a counter. "Nice suit."

Quinndell smiles. He steps to the examining table. "What color are my eyes?"

"Blue." Henry figures the guy is vain about his eyes so why not blow him a little smoke. "About the bluest eyes I've ever seen, make Paul Newman jealous, really." He watches the doctor's eyes a moment longer. "Jeez, you're blind."

Quinndell takes out a linen handkerchief and dabs at the tears collecting around his glass eyes. "I was blinded, yes, that's true, Henry. What do you think of that?"

"How can you be a doctor?"

"Well, Henry, once a doctor, always a doctor. I believe what you mean to ask is how can I practice medicine. And the answer of course is that I can't. Are you curious about why you were brought here, why you're strapped to the table?"

"The deputy said something about some money."

Quinndell smiles. "Of course." Standing there at the examining table he takes some folded bills from the pocket of his pants. When the doctor unfolds the bills, Henry notices that there's a twenty on the top of the stack and a hundred on the bottom. "Forty dollars, correct?" Quinndell asks.

"Yeah," Henry replies, watching the doctor's fine hands as they manipulate the bills. He starts to pull the twenty off the top but then hesitates, turns the stack over, pauses again—and pulls out the hundred-dollar bill, then a second one.

Henry watches with wide eyes.

Quinndell holds the two hundreds in one hand, folding the rest of the bills and slipping them back in his pocket. "Two twenties," he says, extending the hundreds toward Henry. "Right?"

"Right." Henry can't believe his good luck. "Just tuck them there in my shirt pocket, Doc."

Quinndell does. "And why do you suppose I'm paying you forty dollars, Henry."

"Different strokes for different folks, Doc."

"How about *Doctor* Quinndell?"

"Okay."

"And you're under the impression that I gave you those two twenty-dollar bills in exchange for some kind of sexual contact, is that a correct assessment?"

Henry has run across this before, the way some guys got to talk around it and talk around it, trying to talk themselves into it or hoping you'll make the first move, grab their hand and put it on your dick and get the show on the road. Except the way he's strapped down, Henry isn't going to be doing any grabbing, is he?

"Henry? Is my assessment correct, you're under the

impression that I have some sort of sexual interest in you?"

"I don't know, Doc. Doctor. The deputy said you wanted to examine me, so I guess I'm here to be examined. Go ahead, examine me any way you want."

"But why do you think you're in restraints?"

Jesus, how long is this going to take? "Uh, I don't exactly know that either, Dr. Quinndell. Maybe you like guys who are tied up. Or maybe 'cause you're blind you didn't want to take the chance with somebody being brought here from jail."

"Take the chance that you might steal my money and flee and I couldn't do anything about it because I'm defenseless—having been blinded has rendered me defenseless, is that what you're saying?"

"Something like that. Except I wouldn't take advantage of you."

"You wouldn't?"

"Not me, Doc. Doctor. Some guys, yeah, but me, I always treat people straight and expect to be treated the same way myself."

"An honest man."

"Yeah, I am." Then Henry begins a rambling story about this time he stopped at some woman's house and agreed to do a little yardwork in exchange for a few dollars but then when he found out the woman's husband had been killed a few months before in a trucking accident and she had three kids, Henry went around and fixed up all the stuff that was wrong with her house, a leaking roof and replacing a broken window—he bought the new pane of glass with his own money—and twelve hours later he settles for a home-cooked meal, won't take any of the woman's money. In fact, before he leaves he puts a dollar bill in each of the kids' hands, his last three bucks. "Lot of guys would think I'm a chump for doing something like that but me, I figure—"

He's interrupted when the doctor throws back his head, opens his mouth to reveal tiny yellow teeth, and begins heaving his shoulders up and down: it would be laughter except for its eerie silence.

8

LYING FULLY STRETCHED OUT, AS IF IN A COFFIN, THE body is completely covered by a transluscent white cloth, a kind of elegantly silken cheesecloth that clings so intimately to the body's features that Lyon can see that it is a black woman—he can see her breasts, the deep swollen purple of their large nipples, the dark plane of her stomach, and an even darker triangle of pubic hair, some of which sticks up through the shroud's open weave. But he can't make out her face, doesn't know who it is.

Claire Cept? Impossible. But one part of Lyon's mind is insisting he should lift the cloth to find out.

No.

He leans back from his kneeling position, gingerly closing the top of the crate, his heartbeat so strong he can hear it on his eardrums. He gets to his feet and walks around the kitchen with one hand over his mouth, astonished and baffled and absolutely convinced he cannot spend the night in this cabin, not with that crate and whoever's inside it waiting there on the kitchen floor.

Here's what he'll do, he'll get in the car and drive to town, contact the sheriff or state police, report this . . . There's going to be all kinds of questions Lyon doesn't want to answer, but he can't *not* report finding a body. Who put it here? And why is it here—to scare Lyon off? It's doing a damn good job of that but if Quinndell is behind this, maybe there *is* some substance to Claire's charges against him.

For now, just get the hell out of here, Lyon tells himself as he hurries to the rental car and drives off.

Twenty minutes down the mountain road he discovers he can't find any of the turnoffs in the dark. There must have been a half dozen of them, two rights, a left . . . The turnoffs were marked with red paint on certain trees, easy enough to see driving up here in the daylight but now Lyon has already made three turns —guessing—and hasn't seen a goddamn painted tree yet. Even the map Lyon was given, which he left at the cabin, wouldn't do him much good in the dark, the county road and logging trails and private lanes all becoming a maddening maze.

He swings around a bend and sees that a massive tree has been cut down to block the road fifty yards or so ahead. Lyon drives right up to it and then sits there in the car with both hands on the steering wheel. That tree obviously wasn't blocking the road when he came up the mountain. This can't be the county road, he must have turned onto some private road. Lyon keeps staring through the windshield at that tree as if expecting to find an answer among its green leaves.

He finally opens the door and emerges into an absolutely black night. Except for the area illuminated by his headlights, Lyon can't see anything—no lights from town or from a farmhouse, certainly not from the kerosene lantern he left burning in the cabin, which is somewhere behind him or off to the left, he has no idea, he's lost.

The choices are to sleep here in the car until morning or turn around and try to find his way back to the cabin. Lyon doesn't like either of them.

He is just about to get back in the car when he hears someone walking off in the woods to his right. Maybe two people. He freezes, listening as carefully as he can. Probably nothing more than some deer or possums. Or bears. Or Bigfoot for all Lyon knows, he doesn't have a clue about what could be out in these woods in the middle of the night.

Should have stayed in New York and taken my chances at Bellevue, he thinks.

The rustling footsteps stop. Now whatever it is out there is standing still, *watching* him.

Lyon slips into the car and backs up. He gets turned around and drives a few yards before hitting the brakes: someone standing in the road.

Too far away for Lyon to get a good look, the figure is tiny—small enough to be a boy. He's holding something, a stick or a gun.

Lyon's mind is racing. Maybe this is just some local boy out hunting.

In the middle of the night?

Or maybe he cut that tree down to trap me and now he's going to rob me and put a bullet in my head.

Or maybe, Christ, maybe he's got dogs with him.

Lyon was five years old when he was attacked by a neighbor's dog, chewed up bad enough to land in the hospital, and ever since then his fear of dogs has been absolute. When he has nightmares they take canine forms.

Lyon quickly checks that all the windows are up, all the doors locked. Then he eases the car forward. Just going to drive right past him. And if he raises that gun, assuming it's a gun, I'll floor the accelerator and . . .

When Lyon is within fifty yards, the figure turns and walks off the left side of the road into the woods. Lyon continues driving slowly, stopping when he reaches the spot where the little man—or boy—was standing. Lowering the driver's window halfway, his foot ready to jam the accelerator, Lyon searches among the dark trees, seeing nothing, hearing nothing.

He's about to ease forward again when he senses he is being watched by something *close*. He turns suddenly to his right and there it is, looking in the passenger window—a dog's head, a head the size of a bear's, those dark eyes just *looking* at Lyon. He never even heard the creature put its paws up on the car and now there it is, neither growling nor panting, just *looking*.

Lyon's foot can't hit the accelerator fast enough, the tires spinning so hard on the dirt road that for an instant the car doesn't go anywhere, just sits there spinning, the dog somehow managing to stay up on the door, still looking in on Lyon with its intense stare, looking right into Lyon's eyes as if it has a message for him, a message Lyon doesn't want to receive. And meanwhile he is pressing so hard on the accelerator that his entire body is twisted, putting all of his weight behind that foot, *go, go, goddamn it please GO!* The dog is screaming, the fucking dog is screaming like a man!

No, it's Lyon screaming, he doesn't realize it's him until he stops screaming a couple hundred yards down the road, still jamming that accelerator, sideswiping a tree but not letting that slow him down, both hands in a death grip on the steering wheel, constantly glancing at the passenger side window as if he expects that dog to still be there, *looking at him.*

It takes an hour to find his way back to the cabin, and in that hour Lyon still hasn't recovered his composure. He stops as near as he can to the cabin's porch, not sure he wants to chance walking from the car to the front door because maybe that dog has somehow followed him here.

Lyon looks all around, seeing nothing. The yellow glow from the kerosene lamp shows through the kitchen window in a way that is particularly uninviting, especially since Lyon knows what's waiting for him on the kitchen floor. But there's no way he can possibly stay here in this car and keep watching the passenger window all night, watching for that dog to put his head up there again.

What's it going to be: slowly opening the door, looking around, then easing his way to the cabin—or making a dash for it?

Lyon chooses to dash. Out of the car, up on the porch, into the cabin, slamming the door behind him and jamming the dead bolt shut.

Now I have to go around and secure all the windows, he thinks. Make sure everything is closed and locked. Including the back door off the kitchen.

But as soon as Lyon steps through the kitchen doorway he sees that in his absence someone, something, has reopened the crate, the edge of its hinged lid now resting on the floor, the shroud torn loose to expose part of the woman's face and one bare breast.

9

HENRY IS SMILING NERVOUSLY THE WAY YOU DO WHEN someone is laughing at a joke you don't get. "What?" he finally asks Quinndell, who is just now recovering from his silent laughter.

"Henry, you're a stitch, you really are." The doctor has taken out his handkerchief again, wiping the tears from his glass eyes.

Henry waits for whatever is next. He doesn't want to do or say anything that might jeopardize those two hundred-dollar bills in his shirt pocket.

When Quinndell is composed he asks Henry to describe himself. "Not your undying commitment to honesty. I want a physical description."

Here's where we get down to it, Henry thinks. "Okay, I'm forty-three years old, just under six foot, brown eyes, brown hair, a mustache, and I got a—"

"Brown eyes?"

"Yeah."

"How's your vision? Do you wear glasses?"

"Twenty-twenty in both eyes. Hey, when I was in the army I—"

"Please, Henry, no more of your pathetic stories, just answer my questions. What do you think about the fact that you have perfect vision while I'm blinded?"

"Well, I—"

"That you, part of society's debris, a thoroughly useless man, you use your eyes to find items to steal—"

"Hey, I wasn't stealing them tools, I told the deputy, I was going to use the tools to fix up the barn and then ask the people if they wouldn't give me a meal and a few dollars in exchange—"

"That you go through life with no appreciation of what you see, that you don't visit museums, have doubtlessly never seen an original painting, that you never sit and just look at a tree, at the total perfection of a tree, that you can't examine a sick child and determine what's wrong with her, and then correct that problem, that on you, Henry Robarts, vision is a total waste while *I . . .*" And here the doctor taps himself on the chest. "*I,* a man of education, cultured, a man who appreciates the finer things in life, a man who at the age of eighteen *wept* when he saw his first Matisse, a *doctor* who has been trained in the art of healing, of healing *children,* Henry—what do you think of the profound *inequity* of a God who would blind me and yet allow you to have your twenty-twenty vision?"

Henry thinks about this a moment and then says, "Jeez, I don't know, Doc."

"Doctor."

"Yeah, I don't know what to tell you, Doctor. Life's fucking unfair, ain't it?"

"God is unfair."

"Seems that way sometimes, don't it?"

"If God's justice is unbalanced, how might we correct it?"

"I don't catch your meaning."

"I've been blinded, you have vision. My blinding is a terrible loss, your vision is a waste. How can we balance that injustice, how can we put the scales right?"

"I still don't—"

"Henry, stop being stupid, I'm asking a straightforward question. You can see, I can't. That's not right, that's unequal, out of balance. Now how do we *make* it right?"

"You get your sight back?"

Quinndell smiles. "Good, good. That's *one* way the scales can be balanced, the restoration of my vision. Unfortunately that simply is not possible. Can you think of another way to balance the scales?"

Henry thinks. "Not really."

"Come on, Henry, come on, the inequity is removed if we both can see *or* if we both . . ."

"Are blind?"

"Yes!" Quinndell exclaims. "Excellent, excellent insight, Henry."

Nervous now, the man on the table pulls against the restraints around his wrists and ankles.

"And yet," Quinndell continues, "even if you were blind the scales would *still* be out of balance, because what about all the pain I've suffered these past five years, the richness of my life being blunted, the cruel irony of finally achieving wealth and then being robbed of the opportunity to enjoy that wealth fully, how do we balance that out?"

"Hey, all I know, Doctor Quinndell, is that the

deputy said I could earn forty bucks if I came over here and let you examine me."

"The two twenties I put in your shirt pocket."

"That's right, so go ahead and examine me if you want—"

"Not the two *hundreds* I put in your pocket."

"What?"

"I might have put two hundred-dollar bills in your pocket instead of two twenties."

"Really? Jeez, I wasn't even watching."

"So you're not sure if you have forty dollars or two hundred dollars in your pocket?"

"Absolutely no idea, take 'em out and let me see."

Quinndell pulls the bills from Henry's pocket.

"Well fuck me, Doctor, those *are* hundreds! I wasn't paying attention, really. Hey, take 'em back and give me the twenties." But as Henry continues watching Quinndell's face, that yellow-toothed grin, that look of amusement, he changes his mind. "Hell, you keep your money. Just give the deputy a call and let him take me back to that cell, we'll just write this whole thing off as a misunderstanding."

"I have a better idea," Quinndell says, stuffing the hundreds back into Henry's pocket. "You keep the money, you'll earn every cent of it before the evening's over, believe me, you will. Correcting God's inequities is tough work." Then the doctor turns and points toward a cabinet in the corner of the room. "Do you know who lives in there?"

"Lives in there?"

"Mr. Gigli lives in there. And do you know what Mr. Gigli's job is?"

Henry pulls again on the restraints, working himself into a sweat.

"Mr. Gigli's job is to balance the pain, to make you

hurt *physically,* because that's the only type of pain someone as spiritually numb as you would understand, to make you hurt physically as much as I've been hurt spiritually." Quinndell steps very close to the table and takes a heavy tablespoon from the pocket of his suitcoat. "This spoon has a job too, Henry. Its job is to balance the vision inequity."

"Hey, mister, you get that fat deputy on the line, I'm not kidding!"

"Oh, I'm not kidding either. By the time Mr. Gigli and Mr. Spoon finish their work this evening, the scales might not be in *complete* balance but they will have moved one small notch in that direction."

"I don't know what the fuck you're talking about, I really don't."

"Let me explain then. In Mr. Gigli's case I'm talking about the amputation of your hands and feet and in Mr. Spoon's case I'm talking about enucleation."

Quinndell moves to the head of the table, grasping the man's forehead tightly with one hand as he grips the tablespoon in his other, moving the spoon across the bridge of the man's nose, raising the spoon and placing its tip against the outside corner of the man's left eye. "Can *you* say enucleation, Henry?"

10

PEOPLE HE WORKS WITH, ESPECIALLY THOSE WHO SNEER-
ingly refer to him as *His Lordship*, wouldn't recognize
John Lyon now, ashen and trembling and sucking
down a mouthful of Scotch right from the bottle. He's
so rattled he drinks too quickly and gags, forced to
spit up in the sink, no dignity left in this man, it's been
frightened out of him. He tries to wash away the mess
in the sink but nothing comes from the tap. Lyon
remembers too late that the electricity powering the
water pump won't be turned on until tomorrow.

Walking around the perimeter of the kitchen, giving
the open crate a wide berth, in fact refusing even to
look at the corpse, Lyon keeps glancing out the
kitchen window, still expecting that hell dog to appear
there.

He finally steps right up to the window and looks
into the clearing.

No dog, but Lyon is surprised by how light the night
has become, the moon having finally risen high

enough to top the surrounding hills. He glances at his watch, almost midnight.

Not trusting himself to carry the kerosene lamp without dropping it and catching the entire cabin on fire, Lyon takes a flashlight from the box of supplies and uses it to find his way through the living room, the dark bedroom, and into the bathroom. After peeing he flushes the toilet, but of course there's no water to refill the tank. Next time will he have to pee outside? Where that dog is waiting for him and probably snakes too.

Back in the kitchen he finally gets enough nerve and Scotch in him to stand at the crate and look at her. Someone obviously entered the cabin while he was gone, opened the lid, and pulled the shroud loose. Whoever did that *wants* him to look. They're aware of Lyon's emotional instability and are trying to push him over sanity's edge.

Time passes, Lyon sipping Scotch into an empty stomach, trying to convince himself to kneel at the crate and remove the cloth from the rest of her face. It's not Claire. Lyon can tell even from her partially exposed face that the woman is much too young to be Claire. He finally kneels there on the floor, images from a dozen horror films leaping to mind, the corpse coming suddenly to life, bolting upright to grab him.

He waits for it to happen, for *something* to happen.

Then with the finger and thumb of one shaking hand he delicately pinches the top edge of the cloth and s-l-o-w-l-y pulls it from her face.

Seeing her, he breathes more easily, placing the Scotch bottle on the floor, staring at her face and exposed breast, surprised by his sudden sexual arousal.

The white cloth looks more like a negligee than a

shroud, a negligee that's been pulled aside by a lover to expose that breast. The woman's face is beautifully exotic, her skin deeply black, big eyes gently closed, flared nose, prominent cheekbones narrowing to a delicate chin, her mouth wonderfully large, lips full and still tinged with a lifelike pinkness—looking nothing at all the way Tommy Door looked in *his* coffin, mummified and overly made up and resolutely *dead*. Ever since seeing Tommy like that, Lyon has been in mortal fear of ending up the same way. But what's the alternative?

He again pinches the top edge of the cloth between finger and thumb, pulling it down far enough to expose the other breast. He wants to touch them. What would the breasts of a dead woman feel like— and why is Lyon even thinking along these lines, what's wrong with him? Maybe he should cover her back up again. But Lyon doesn't *want* to, he can't stop looking at her.

Most of the black women he knows back in New York are, for want of a better term, *American* blacks, skin the various shades of light coffee, features narrowed and homogenized by the white blood in their ancestry. Not so the face into which Lyon now stares, a face shining with the heart of Africa, ebony black, racially pure, black-to-the-bone black.

She's only a girl, can't be much more than twenty.

Before Claire stepped in front of that cab she vowed she would send someone to help Lyon, that her soul would be watching over him—he wouldn't be alone, she promised.

Lyon rubs his face with both hands.

Then he gets up and again walks unsteadily around the kitchen, glancing nervously at that window, worried he might be so totally crazy he's not even aware of *how* crazy he is. He has dedicated his entire life to maintaining control, never letting anyone know how he feels deep inside, keeping his interior a secret for so long now that he doesn't know what's in there himself, all those protective layers poured like concrete over his soul: no wife, no children, living alone, selfish, independent, tough, can't-touch-me, no social or financial debts, an island. And now that concrete is breaking up and whatever it is coming loose deep inside Lyon, that's what's scaring him worse than this corpse or that dog or anything else that's happened to him this past week.

Lyon returns to kneel at the crate.

Her breasts are plump and high on her chest, a young woman's breasts topped with deeply purple nipples so richly swollen that Lyon can too easily imagine them in his mouth, imagine tasting that soft black flesh, chewing it gently, his arousal returning as he sees all too vividly in his mind how he could bend over right now and suck that nearest nipple between tongue and palate.

He actually dangles one hand over the side of the crate.

She appears to be only sleeping. Lyon argues to himself that it's perfectly normal to be aroused by the sight of a beautiful young woman, half-naked and asleep. He has come upon her in bed, a silken sheet slipped to her waist, and here she sleeps in front of him. He can stare at her without censure, even venture to touch a breast without awakening her. John Lyon tries hard to justify this rancid desire he's suffering, his dangling hand moving closer and closer until the knuckles of that white trembling hand brush across one black nipple.

He's not horrified to be doing this, her flesh feeling

cool but not dead, however dead might feel, certainly not repulsive. Lyon moves his knuckles across the nipple a second time, his arousal setting itself like a steel bolt, urging him on, go ahead and take that black breast in your hand, who's to know, you're isolated out here and when you bring the police back in the morning *she* certainly can't tell them what you did, go ahead and do it, lean your head down, John Lyon, and suck that nipple, go on, see what it tastes like, you're the only one who will ever know what you've done and you can handle it, suck both of them, *do it*, why not?

Torn up inside by desire and by the self-hatred that desire is creating, Lyon lowers his forehead onto the edge of the crate so he can't see what his hand is doing, covering her breast and gently kneading it.

Past midnight now, John Lyon stands at the kitchen window and stares out, waiting for what he isn't sure.

He turns toward her again, the lust he was previously feeling replaced now by shame. He can't tolerate looking at her. Hurrying to the crate, intending to replace the cloth over her body, he notices that her right wrist, the one nearest him, is tucked down toward the bottom of the crate and is bound in a thick leather cuff apparently anchored to the crate. Leaning over, he finds that her left wrist is similarly cuffed.

Maybe the woman was alive when she was placed in the crate, alive and struggling so that she had to be strapped down. *She's alive now.*

Lyon freezes. Of course she's alive, her nipple puckered under his touch, *of course she's alive,* he's been repressing that knowledge so that he could . . . Oh Jesus. And now Lyon is nervously reaching down next to her hip, pulling loose a leather thong that is laced through that cuff, taking her slender black wrist in his hand.

Just as the tips of his fingers touch the underside of her wrist, Lyon's peripheral vision catches a movement. Lyon turns—Jesus God, *at the window.* He drops her hand and jerks around on his knees just in time to get a good look before it ducks down out of sight beneath the window's ledge.

11

THE SCREAMS CAUSE MARY AURORA TO BOLT UPRIGHT
in bed. She had no idea the doctor was doing this
tonight. Mary lowers her head to her knees and covers
her ears with her hands and then with a pillow, but of
course nothing can shut out the screams, because once
you hear screams like that, you hear them *inside* your
head. Inhuman? Of course they are inhuman, or at
least like nothing a human should be capable of
producing, like no scream-shriek-bellow Mary has
ever heard before she came to live in Dr. Quinndell's
house. Surely neighbors can hear them, what do the
doctor's neighbors do, roll over in bed and put more
pillows on their heads? Just like me, Mary thinks—
cover your ears and hope the monster doesn't come
visiting *you*.

Then after the initial screams, after shrieks have
injured the vocal cords, after the volume has gone as
high as it can go, then come the more pitiful sounds:
the moans, the begging for death, for release, and

finally a long, low, wordless pleading. If you could hook a microphone to a soul in hell, it would sound like what Mary is hearing right now.

I'm not doing this for the money, Mary tells herself. I'm *not*.

The sound stops abruptly. Now Mary waits in dread. Will he come up here? And if he does, will he—

Footsteps on the stairs, Mary bundling herself into a ball on the bed, arms hugging her legs, shivering and praying and then ashamed of herself for praying but praying some more.

The door to her bedroom is pushed open, Dr. Quinndell lighted from the hallway lamp. "Oh Mary," he says, "it was *awful.*" His suitcoat off, sleeves rolled up, that pristine white shirt splattered black with blood, he comes to her.

Mary makes room for him on the bed, less an invitation than an effort to avoid his touch.

"Mr. Gigli was *especially* voracious tonight." The doctor finds her shoulder with one bloody hand, moving the hand down to her breast. "I need you."

"Yes," she tells him, hating whatever it is inside her that allows her to say yes to him.

"I need you to give me an injection."

She's relieved. Maybe once he gets his shot he'll go away and leave her alone. Mary's not sure what he puts in the syringes. From his reaction she guesses it is some mixture of amphetamine and cocaine, something that enhances his madness without greatly impairing his speech or the function of his hands—which are moving down her stomach, digging between her legs.

After receiving the shot, Quinndell stands and walks around her bed, hitting the base of his palms together in silent applause, describing what he did to the man, Mary wounded by the details of this account but hoping that if he continues talking maybe he'll talk himself out, exhaust himself, work through the effects of the injection and then go to sleep.

"When you go down there and *see* what I've done, you'll appreciate what I'm telling you."

Mary says nothing.

"I want you to clean up the mess. Pick up the pieces, so to speak."

"Carl always does that."

"Tonight *you're* going to do it."

"Please."

"Turn over."

She does, Quinndell standing now at the edge of the bed, standing between her legs.

"Don't make me go down there," she begs. "Carl'll do it."

He unzips his pants and lies on top of Mary, prodding her. "You like it this way?"

"Sure."

"Sure?"

"Yes, I like it this way, I do."

"Convince me you like what I'm doing," he says, pushing against her, "convince me that you're not just tolerating it but that you're really enjoying it, that you adore it, that you want it—convince me of that, Mary, and I'll call Carl and make him bag up the parts, clean the room, you won't even have to see it. But if I detect one false tone, one faked response, then *you* are going down there and clean up what's left of Mr. Henry Robarts."

Her lower lip is between her teeth.

"And although I can only *listen* for your duplicity," Quinndell continues, reaching into his pants pocket and taking something out, laying it in the small of her back, the wet-flesh clamminess of it causing Mary's skin to crawl, "Henry will be keeping his eye on you."

Mary bites her lower lip as the doctor pushes harder against her, holding her hips with his bloody hands.

"You *like* that, don't you?"

She says she does, moving her ass against him, arching, purring, saying things that take small bites out of her soul.

12

NOT EVEN HUMAN. TINY, ANCIENT. BOTH EARS PERFECT-
ly round and cupped, sticking straight out from the
sides of its head like two halves of a china teacup.
Large black eyes, a bulblike forehead, chinless—
spying in on Lyon with an idiot's grin.

Nature is supposed to prevent something like that
from being born. When something that monstrous
forms in the womb, nature is supposed to ensure it is
aborted before it can be carried to term. What Lyon
saw at the kitchen window—something like that is
not supposed to live.

After he gets over the initial shock, Lyon scrambles
to his feet, stumbling backward, reversing so hard into
the kitchen stove that it rears up on its back two legs,
Lyon's eyes flashed open and his heart full of such
terror that it feels as if it's trying to escape his chest,
having already crawled up into the base of his throat,
cowering there as it pounds out its fear.

Lyon wishes he had a gun. Yes, this New York

liberal who has broadcast commentaries in support of restrictions on the purchase and ownership of handguns, now *he* wants a big ugly pistol in his hand—or an automatic assault rifle, something that fires the most powerful and deadly projectiles ever manufactured, and Lyon wouldn't care if the weapon was unregistered, stolen, serial number filed off, used in heinous crimes, inappropriate for hunting, the more of a man-killer the better. He would sign a lifetime membership to the NRA and appear in their magazine ads and tithe to them ten percent of his income, do *anything* right now to have in his hand a big goddamn loaded gun.

Unarmed, he waits for that face to appear again in the window. Maybe it's Quinndell.

No, that face does not belong to a doctor, not even one who butchers babies.

It's the hunter, that little man Lyon caught in his headlights, the one holding the rifle—which means that the dog is out there with him.

Lyon waits.

Nothing happens, no face at the window, no sound from the porch, *nothing.*

He picks up a sturdy wooden kitchen chair and advances carefully toward the door, trying to convince himself he shouldn't be afraid of someone so small. Lyon himself is six one, two hundred pounds, though nearly twenty of those pounds is carried in a gut he's put on in the past five years. Still, he is broad-shouldered and strong, has been since high school, a man whose size and strength has always made him confident around other men, unintimidated. I'm *twice* the size of that little creature out there, he tells himself.

Except *he's* got a gun and a dog.

But Lyon has to do something, he can't simply wait for the creature to keep popping up at windows.

Holding the chair in front of him, Lyon makes his way to the door. He looks out into the clearing in front of the cabin and, *yes*, there it is, standing a hundred feet from the cabin, just standing there looking back at Lyon. No gun, no dog.

"What do you want!" Lyon hollers through the door. "What're you doing here!"

No response.

He's retarded, Lyon decides. Just some local retard who gets his jollies peeping in windows.

Lyon unlocks and opens the door. "Hey there, listen to me! I want you *off* this property!"

Illuminated eerily by moonlight, the little figure stands unmoving like a statue from a horror film, awaiting animation.

Bringing the chair with him, Lyon steps out onto the porch. "All right, if you don't leave I'm going to come out there and break this fucking chair over your head!"

Back across the clearing comes a tiny but resolute voice, "I think not."

Lyon is trying to figure out what the hell that means when he once again senses eyes on him. Looking down he sees that *the dog*—huge, black—has been sitting there the entire time, right here on the porch, just to the other side of the door, sitting and looking at him.

It's the same dog that was up at the car window, staring at Lyon the way it's staring at him now, a steady and urgent stare, waiting for something, for a response from Lyon, for an answer to some question those dark almond eyes are asking.

Lyon eases the chair between himself and the dog, although the chair affords little comfort because the dog—some kind of cross between wolf and German shepherd and hound from hell—looks as if it could easily rip the chair apart and then turn those jaws on Lyon. The horror he feels is not only that the dog will kill him but that it will actually consume his flesh.

In his peripheral vision, Lyon sees the little man moving, turning from the cabin and heading for the woods at the edge of the clearing.

"Hey, what about your—"

But Lyon is interrupted by a low, rumbling growl that seems to vibrate the porch's floorboards. And when Lyon finally manages a quick glance at the clearing, he sees that the little man is already gone.

Now what?

Lyon takes one hand off the chair, reaching around behind him to find the door handle, opening the door, easing backward into the cabin—and all this time the dog doesn't move, doesn't avert its eyes from Lyon's. No one, not mother or lover, has ever looked at Lyon with such intensity, such intimacy: no one has ever looked at him as a meal.

Once inside the cabin, the door locked behind him, Lyon turns into the kitchen to confront another horror, to see in the soft yellow light of the kerosene lamp that the woman's right hand, which he had uncuffed, has moved, her right arm lying now completely across her bare stomach, her fingertips grasping the leather restraint that still holds her other wrist. Although the woman is rigidly still, is once again comatose, it's obvious what she was trying to do, *trying to escape.*

13

WILL SHE BE ABLE TO REMEMBER WHAT I *DID?* LYON wonders as he struggles to get her out of the box and then, in a panic of shame and fear and concern for the woman's life, carries her quickly through the cabin, careful not to bump her head in the doorways, rushing her into the bedroom. She feels impossibly light in his arms.

Lyon places her gently on the bed and then works the summer blanket and top sheet from beneath her body, pausing briefly to marvel at how black and small she appears lying on the starched white bottom sheet. He covers her with the top sheet, bundling the summer blanket in his arms and tossing it on a nearby chair. He reaches under that top sheet to find the young woman's wrist, checking her pulse and finding it strong and steady. For a long time he sits on the side of the bed watching her face.

Finally he leaves her and stands by one of the

bedroom windows to await dawn and deliverance. And if not deliverance, then surely dawn.

Some hours later John Lyon is at the cabin's locked front door, looking out at the porch and then the clearing and then back at the porch. The night has turned dark again, the moon having dropped below the surrounding hills, but Lyon can see enough to confirm that the dog is gone.

He steps into the kitchen, searches through the crate for documents or messages (finding none), and tries to get a drink of water at the kitchen tap but of course the electricity is still off. The taste in Lyon's mouth is so horrible that he keeps fighting the urge to swallow.

He returns to the bedroom and stands by the bed looking down at the young woman who appears now just as she did in the crate, peacefully asleep. He takes her pulse again and has just put his hand to the side of her face to check for a fever when he is startled by the overhead light coming on.

Glancing at the doorway to the tiny bathroom he sees that the light there is on too. He can hear water running, filling the toilet tank. And when he listens carefully he can also hear the distant hum of motors working elsewhere in the cabin, pumping, pressurizing, heating, cooling.

These various indications that Lyon has once again been connected to the grid of civilization comfort him enormously.

In the morning when he brings people here and tells them what happened, shows them the comatose woman, Lyon will act in a manner that is bloodlessly professional. No tears, no quavering voice; he won't rant and rave about hell dogs and misshapen little man-creatures peering in the kitchen window. Lyon will simply relate what happened, tell the police he has absolutely no idea what these bizarre occurrences mean, and then offer to cooperate however he can in the investigation. He certainly won't mention that he fondled the woman while she was in the crate, while he was still operating under the belief she was dead. And he's assuming her coma is deep enough that she won't be aware of what he did either. In other words, no one'll ever know. The craziness is over. He slipped his moorings during the night but Lyon is confident that daylight will find him once again tightly secured. There's a *story* here—who cuffed that comatose woman into a crate and brought her to the cabin, *why* was it done, who *is* she, and what does this all have to do with Dr. Mason Quinndell and Claire Cept's accusations against him? From now on Lyon's only connection to the young woman and to this entire mess he finds himself in will be as a reporter getting answers to questions, doing his job, resurrecting his career.

When he steps to the bedroom window, Lyon nods slightly, approvingly, at the arrival of dawn.

14

BUT DAWN BRINGS NO COMFORT TO THE HERMIT ARRIV-
ing just now at his shack, located on the far side of
Rosebush Ridge, a hard three-hour hike from the
rental cabin where John Lyon is staying. As soon as
the hermit steps up on his rickety porch he hears the
baby crying, crying in that tired, voice-worn-out way
that means she's been crying most of the night—
maybe ever since he left. *What's wrong with her?* The
hermit looks down at his black dog but it doesn't have
any answers either.

He's tried everything, different formulas and special supplements, vitamins, and just about every kind
of baby medicine you can order, that beleaguered
UPS truck grinding its way to the hermit's shack
two or three times a week with something new for
the baby. But whatever's wrong with her is getting
worse.

For the first three months she was fine except for

that place on the bottom of her spine, and of course her head, which never did seem to be exactly the right size, but at least she ate well and slept through the night. Then a few weeks ago she went off her food and started crying too much. And now the past ten days or so, it's like she's dying.

He hurries into the shack, puts his shotgun in the rack, and run-trots into the back room to change the baby's diaper and offer her a bottle. She drinks less than a third of it before spitting up and resuming her incessant crying. The hermit fusses over her but nothing seems to help. He pinches a bit of skin on her tiny forearm, watching how long it takes the skin to smooth out. She's dehydrating.

He tries to be hard-hearted about these matters, having buried four of these babies on his property in the past five years—and now this one's time has just about come too. In fact he's already thinking about where he's going to put her, maybe under that big cedar on the ridge behind his shack. Or did he already bury one there?

If anyone ever finds out what he's done to these babies, he'll be taken back to the institution and put in that little locked room, spend the rest of his life there, he knows that much. He thought maybe if he kept this last one alive, he could explain what's been happening the past five years. But explanations don't come easy to the hermit.

He's carrying the baby girl around the shack, patting her on the back. He loves the way babies smell. But how would he explain *that,* for example? She's quiet now but he continues carrying her up on his shoulder, still patting her back, humming more to himself than to the baby as he thinks about which of her new outfits he'll dress her in when it comes time to place her deep among the roots of that big cedar tree.

It was the UPS driver who told him about this famous man everybody in town was saying had rented that cabin on the other side of Rosebush Ridge. The hermit can't get television reception where he lives but he knows what TV is of course, he used to watch it all the time back when he lived in the institution and he remembers how men on TV were always explaining things, so the idea was he'd hike over to that rental cabin and see if the famous man couldn't help him explain to people about these babies the hermit's been burying on his property. To the hermit's way of thinking, if it was all just *explained* right then maybe they wouldn't take him away and put him in the little locked room, maybe they would let him stay on his property for the rest of his life. He'd promise people he'd never cause trouble again if they would just make sure no more babies came his way.

But after that TV man went driving away crazy-like on the logging road, the hermit caught up with him over at the rental cabin and saw enough through that kitchen window to realize the famous TV man had his own problems. At least the hermit never touched the babies after they were in their burying boxes, not like that TV man was doing to that black woman in *her* burying box—touching her with one hand and touching himself with the other hand. Mother always said you'd go to hell for doing something like that.

He puts the baby in her bed in the back room and then collects the dogs' bowls and begins his morning chores.

He's tired of burying babies and scared that he's

either going back to the institution or going to hell. One thing he'd like to have explained to people, one way of looking at it, you could say he's just giving those babies back to God. But even if he had a TV man doing the explaining, the hermit is almost sure people *won't* look at it that way.

15

DRIVING OUT OF THE MOUNTAINS THAT MONDAY MORN-
ing, July 2, easily finding each of the turnoffs marked
by a tree with red paint on it, John Lyon is buoyant.
The visuals on this story are going to be terrific, all
these ridgelines and hills that fold in on you, giving
this area a hidden enchantment that exactly matches
the otherworldly events of last night—*perfect*. Lyon
can *see* the segment's opening (hell, the network might
even make this into a special): a shot of the cabin at
twilight, kerosene lantern flickering in a window, a
hand-held camera walking the viewer up to the cabin's door, into the kitchen, a lingering close-up on the
closed crate while Lyon delivers the voice-over, describing how it felt to be all alone in that cabin with a
mysterious crate which he finally opened to find a
comatose woman. Dynamite stuff.

And now that Lyon is hot on a story he feels none of
the inner turmoil or bitterness or world-weariness that
seemed to be dominating his life just one week ago.

He's not going to bust out crying or laughing anymore, by God, he's a *journalist* again. Lyon drives all the way off the mountain without coming to any tree blocking the road, realizing again how truly lost he was last night.

It's 8:00 A.M. when Lyon reaches Hameln, a mean little coal town with outskirts of shacks and trailers perched on hillsides, the main residential area a tight collection of formerly grand (and formerly white) houses on small lots at the bases of the surrounding hills, the three-block commercial strip almost entirely boarded up—a town where a rental car with New York plates causes people to stop and stare.

Hameln is, however, the county seat. The sheriff's office is in the basement of the only major structure in town with its windows not broken out—the county courthouse.

Lyon finds a public telephone in one of the courthouse corridors and places a call to a network producer he's worked with half a dozen times. When he finally gets the producer on the line, Lyon describes as coolly as he can the events of last night, Claire Cept's charges against Quinndell, and Lyon's plans on how he's going to start an investigation into those charges. The producer says "uh-huh" a lot.

"I know what you must be thinking," Lyon tells him, "considering my performance a week ago Sunday and then my sudden disappearance, but after I talk with the sheriff I'm going to fax you his report on that woman who's in a coma—she's still out there at the cabin—then I'm going over to the county hospital and talk with people who knew Claire Cept and Dr. Quinndell. I'll dig out all the old records, interview the mothers of those children who died under Quinndell's care—"

The producer interrupts to say he doesn't think it's a very good idea for Lyon to be going around representing himself as on assignment from the network when that is not, in fact, the case.

"All I'm asking from you right now," Lyon replies, "is to keep an open mind. If I come up with something solid to go on, make your judgment then whether any of this is worth pursuing."

Lyon continues pressing his case with such unemotional clarity and logic that the producer finally agrees to "kick it around" with a few people and find out if the network can commit any resources to the story. "But first, John, I'll need to talk to the sheriff myself. After you file your report and after he looks into the matter. You understand, don't you? I mean, this whole thing's going to have to be *confirmed.*"

That hurt, to hear how totally his credibility has been destroyed. But he suspects the real reason he's not trusted now is that he was never liked or particularly trusted in the past, even when his reliability was absolute. Always too much of a loner, too private. But Lyon tightens up and doesn't let the hurt show in his voice. "Absolutely," he tells the producer. "I understand totally."

"Why didn't you bring her in with you?" is the first question Sheriff Stone asks after listening to Lyon's account.

Lyon doesn't have an answer. In fact, he can't even manage to speak and knows he must be looking at the sheriff with a dumbfounded expression.

Sheriff Stone uses Lyon's silence to press the matter. "If that woman was in a coma or drugged, seems to me you'd want to get medical attention for her ASAP. I can understand you not being able to drive her to a hospital last night, heck even I get lost in those mountains—but why didn't you bring her in with you this morning?"

Why *didn't* I? That would've been the logical thing to do, the right thing. It didn't even occur to me to put her in the car this morning. Because I was more interested in getting to work on *the story.*

"Mr. Lyon?"

His mind is in such a muddle over this that he can do nothing but continue staring dumbly at the sheriff.

At first Lyon was relieved to discover that Sheriff Mike Stone was not beer-bellied or heavily armed or beetle-browed, that he was in fact a transplanted Washington, D.C., yuppie with sandy-blond hair, clean fingernails, and an obvious affinity for L.L. Bean. But now Lyon feels intimidated by the sheriff's bland good looks and relative sophistication.

"You all right, Mr. Lyon?"

Last time someone asked him that, he was sobbing on the set and couldn't answer. I'm *not* going to lose it again, Lyon tells himself. "Yeah, I'm fine. I *should have* brought her in with me this morning. Why don't you make arrangements for an ambulance and we'll continue talking on the way out to the cabin."

"Sure." But now it's the sheriff who seems in no hurry to get the woman to a hospital. "All that stuff that happened to you last night, is it connected to some story you're working on?"

Lyon hasn't told Stone about Claire Cept or her accusations against Dr. Quinndell. "I can't really go into the details of that right now. Maybe you should be calling an ambulance, it'll take a while for us to get to the cabin and if the woman does need medical help—"

Ignoring this, Stone says, "I told you I wasn't a

native. Followed a girlfriend down here from Washington and then decided to stay on. What I didn't tell you is that I was in the Reagan White House."

"Really?" Lyon tries to act suitably impressed but is distracted by his belated concern for that woman lying in a coma out at the cabin.

"Yeah, worked on speeches, position papers. I wasn't even thirty yet and I was impacting on domestic policy and international relations. Heady stuff. We called ourselves the Conservative Corps, those of us who were under forty, true believers. We thought we were going to change the world. Then the Bush people came in." Stone makes a sour face.

"Must have been fascinating. Maybe we can talk about it on the way—"

"You know how I got elected sheriff, an outsider running in the primary against a couple good ol' boys? One thing and one thing only did the trick—my slogan. *Mike Stone: Hard On Crime.*" He laughs. "Talk about your subliminal messages! Of course this job doesn't pay enough to live on so I'm still doing income tax returns, but I *am* on the bottom rung of a ladder that I expect to climb all the way to Congress. Hameln's the place to start 'cause there's no competition here. The point being, Mr. Lyon, someone like you, connected at the network and all, I'll really bend over backwards to cooperate with you any way I can. Then maybe I could ask *you* for a favor someday. But first I have to know what you're working on, why you're here."

Lyon can't figure out if Stone is dumb—laying out that business about doing each other favors in such a crude fashion—or if he's only playing dumb. Lyon finally decides he has to tell the sheriff *something*. "I'm here looking into some charges against one of your local doctors. And if you can help me, I could see you getting some significant air time, definitely."

Stone doesn't miss a beat. "Dr. Quinndell, right?"

Lyon nods. "You know what he's being accused of?"

"Sure, killing babies," Stone replies quickly, almost jocularly. "I can't imagine how you got interested, though. It's an old story, it's been investigated, and as far as I know there's nothing to the charges." The sheriff pauses, staring at Lyon. "I saw you on TV a week ago this past Sunday."

Lyon decides to brass it out. "I had a breakdown. But that's all over with now."

"Miracle recovery, huh?"

Before Lyon can reply, the sheriff stands and announces he's going to another room to call the volunteer rescue squad. "Soon as they get assembled they'll swing by here and follow us out to your cabin."

It's only after the sheriff leaves that Lyon wonders why the call has to be made from another room. He notices one of the lights on the sheriff's telephone blinking on. After fifteen or twenty seconds it goes off and then comes on a second time, staying on for over a minute. Why two calls?

When Stone returns, Lyon immediately asks him, "Did you have trouble reaching the rescue squad?"

"No." Stone appears confused by the question until he returns to the chair behind his government surplus desk and glances at the row of lights on his telephone —then he looks up quickly at Lyon.

Lyon is smiling at him.

Stone acknowledges the smile with one of his own, then asks, "How'd you come to rent that particular cabin?"

"It was recommended by a friend."

"What was her name?"

"I didn't say it was a woman."

The sheriff nods and Lyon understands for the first time how much Stone is enjoying all this cat-and-mousing.

"You know I'm kind of surprised the network didn't put you on medical leave after what happened right there on camera and everything. Why don't you give me the name of someone I can call at the network, you know just to confirm you're down here on official assignment—all right?"

Determined not to be intimidated, Lyon replies, "Why don't we go out to the cabin and make sure that woman gets safely to a hospital, then I'll have my producer call *you*—all right?"

Before Stone can speak, a rescue truck with various of its lights flashing pulls into the parking lot and stops near a window to the sheriff's basement office.

On the way to the cabin Stone tells various anecdotes about the adventures he's had being a sheriff. "I have a deputy working for me," Stone is saying at one point, "and, Mr. Lyon, if you had a stereotype in mind of a rural county law enforcement officer, I guarantee you that Carl fits it to a tee. I mean, we're talking *Deliverance* material here. One time Carl stopped an out-of-stater for speeding on a county road. Guy was a businessman, going five or ten miles over the limit, but Carl approaches the car like it's filled with Colombian drug dealers. Asks the businessman where he's from and the guy says Chicago. Upon hearing that, Carl draws his sidearm and tells the guy to get out of the car and assume the position. The businessman, terrified, he asks what's the problem,

Officer, and Carl says, 'You say you're from Chicago, huh?' Businessman tells him that's correct. Carl says, 'Okay then, asshole, what's them Illinois plates doing on your car?' "

When he turns to Lyon to get his reaction, Stone sees that Lyon has fallen asleep. The sheriff doesn't awaken him until they're pulling into the clearing in front of the cabin.

Lyon apologizes. "Got no sleep last night, zero."

"No problem." Stone stops the car, gets out, directs the rescue truck where to park, and then instructs the three-man medical crew to stay on the porch until he has had a chance to check out the cabin.

When Lyon starts to enter the cabin with the sheriff, Stone tells him, "I want you to wait out here too, Mr. Lyon."

After Stone goes inside, the three rescue workers talk among themselves, occasionally laughing, keeping their distance from Lyon, who is sufficiently baffled by their thick country accents that he can't follow what they're talking about. If the three men recognize him from television, they're acting pointedly unimpressed.

When Stone returns to the porch his face is so grim that Lyon knows immediately what has happened: the woman's dead. *I should have brought her into town with me this morning!* "She was alive when I left," he tells Stone urgently. "Her pulse was strong, she was breathing just fine, I assumed—"

"What did you do with the crate?"

"The crate? I didn't do anything with it, left it in the kitchen—why?"

"And the woman was in the bedroom, right?"

"Yes! What's—"

"Well she's not there now. No sign of any crate or coffin in the kitchen either."

Lyon brushes past the sheriff and rushes into the kitchen. No crate. He turns and runs back past the front door, through the living room, into the bedroom.

When the sheriff comes in he finds Lyon standing there looking at the empty bed.

"Wait a second," Lyon says. "I locked the front door when I left this morning but you walked right in. Someone's been here, took the woman *and* the crate."

"Who? That little man you told me about, the one who was peeking in the window?"

"Yes! I guess. I don't know." Lyon is becoming frantic. "Someone's trying to discredit me and . . . did you look in the bathroom, the closets? Maybe there's a—"

Stone takes him gently by the upper arm. "I checked everyplace, Mr. Lyon. No woman, no crate. You know, if you're not used to these mountains, staying out here by yourself, your mind can play tricks on you. You'd be surprised the reports I get from city people who are camping and think they—"

"There was a woman here, goddamn it! And some little guy with a weird face *did* look in through the kitchen window. He had this huge dog with him, some kind of fucking wolfdog—"

Lyon is interrupted when one of the three rescue workers who are crowded in the bedroom doorway laughs.

"I'll check the county hospital," Stone says softly. "See if a young black woman was brought in this morning. She didn't have any identification on her?"

"She was naked!"

Two of the rescue workers laugh at that.

"Come on then," Stone tells Lyon. "I'll give you a ride back into town."

As the sheriff and Lyon pass through the bedroom doorway, the rescue workers making way for them, all three of the men openly smirk at the famous John Lyon.

16

ON THE WAY BACK TO HAMELN, LYON PRETENDS TO BE sleeping so he won't have to talk to the sheriff, then as soon as they drive onto the county building's gravel parking lot, Lyon "awakens," thanks Stone, and gets out of the patrol car without further comment.

He's just reaching his rental car when the sheriff calls to him. "Hey, were you in a wreck? Looks fresh."

Lyon glances down at the dents and scrapes where he sideswiped a tree last night trying to get away from the staring eyes of that dog. "Hit a tree," he tells Stone.

The sheriff walks over and stands next to him, both men now examining the damage. "You do it coming in this morning?" Stone asks.

"No, last night. When I was trying to get off that mountain."

"You didn't tell me about that, John. Leaving anything else out?"

Since when did it become *John*, Lyon wonders.

And, yeah, he thinks, I'm leaving out the part where I fondled the woman while she was still in the box, while I was still thinking she was a corpse—I lied to you, *Mike,* when I said I knew the woman was alive all along, because for the longest time I assumed she was dead but I *still* fondled her breasts, kneeling there on the kitchen floor feeling her up with one hand and jerking off with the other like the true necrophiliac I apparently am. Lyon experiences a clenching deep in his gut, a sudden anguish.

"John?"

"No, Sheriff, I'm not leaving anything out."

"What're your plans now?"

"Get something to eat."

"There's a diner just up the street. Why don't you check back with me after you have breakfast, huh? I'll give the state police a call, talk to the hospital, check with some local doctors—see if anyone has a line on a young black woman who's been in a coma or has been reported missing, whatever. Okay?"

"Sure."

"Take care now."

Lyon bites back the impulse to break down and confess everything.

The day's already hot, Lyon sweating as he walks three blocks to an old-fashioned greasy spoon containing four booths and a six-stool counter. He orders the kind of breakfast he hasn't eaten in more than a decade: fried eggs, sausage patties, home fries, buttered white toast, a large glass of whole milk, and cup after cup of strong, black coffee. Looking at the breakfast when it arrives on the bone-gray oval plate, Lyon figures that if the food were scraped into a winepress and squeezed dry, it would easily yield a full cup of grease. But he's so famished he eats the breakfast the way the four other men in the diner are eating theirs, leaning over his plate and forking it in without looking left or right.

When he's done, his stomach feels as if it's been inflated like a basketball. Lyon looks around and notices that the four other patrons, finished with their breakfasts too, have lighted cigarettes and are openly glaring at him. Lyon is accustomed to being recognized of course, but these stares aren't the usual ones, these are more hostile than curious.

It's easy enough to catalog the differences between Lyon and the four men watching him. In spite of the duress he was under this morning, Lyon took time to shave and then to comb his seventy-five-dollar haircut; the four men are all bearded and have long hair sticking out from ball caps displaying the logos of farm equipment and cattle feed. Lyon is wearing Dock-Sides without socks, chinos, and a hundred-dollar white shirt; they have on work boots made in Korea, jeans from Mexico, and Taiwan workshirts. Whether they recognize him from television is not the issue—John Lyon is a stranger from the city and, in this part of West Virginia, city strangers have always come here looking for something to *take*. They've taken these men's land, the coal under their land, the timber growing *on* their land, taken their labor and their way of life. City strangers mean trouble from the law and from the government. The four men in that diner know instinctively that whatever has brought John Lyon here, it's not going to do them any good.

Lyon wants to leave—now even the waitress is standing behind the counter with her arms crossed, staring at him—but he hasn't decided what to do or where to go next.

Sipping his coffee, which has a grease slick over its entire surface, Lyon figures there are two ways of looking at what's happened. First, assuming that Dr. Quinndell is behind the placement of that woman in the cabin and then her removal, this probably means Quinndell is guilty of *something,* is running scared, and it's all going to make for a hell of a story when Lyon finally gets to the bottom of it. The second way of looking at it, however, is that the woman's disappearance has effectively blocked Lyon's investigation, because he can't bring in the resources of the network until Sheriff Stone or some responsible third party confirms what happened last night.

As he downs the last of his greasy coffee Lyon realizes there's a *third* way of looking at his situation: that he's lost his mind.

When Lyon finally moves out of his booth, the diner's four customers and the waitress suddenly find other places to put their eyes. The bill comes to under four dollars, tax included. Be lucky to get a cup of coffee and bagel for that in New York, Lyon thinks.

As he waits at the counter for his change, Lyon notices a local telephone book, which strikes him as a child-size version of a "real" phone book, not big enough to list New York City's podiatrists. He flips through the pages, finding three names under *Q,* the last of those "Quinndell, Dr. Mason, 650 S. 16th St."

After the waitress hands him his change, Lyon gives her back a dollar tip and asks, "Can you tell me where six-fifty Sixteenth Street is, can I walk there from here?"

"We don't go by street numbers."

"Dr. Quinndell's house."

She looks momentarily panicked, glancing at one

particularly hairy customer sitting three stools down from the cash register—then the waitress shakes her head and turns away from Lyon.

He leaves the diner and stands out on the sidewalk looking for street signs, seeing none. When someone grasps his arm, Lyon whirls around to confront the heavily bearded, shaggy-haired man who was sitting at the counter. "Don't put your hands on me," Lyon says, unsure why he's reacting with such hostility.

The man immediately releases Lyon's arm. "Sorry." He seems to be about forty years old but it's difficult to tell for sure with all that hair coming down to his eyes and then the bushy beard covering the lower part of his face.

"What do you want?" Lyon asks, his voice still edged.

"People in there ain't going to help you. Quinndell's got 'em buffaloed. You're here from TV, right?"

Lyon nods.

"I'd like to see you hang that bastard out to dry. Hell, I was even rooting for the nigger woman to nail his ass. He raped my daughter."

"Quinndell?"

"Yeah Quinndell. She had a job working for him, stopping by after school cleaning his house, and he got her cornered in a room one afternoon, ripping her clothes and getting her down on the floor. Then after he did it he warned her if she told anybody he'd ruin her. That's the way he operates. She told her mom anyway and her mom told me. We're separated. She was only fourteen."

"Did you bring charges?"

"Well, first I went over to see him my own self and he came at me with a spoon."

"A spoon?"

The man pushes back his cap and lifts the hair from his forehead to show Lyon a vivid scar just above his right eyebrow. "You wouldn't think a spoon could do so much damage, would you? If you let him get close enough he'll go for your eyes ever time." The man releases his hair and pulls his cap down low.

"Why didn't you report this to Sheriff Stone?"

"I *did*. But Quinndell got to Stone first, accused me of attacking him, said he had to defend himself. Stone never even arrested him for what he did to my little girl and then I was the one ended up doing thirty days on the county, lost my job and was out of work six months because of it. I say go get him, mister—put his ass on TV and make him sweat. His street is four blocks down, then hang a right and his house is that big three-story white job in the middle of the block, red shutters, you can't miss it, only house in town with a fresh paint job."

The man turns to leave but Lyon stops him. "I'll have a camera crew here in a few days, if you'd give me your name perhaps we could—"

"I ain't going on TV, not against Quinndell I ain't. I got to *live* here."

"Let me ask you about something else then. Last night I was staying at a rental cabin about eighteen miles—"

"Yeah, I know where you're staying, everbody in town does. Man at the hardware store been talking about it for a couple of days now. That cabin was owned by the nigger nurse who went after Quinndell."

"Claire Cept, it's *her* cabin?"

"Used to be. She lost it when she went bankrupt, lost everything when she and Quinndell was suing each other back and forth, hell he sued her black ass three or four different ways."

Lyon takes a moment to digest this but then speaks quickly when he notices that the man is nervously shifting his weight, eager to leave. "Do you know anything about a strange little man who lives out in those mountains? He—"

"Randolph Welby."

Lyon is astonished. "Does he have any connection to Claire Cept or Dr. Quinndell? Can you take me to his house?"

The man laughs. "Mister, you don't want to be visiting that old hermit, guarantee you don't. He'll feed you to his dogs."

"But I think he might have been sent to the cabin to harass me—and maybe Dr. Quinndell was the one who sent him."

"I don't know about any of that." The man pauses, weighing a decision. "But I know who might know. Come on, Charlie's place ain't far from here, I'll take you there."

"Charlie?"

"Yeah," the man replies, laughing, "he'll tell you all about Randolph and the owl eaters."

17

THE DIRT YARD IN FRONT OF THE TRAILER IS POPULATED with a wild variety of concrete figures: tiny deer with ears missing, garishly green frogs in decidedly unfroglike poses, somewhat realistic poultry (chickens, ducks, geese), and thirty different species of malevolent gnomes and evil dwarfs that look like they might have been created by Walt Disney during a particularly nasty acid trip.

To find this place, Lyon and the man from the diner walked down to a dry creek, following it for a hundred yards before making their way up the other side, through waist-high weeds, crossing several empty lots, coming finally to this tiny trailer set high on concrete blocks.

"He'll sell you anything in this yard," the man tells Lyon, "except for them gnomes and dwarfs, which he collects for himself."

"And this man's name again?"

"Charlie Renfro. He's an old fart and he don't always make sense to talk to but he knows them mountains where Randolph Welby lives better'n anybody. Some people say Charlie is an artist in concrete, I don't see it myself."

The man who opens the door to the small trailer is in his eighties, short and round and white-haired. He listens carefully—head tilted, eyes cast down—as he's told who Lyon is and why he's been brought here: to get information on the hermit Randolph Welby.

The old man finally looks at Lyon and then nods to indicate that he both understands the assignment and is accepting it. After Lyon's guide leaves, Charlie hauls two plastic-webbed lawn chairs out of the trailer, sitting in one of them and pointing to the other for his guest.

But before Lyon can ask a question, the old man launches:

"Randolph Welby! Yessir, I know him better than most. He's a full-blood hermit. Lives so far back in them hills he has to have his sunshine *piped* in."

Charlie Renfro pauses, looking slyly at Lyon with a half-grin, the old man's nearly transparently blue eyes glistening—Lyon finally understanding that he's supposed to laugh at the witticism. He does.

Charlie continues. "I expect you want to know about Randolph Welby and the owl eaters."

"Owl eaters?"

"Randolph Welby is old enough that he knew Caesar when Caesar was a corporal." Charlie waits for his laugh before continuing. "He's so old and wrinkled and ugly and *little* that I could set him down in this yard here and tell him not to move and you wouldn't be able to tell him apart from my art."

"Your art?"

"I make everything you see here and everything you see here is for sale except the gnomes and dwarfs. I collect 'em."

"Yes, that's what—"

"Randolph Welby owns something like three hundred acres, most of it logged over and too steep to farm, I grant you, but even at a hundred dollars an acre, you figure it out—where does he get all that money?"

"Do you know if he has any connection to—"

"Word is he was left a fortune by his high-tone mother. Or he's some kind of insane genius, made a bundle inventing weird stuff for the space program or the H-bomb and then moved out into the mountains to get away from people 'cause they was always making fun of his size and the way he looks. Or maybe he runs a still or grows mari-ja-wanna or raises a particularly fierce line of bear dog and sells them down to Kentucky."

"I think I might have seen one of those dogs last—"

"I myself however am of the opinion—generally ridiculed in other quarters I grant you—that Randolph Welby acquired his fortune by setting up trade with the owl eaters."

"The owl eaters?"

"Many have gone looking for Randolph's shack but few have found it and fewer still have lived to tell the tale."

Lyon smiles, realizing now that he's hearing a story that is part of the old liar's stock and trade. Before Lyon can decide if it's worth listening to any more of this nonsense, Charlie launches again.

"Even deer poachers—meat hunters, they're called, freezer fillers, not sportsmen—avoid Goose Creek, the Rosebush Mountain area where old Randolph owns all those vertical acres of his. First off he knows them hills and hollers and sink holes and all them limestone caves better than any man, snake alive. Especially the caves. Word is he's got them all mapped out and memorized in his mind so that if he wanted to he could walk one of his dogs down to Kentucky without ever seeing the sun. Even goes into those caves without a light, doesn't need one, and he's tunneled into the abandoned coal shafts that snake through this whole area, making it possible for Randolph Welby to proceed underground just about any-place he pleases hereabouts, even to popping up outside your window one night and slitting your throat so's you wake up dead the next morning." The old man cackles.

Wearying of this and put off by the reference to Randolph Welby popping up outside his window, Lyon tells Charlie he appreciates the information but he's running late and must—

"A confirmed black powder man, Randolph fills that old muzzle-loading shotgun of his with bent nails and rusty bobwire so that if the shooting doesn't kill you, lockjaw will. Fond of booby traps too, wire snares and iron jaws. Once he catches you he'll truss you up like a Christmas turkey and tuck you away in some cave where you won't be heard of 'til come Judgment Day or maybe he'll feed you to them bear dogs of his, a couple pounds of your tender meat at a time. I'll sell you one of them Heartsick Frogs for twelve-fifty and I don't charge tax either."

Lyon laughs. "Actually, Mr. Renfro, what I really wanted to find out was if there is any connection between Randolph Welby and Dr. Quinndell."

"Quinndell kills babies, everybody knows that."

Lyon is stunned to hear this declaration—but then

wonders what he can possibly do with it. Tell his producer he has two sources now, one of them a woman who handed Lyon a voodoo doll before killing herself in front of a cab and the other source an old man who makes concrete frogs? Besides, Charlie is undoubtedly just repeating the accusations that everyone here knew Claire had lodged against Quinndell. Still, Lyon feels obligated to ask "What makes you think Dr. Quinndell kills babies?"

"The hermit Randolph Welby gives them babies to the owl eaters and in exchange the owl eaters give ol' Randolph tree moss ferns, ginseng, mushrooms, roots, herbs, and other forest products that the hermit sells via UPS to regional dealers, thereby making enough money to buy all those up and down acres of his."

"So you're saying there *is* some connection between Randolph Welby and Dr. Quinndell? Quinndell kills the babies, gives the bodies to the hermit for disposal, in those caves—is that what you mean?"

After listening carefully to Lyon, Charlie resumes his own story, apparently unaware of any link between what Lyon is asking and what he, Charlie, is relating. "Them owl eaters haven't even full evolved yet into human beans or else they have kinda reverted, wearing animal skins and eating owls, they're such little people you could snip off both hands of a owl eater with a pair of your grandmother's sewing scissors, put both of them hands in a shot glass, pour in the whiskey, and still have plenty of room to get drunk. If it wasn't for getting those little hands of theirs on other people's babies them owl eaters wouldn't be able to perpetrate themselves."

As he stands, Lyon says, "Okay, then, Mr. Renfro. Thanks again for all the information. I have to be going now." Lyon reaches down and shakes the old man's hand.

Charlie Renfro is smiling, his transparent blue eyes still looking happy and eager. "You ain't going to buy anything from me, are you?"

You old fraud, Lyon thinks. Making up tales for the tourists, charming them into buying your concrete art. What the hell. "I'll take the smallest frog you have."

"Twelve-fifty, don't matter the size when it comes to frogs. That one over there I call Heartsick. See how he's got his little hands folded over his heart. He's pining for lost love. I could tell you his story too."

"That's all right." Lyon gives the old man two bills, a ten and a five.

Charlie quickly pockets the fifteen bucks, saying, "What with tax and handling and all, that'll just about do it."

Lyon laughs, walks over and picks up the hideous little frog, surprised by how heavy it is. When he turns to tell the old man goodbye one last time, Charlie says:

"Three things a body would never want to do. Never kill a owl anywhere near where Randolph Welby lives. And *never* go into a cave with that little hermit."

Lyon waits a moment. Then bites. "What's the third?"

"Huh?"

"You said there were three things a body would never want to do."

Charlie looks up as if searching the sky for what that third thing might be. He apparently finds it there, telling Lyon with some authority, "Never try to get information out of a UPS man."

"What?"

"Word is that the UPS man is the only outsider ol'

Randolph ever sees or talks to, them shit-brown trucks making deliveries to his shack 'bout ever other day, God knows what the little dwarf is ordering. Maybe elevator shoes."

Lyon laughs.

But the old man has turned suddenly serious. "So what you're thinking is, if you could ever find out what the UPS is delivering to Randolph, you'd know the answer to the hermit's secret. And you are absolutely right about that. But never try to get information out of a UPS man. They wear uniforms and are trained to withstand torture."

18

MAYBE IT'S SOMETHING IN THE WATER, LYON THINKS AS he tries to find his way back, walking through weeds and empty lots.

The day has become seriously hot, an amazing array of bugs tormenting him as he finally reaches the dry creekbed, crossing it however at a spot he doesn't recognize. More junky lots, more bugs, more sweating —but then he eventually reaches a residential neighborhood.

Lyon continues walking, heading in what he believes is the general direction of the diner and the county building. He feels foolish carrying the thirty-five-pound concrete frog and thinks maybe he'll leave it in someone's yard. He's just about to do that in fact when he notices a house in the middle of the block: three stories, painted a brilliant white, red shutters. Quinndell's place.

Lyon approaches it with a mixture of curiosity and dread. He certainly doesn't want to bump into the doctor *now,* before Lyon has had a chance to talk with anyone at the hospital or has identified the comatose black woman. The thing to do is cross over here and pass the house from the safety of the other side of the street.

Still carrying the concrete frog, Lyon is just stepping into the street when a woman comes from around the corner of Quinndell's house. She's tall, blond, wearing very short red shorts and a white halter top; she's dragging a watering hose.

When she catches him staring at her, the woman gives Lyon a friendly wave and cheery "Hello!"

He says "Hi" back and thinks, nice legs.

With Lyon now in the middle of the quiet residential street, the woman drops the hose and comes to the sidewalk. "Nice frog."

Looking down at the concrete creation in his arms, Lyon can't figure out how to explain it.

She's motioning for him to join her on the sidewalk. "Would you like to see Dr. Quinndell now?"

Lyon is nonplussed.

The woman is still smiling broadly. "Sometimes a car comes down this street."

Lyon checks both ways and then, red-faced, goes to the sidewalk. Up close, the woman looks hard-edged and too carefully made up for yard work— looks in fact like an aging model who used to work industrial trade shows. Fine lines radiate from those green eyes and her neck has begun to go crepey, and you can tell by the way she makes up her face and keeps her hair too blond and too fluffed that she's still trying to hold on to an image she had of herself a decade or so ago when she wowed conventioneers by being named that year's Miss Crescent Wrench.

Her smile, however, seems genuine enough. "Come on in, Dr. Quinndell is expecting you."

Lyon finally finds his voice. "I think you're mistaken. I didn't make an appointment. I mean, I'm not a patient."

"Oh, Dr. Quinndell doesn't have any patients."

They both laugh.

She steps closer to him. "Come on, I'll show you the way, Mr. Lyon."

"You recognize me," he says—a statement, not a question.

"Sure. And Dr. Quinndell *is* expecting you."

"But he can't be, I haven't talked to him."

"You'll have to take that up with the doctor," she says, linking her arm with Lyon's and leading him toward the house. "Do you take your frog with you everywhere you go?"

"I just bought it," he mumbles. When they reach the porch, Lyon says, *"Wait.* I can't go in."

The woman flashes him another of her bright smiles. "Why not?"

"I don't . . . uh, I'm not . . ."

"You're in town to interview him aren't you?"

"Well, that's something I'm really not—"

She tugs good-naturedly on his arm. "Come on, he just wants to meet you."

He allows himself to be taken into the house and down the central hallway, panicking when the woman stops by a set of dark mahogany doors. He realizes he is indeed about to be introduced to the doctor. "I'm not prepared to meet Dr. Quinndell just yet. *Please.* I'll call and make an appointment. What's your name?"

"Mary. Mary Aurora. I work for the doctor."

"As?"

"As chauffeur, secretary, traveling companion, reader—"

"Reader?"

"Sure." She reaches for the door. "He's right in there waiting for you."

"He *can't* be waiting for me, I haven't made an appointment to see him. I shouldn't even have come in here with you." And to emphasize that, Lyon pulls his arm away from hers. "I'll call—"

He's interrupted when a deep voice comes from somewhere behind those double doors. "Mary? Who's out there with you?"

Lyon frantically shakes his head, a signal Mary blithely ignores. "It's John Lyon."

"Well by all means show him in!"

Lyon's heart sinks as Mary opens one of the double doors and holds it for him. The room is completely dark, but Mary is standing there still smiling, nodding encouragement. "Go on," she says as if speaking to a shy child.

As soon as Lyon takes a step into that dark room, the door closes behind him.

"I hope you don't mind," comes a honeyed voice somewhere in the room.

A faint light showing around the edges of a heavy set of curtains helps Lyon make out certain shapes, bookcases and tables and a few overstuffed chairs, but he still can't see who has spoken. "Dr. Quinndell?"

"I feel more comfortable, at less of a disadvantage, if the first few minutes of our meeting can be conducted like this, but if you find it absolutely unbearable I will of course turn on the lights."

The voice is pleasant, almost theatrical in its resonance, and cultured in the fashion of a courtly Southern gentleman.

Lyon takes a few tentative steps toward the voice, putting his hand out until he comes to the back of a large chair. He rests the frog there. "How could you have been expecting me?"

The voice chuckles. "Well, I'm tempted to say, 'Elementary, my dear Watson,' but I'll resist that particular cliché. I was informed you had rented a cabin—a cabin once owned by someone I think we both know—and I *assumed* that I am the reason for your visit to our area. Is that assumption incorrect?"

Lyon's not sure what to say. "Normally I would have called for an appointment."

"But you just happened to be in the neighborhood?"

"Yes!" Lyon replies too quickly. He laughs nervously. "I was walking by and—"

The lights flash on, causing Lyon to squint toward the back of the room where Dr. Quinndell is standing behind a large desk.

Mason Quinndell looks like one of the Barrymore men in their glory days, a jutting chin and a long straight nose, black hair combed back, his face so dramatically handsome that it's almost a caricature of an old-fashioned matinee idol.

He's dressed in an expensive pinstriped suit, his shirt very white and heavily starched. His black hair curls fashionably at the shirt's collar, and he's wearing onyx cufflinks. The doctor's presentation is so perfect that Lyon—still sweaty from his walk, standing there balancing that thirty-five-pound concrete frog on the back of a chair—feels awkward and inferior.

"Mr. Lyon?"

When he notices that the doctor is holding out his hand, Lyon lifts the frog from the chairback and hurries to the desk. While shaking hands with Quinndell and trying to figure out how he's going to explain the frog, Lyon sees that the doctor's unnaturally blue eyes don't quite focus on him.

"Surely you knew I was blind."

Lyon doesn't reply.

Quinndell laughs. "Goodness, Claire must be slipping, she's usually more than eager to explain how my blindness is the result of God's vengeance. She didn't go into that with you?"

Lyon still doesn't reply. When he tries to withdraw his hand, Quinndell won't release it. The doctor is grinning, showing his one physical flaw: teeth so small they look as if they should be in a child's mouth, as if they've been filed down, the enamel stained yellow.

When Lyon again tries to get his hand free, Quinndell holds it all the more tightly. "I'm going to have to insist that you answer me aloud when I ask a question, Mr. Lyon. Head shaking, chin nodding, face making, eye rolling—all lost on me I'm afraid."

Then the doctor waits.

"Of course, I'm sorry."

Quinndell releases his hand. "You're sorry?"

"I mean I understand."

Quinndell sits behind his desk and Lyon takes a straight-backed chair in front of the desk, placing the concrete frog at his feet. At least I don't have to explain the frog, Lyon thinks.

"We'll see if we can't get through this as painlessly as possible," the doctor says, as if reassuring a patient on whom he is about to begin some potentially troublesome procedure.

Lyon nods but then quickly adds, "All right." He

senses he has already relinquished control of the conversation.

"Claire must have made a deep impression on you because you're the first one actually to come here and visit me in person." Quinndell again offers his yellow, tiny-toothed smile.

"The first one to visit you in person? I don't—"

"It's all in here," Quinndell says, lifting a thick folder from his desk and holding it out to Lyon. "In the past five years Claire has managed to convince three individuals to look into those ghastly charges she has lodged against me. Two newspaper reporters and one gentleman from a Charleston television station. Their names and telephone numbers are in the folder. None of them got past making a few calls before dropping their so-called investigations. The results of their initial inquiries were so conclusively in my favor that two of the three wrote me letters of apology. Copies of those are in the file too. You're the first of Claire's contacts who ever bothered to visit me in person. What *did* she say to you, Mr. Lyon?"

Lyon is still staring at the doctor's impressive bearing and perfect clothing. Claire's file says that Quinndell is sixty-one but he looks a decade younger, Lyon's age.

"Mr. Lyon, please—your silence is rude."

"I'm sorry. I'm wondering if you could give me a little background on—"

"Absolutely not," comes the immediate reply. "Everything you need to know is in that file. Please try to understand my position, Mr. Lyon. I devoted my life to a pediatric medical practice and *that woman* has accused me of *murdering* children. It's obscene. I've tried to feel compassion for her, considering her insanity, but—"

"Her insanity?"

"It's all in the file, Mr. Lyon. The woman is a classic paranoiac, accusing me of murdering children, accusing another doctor of drinking blood."

"Drinking—"

"Surely you've looked into this matter before coming down here. You *are* aware that in the past five years that woman has been fired from *seven* nursing positions at hospitals in Baltimore, Washington, D.C., and New York City."

"No, I wasn't actually—"

"Unforgivable." The doctor pronounces this the way a judge might pass a harsh but justified sentence. "I suppose then you're also unaware of why it was under *my* care that those poor children died." Quinndell pauses but then continues before Lyon can say anything. "All eighteen of the infants Claire cited in her original accusation were the children of destitute families or unwed *girls*. Not women, Mr. Lyon, *girls*. And why was I caring for those infants? Because I allowed the mothers to pay whatever they could afford, usually writing off my fees entirely. The poorest of the poor were among my clients. And who are the victims of this country's abysmal child mortality rate? The poorest of the poor, Mr. Lyon. Their babies do not receive proper nutrition or medical care, and when those babies are brought into the hospital, the situation usually is so acute that it's long past reversal —so of course many of those infants died while officially under my care, even though my care was being offered without charge and usually consisted of a few desperate moments of emergency procedures.

"Five years ago while I was in the middle of defending myself from Claire's obscene charges I was blinded when my optic nerves were damaged during the removal of a brain tumor. Do you know what that woman did when she heard about this? She called me and said she was *glad* I was blind, that God had blinded me but that she wasn't going to give up until the world knew what I had done to those eighteen children. Can you imagine?"

Lyon feels like apologizing but Quinndell doesn't give him a chance.

"Well at least she has an excuse, she's insane. But *you*, Mr. Lyon, what's your excuse? Coming down here to root around in my affairs without having bothered even to make a few rudimentary inquiries into the substance of Claire's charges, unaware that Claire has accused other doctors of outlandish atrocities, unaware that she is too mentally unbalanced to hold a job—Mr. Lyon your presence here is a disgrace. I know you won a Pulitzer as a young man but your actions in this case surely qualify you for a prize as the World's Worst Reporter."

Lyon couldn't agree more. If it were possible for him to melt into a small puddle and then seep back out under those double doors, he would do so immediately.

"Here's what happens next, Mr. Lyon. If you mention to anyone else that you're here investigating me, as you told Sheriff Stone this morning, I will bring legal action against you and your employer. This is not an idle threat I assure you. I have in fact won legal redress against Mrs. Cept but her insane zealotry renders those sanctions quite useless."

Lyon can do nothing but continue to stare at Dr. Quinndell, whose too blue glass eyes are opened wide, alarmingly wide.

"You notice I continue referring to Claire in the present tense. I know of course that she died recently.

But she has been such a constant and destructive force in my life that I keep thinking of her as somehow still out there, still harassing me. And in a way she *is,* causing you to come here, for example."

When Quinndell stands he pulls his suit jacket down and adjusts those snowy white French cuffs. Lyon stands too, surprised that he is several inches taller than the doctor, Quinndell's regal bearing having masked this fact when they first shook hands.

With nothing to say in his defense, Lyon is happy to let the doctor do all the talking.

"If my words have been overly harsh, I apologize, but you have no idea what that woman put me through." Quinndell pauses and then continues in a gentler voice. "I've admired your work, Mr. Lyon. I can only listen to you now of course, but I remember seeing you on television, remember being impressed with your civility, your seriousness. So unlike most of your plastic and fawningly superficial colleagues. In fact I've even thought that you and I are similar in some ways, that we are both *gentlemen* in the best and most old-fashioned sense of that word. Also, in spite of the fact that we are meeting now for the first time, you have a face."

"A face?"

"People I meet for the first time, they are of course faceless to me. I have to *imagine* what they look like. But because I watched you on television before I was blinded, in my mind's eye you have a face. Which I find wonderfully comforting. You always reminded me of an actor, William Holden. Has anyone else ever commented on the resemblance?"

"Yes."

"Well then." The doctor holds out his hand, Lyon hurrying to shake it.

"I'm sorry." To his own ears, Lyon sounds pitiful.

"Nonsense. You were somehow taken in by Claire and she apparently got to you at a very awkward time in your life. I'm guessing that your breakdown while reporting that story about murdered children is what brought you and Claire together. For a man of your dignity to lose control in such a public forum—how I feel for you, Mr. Lyon."

Quinndell sounds totally sincere. First he humiliates Lyon and now he's being so gently sympathetic that Lyon feels as if he might start crying.

"These hills and forests of ours can be wonderfully rejuvenating. Why don't you stay in the area and recuperate? Assuming of course that you have been seen by a doctor and have been assured that your emotional problems are not organic in nature. In any case, don't let it break your spirit. You'll emerge from this experience more *potent* than ever. I know, Mr. Lyon, because I underwent a similar crisis and recovery with my blindness. What does not kill us, makes us stronger—yes?"

"Yes."

The doctor works his way around the edge of the desk. "Come, I'll walk you out."

They're halfway to the double doors when Lyon remembers the frog. "I left something by my chair."

"Your briefcase?"

Lyon is back by the chair he was sitting in, lifting the heavy concrete sculpture into his arms with a grunt before he answers. "No, it's, uhm, a frog."

"A frog?"

Lyon begins laughing. "Yeah, other reporters bring notebooks and tape recorders with them but the *World's Worst Reporter* always carries a frog to interviews." Saying this and then seeing Dr. Quinndell's strange astonished expression cracks up Lyon even more.

"You're laughing at me?" Quinndell asks. His voice sounds hurt but edged with anger too.

"No, it's . . . it's just . . ." But Lyon can't go on. His laughter has become an *attack* of laughter—like what happened when he was back in his apartment looking through those newspapers for information on Claire's death. "I'm . . . I'm . . . I . . ." John Lyon once again having lost control, hugging that goddamn frog and shaking with laughter, feeling terrible that Quinndell thinks he's being laughed at but unable to explain to the doctor what's wrong, Lyon laughing too hard to talk.

Quinndell coolly walks past Lyon and returns to his desk where he touches a button that extinguishes all the lights in the room.

Being immersed into abrupt darkness prompts Lyon to regain some control but he's still chuckling, trying to get his breath, the tears of laughter wetting his face. "I'm sorry . . . I haven't had any sleep and . . ."

Suddenly remembering what the man from the diner said about Quinndell going for your eyes, Lyon wonders exactly where the doctor *is*. Still behind his desk?

"Doctor?"

Silence.

There's no laughter left in Lyon now. "Dr. Quinndell, I wasn't laughing at you."

He thinks he hears movement off to his right, well away from the desk. "I'm going now," Lyon says as he turns and heads for the double doors. He bumps into a chair and then, trying to recover, knocks over a small table.

"Sorry."

Still no answer.

And although Lyon doesn't hear any movement in the room, he *senses* the doctor coming for him, gliding through the blackness, Lyon frightened enough that he leaves the table on the floor and runs for the double doors. *Jesus, he's right behind me.*

Frantically searching for and then turning a doorknob, Lyon gets one of the double doors open and lurches so clumsily out into the hallway that he bumps up against the opposite wall.

He turns around and stares into the darkness of that room, seeing nothing. No, wait. The doctor *is* standing there, just out of reach of the hallway's light, Lyon forced to look hard before he can make him out in the shadows: Quinndell standing there pointing at Lyon, something in the doctor's hand, a small metal object, a heavy tablespoon, Dr. Quinndell standing there eerily silent and pointing that spoon with uncanny accuracy at Lyon's face, right at his eyes.

19

Standing in the middle of the center room of Randolph Welby's shack, Sheriff Mike Stone is surprised by all the books and by how clean everything is. From the stories he's heard about Welby (hates people, possibly retarded, dangerous if he catches you on his land) and from the outward appearance of the shack, Stone assumed the hermit's living quarters would be trash-cluttered and filthy. But the place is in fact tidy, the homemade furniture simple but clean, the wide-board pine floors bleached from repeated scrubbings, all those books—how-to books, gardening books, books on survival and dog breeding and baby care—lined up neatly on shelves along every wall. Only the hermit himself lives up to his billing: dressed in clothes that look as if they've been salvaged from a rag bin, under five feet tall, less than a hundred pounds, his chinless weathered face indeed gnomish, baby-fine gray hair wildly uncombed, both ears sticking straight out from the sides of his tiny head.

Trying to get information out of him is a study in frustration, Randolph either refusing to answer or mumbling something so mangled by his speech impediment that Stone can't understand him.

"Let's try yes or no questions," the sheriff finally tells him. "Did you go over to that rental cabin last night—yes or no?"

Randolph is standing by the door to the shack's back room, his hands folded in front of him, staring at the floor—looking like a contrite, albeit ancient, schoolchild. "I bewieve so," he finally whispers.

"What? You *believe* so? Is that what you said? Excellent! Now we're getting someplace. You heard that John Lyon was staying in that cabin, John Lyon from television, and you went over to speak to him—yes or no?" Stone leans against one of the posts holding up the ceiling.

"I bewieve so."

"Good, good. What did you go over there to speak to him *about?*"

He looks up at the sheriff with an anguished expression: Randolph knows the answer but can't *explain* it.

Stone shifts his weight away from the post. "All right, that wasn't a yes or no question, sorry. Did you go over to talk to the television man about something you found in a cave near here?"

Randolph returns his gaze to the floor. "I bewieve so."

"And what was it you found?" The sheriff unsnaps the strap holding his revolver in its holster. "Come on, Randolph, I know that's not a yes or no question but surely you can speak a single simple word. What was it you found in that cave?"

Randolph knew something like this was going to

happen. Which is why he wanted that TV man to explain things *for him*—because now the sheriff is going to be asking other questions, not only about what Randolph found in the cave but about what he *did* with what he found and then the sheriff will want an answer to the toughest question of all, *why* did you do it?

"Talk to me, Randolph. Do you know who sent me out here, who told me it was you peeking in on Lyon? It's a very important person, someone who can cause you a lot of trouble. *Talk to me.*"

Randolph's mother told him that if he were ever to eat dinner with important people and if Randolph were asked a question, such as would he like some more potatoes or would he care to have his drink freshened, Randolph should not crudely answer yes or no, but should say *I believe so* or *I think not*. And although Randolph has never gone to dinner with anyone, important or otherwise, the only responses he feels comfortable giving people are those his mother taught him.

"Okay then, pal, I'm going to take you in and put you in a jail cell overnight, maybe that'll get you talking."

Randolph looks up at him panic-stricken. "I tink not!"

"Well I *think* so."

When the sheriff takes a step in his direction, Randolph turns toward the door to the back room and beats upon it with tiny fists. The racket causes a baby in there to cry.

"I'll be a son-of-a-bitch," Stone says. "You got your hands on one of those babies!"

Exactly what Randolph wanted to explain.

"Let's take a look."

Randolph opens the door to the back room and lets out two dogs, who immediately sit in front of him and stare up at Sheriff Stone. Then Randolph closes the door; the baby's still crying.

"Nice-looking dogs," Stone says, resting his hand on the butt of his pistol and trying to figure out how to play this. He's heard about Randolph and his dogs of course. "I used to raise Swedish elkhounds but the D.C. weather was murder on them. Looks like some elkhound in your dogs, huh? Norwegian? Except the coloring's different, the shape of the head . . . Actually those look like oversized Karelian bear dogs. Jeez, Randolph, where'd you get ahold of a breed like that?"

The little hermit remains as silent as the two black and white dogs sitting in front of him.

"So you and your dogs are going to stop me from getting in that room, right?"

"I bewieve so."

Sheriff Stone doesn't see any way around it. He could shoot one of the dogs but the other would be on him before he could get a second shot off—and Stone knows that these Karelian bear dogs, developed by Finns and Russians, are pugnacious. Plus, the two dogs guarding Randolph aren't purebreds, they've had other lines mixed in to make them bigger, even more determined.

Stone is easing toward the shack's front door. "You know I'll be back, bring Carl with me and—"

"I tink not!"

"Yeah, I realize there's bad blood between you and Carl but you're leaving me no choice. We'll be back with shotguns and we'll kill every fucking dog you got on the place."

Randolph hurries to an opened window, calls and gestures in ways that make no sense to the sheriff, and then turns toward Stone and just stares at him. The two bear dogs are still sitting near the door to the back room and they're still staring at Stone too.

"You sic your dogs on me, pal, and the first shot goes right between your eyes."

"I tink not."

Stone has his pistol out, holding it at his side, managing his fear. "Yeah, well don't make me prove it."

He backs out onto the porch and works his way carefully across the dirt yard, reaching his car just as Randolph and the two dogs come out to stand on the porch and watch him. Stone doesn't feel truly safe until he's in the patrol car with the door closed. He puts the pistol on the seat and takes the shotgun from its holder on the dash, pointing the twelve-gauge through the open window. "I could blow you away right now, wouldn't even have to go get Carl."

"I tink not!" Randolph calls from the porch.

"Yeah, you *tink* not and you *bewieve* so—we'll see what you have to say when I come back."

Stone relatches the shotgun, starts the patrol car, and turns around, throwing an arm over the seat back so he can see to reverse out of Randolph's rutted drive—turning around in that seat to put his face right into the face of the biggest, blackest, most ferocious dog he's ever seen in his life, a dog that fills the backseat of the patrol car, a dog that makes those two Karelians up on the porch look like toy poodles.

The fright causes Stone to void a small amount of

urine into his underwear—enough for the black dog to smell, inciting him, causing his dark eyes to widen.

Knowing the importance of making no sudden movements, Stone stays frozen in his turned-around position, wondering if he can get a hand on the pistol before the dog takes off his face. Now even Stone can smell the fear seeping out from his groin, from under his arms, filling the car, causing the dog to whine in anticipation.

Stone goes for the pistol at the same time Randolph hollers a command from the porch, the black dog lunging as if he's enraged, not simply attacking Stone but acting as if Stone's very existence is an offense, as if he has caught Stone in his den, strangling puppies and eating his food, fouling the nest, this man needing death in the worst possible way.

Hackles up, snarling, the dog snaps four quick bites on the sheriff's face, tearing flesh, blinding one eye, Stone forgetting about the pistol, screaming and trying simply—desperately, pathetically—to get his hands up to his face, the dog clamping its massive jaws onto the man's neck, shaking him the way a terrier would a rat, up into the front seat with him now, snapping his spine, the two bear dogs from the porch scrambling through the patrol car's open windows, all three animals mad for a purchase of flesh, eviscerating the sheriff, ripping out entire muscles from his thighs.

With the world's saddest eyes, Randolph Welby watches from the front porch. Then he enters the cabin, goes straight to the back room, picks up the infant girl, and pats her gently until she stops crying.

Back on the porch, holding the baby up on his shoulder, Randolph whistles and the three dogs— blood staining their muzzles, blood all the way up their necks—come leaping out of the patrol car's windows, bounding to their master, sitting at his feet. He turns the baby around in his arms to show her the killers.

"Doggie," Randolph says to the wide-eyed girl. *"Doggie."*

20

DAZED WITH HUMILIATION, ANOTHER MIGRAINE GRIND-
ing inside his skull, John Lyon walks through the
ruined commercial district of Hameln, to the county
building's parking lot, to his rental car—opening the
door, easing the frog onto the front seat, tossing in the
file that Quinndell gave him, and then sliding into the
car's ovenlike interior, driving off, unable to decipher
how the air-conditioning lever works, at a loss for
where to go or what to do next.

The sheriff has probably already called the network,
saying that Lyon is reporting nonexistent bodies in
nonexistent crates, boogeymen at his window. Lyon is
sure he no longer has a job. What he's less sure about
is Mason Quinndell. The man seemed so totally
reasonable defending himself against Claire Cept's
charges, explaining the reality of the situation—then
why that business with the spoon as Lyon was leaving?
Does the good doctor hate being laughed at enough to

attack someone? But why in hell would you attack someone with a *spoon?* Maybe it wasn't a spoon. Maybe Quinndell was pointing a pen at Lyon.

"Wanted an autograph," he mutters as he heads toward the state highway that leads to the county road up through those mountains to the cabin. He's going to pack up his stuff and get the hell out of West Virginia.

And the farther he goes, the faster he drives, eager now to put an end to all this craziness, driving those eighteen miles into the mountains at such a high rate of speed that he keeps skidding around corners and twice jams the brakes to stop the car just before it goes over the edge. He watches carefully for the trees painted red but apparently misses one, getting lost, retracing his route, finding the tree, stopping to pee, driving on, the idiot light in the left corner of the instrument panel blinking to inform him the car is overheating, Lyon refusing to slow down, recognizing now the final mile of road leading to the cabin, racing into the clearing and bringing the car to a sliding, sideways halt with all four wheels locked.

He gets out of the car. This tucked-away hollow is all hushed up with twilight, where did the day go? Lyon feels as if he has been returned to a high-sided nest where time runs differently than it does in the outside world. Walking up to the porch he flashes on the idea that the crate will be back in the kitchen. Of course. That's how *they*—Quinndell or whoever it is—plan on driving him insane: allowing Lyon to make these weird discoveries whenever he's by himself but then removing the evidence before he can confirm it with a third party.

He walks to the porch, steps to the door, hesitates a moment, then enters, turning to his right and looking into the kitchen. No crate. The room looks exactly as it did when Lyon was here with Sheriff Stone.

Nothing out of place in the living room either. Lyon walks toward the bedroom, thinking, she's going to be lying in bed just as I left her this morning.

Then he decides, no, she's gone and won't be back. Whatever happened last night was a onetime phenomenon.

He stops at the bedroom doorway. She's going to be waiting for me, lying in that bed, I know she is.

He steps into the room.

She's not there.

And Lyon can't figure out if he's disappointed or relieved.

He returns to the kitchen, turning on all the lights as he goes, thankful for electricity. Lyon is hungry and ready to fall asleep on his feet. He won't get very far driving in this condition, better have something to eat and take a nap, still got a couple hours of light, plenty of time to . . .

Lyon killing time, waiting for her to show up again.

Operating on automatic pilot, he looks through his box of supplies, opens a can of soup and puts it in a pan on the stove, moving orange juice and lunch meats into the refrigerator, wondering how much of his food has spoiled.

When he opens a tap over the kitchen sink, the water spits out red and then brown, finally running clear enough for Lyon to wash his hands and face. He eats the hot soup right out of the pan, pours a glass of Scotch and carries it into the bedroom with him. He takes a cool shower and then opens the tiny bathroom's door, expecting to see her in bed waiting for him, but of course she's not there, his bed is empty.

With only a towel around his waist, Lyon walks back through the cabin making sure all the windows are down and locked. The place is stifling but he's not taking any chances on what's-his-name, Randolph Welby, crawling in some opened window, Lyon not wanting to wake up from his nap to see the little hermit standing there by his bed, idiot-grinning at him.

Looking through kitchen drawers, he finds an impressive butcher knife and brings it with him to the bedroom. Lyon removes the towel to sit naked on the bed. When he finally lies back, he notices for the first time that directly above the bed is a small skylight—and in that skylight there's already a promise of night.

Although bone weary, he doesn't fall asleep. Thinking too much. Lyon begins reading through the folder of information Dr. Quinndell gave him, his heart sinking with each report on Claire Cept being fired from another nursing job, Claire Cept accusing another doctor of being a vampire, Claire Cept testifying to strange baby-murdering plots, Claire Cept forcibly removed from one hearing for bringing voodoo paraphernalia in with her. Wonder why Quinndell didn't mention the voodoo.

Depressed, Lyon puts the folder on the floor, sets his travel alarm for an hour, takes one last sip of Scotch, and falls rocklike into sleep.

He awakens in a room lighted only by the moon in the skylight directly above him. What happened to his alarm? And didn't he leave all the lights on? Lyon turns his head toward the bedside table; the clock is facing away from him. He keeps blinking. He *is* awake, isn't he?

He senses what's wrong as soon as he moves, intending to reach over and check the time, making only a half turn before he feels it: something in bed with him.

21

SHE'S LYING ON HER BACK, THE WHITE SHEET PULLED TO just below her breasts, her long black arms outside the sheet and resting along the sides of her body, eyes closed—either still in a coma or still faking it or dead now for real.

Lyon's surprised but not terrified. This is what he's been waiting for, this is why he came back to the cabin and then went to bed instead of leaving before it got dark: hoping she'd be returned to him.

Carefully he moves toward her, staring at those breasts round and high on her chest, topped with those fleshy purple nipples, remembering touching her right breast, recalling how it felt—full—in his hand. Does *she* remember?

He reaches over and finds the inside of her right wrist, the woman's pulse strong and steady.

She came to bed on her own. No one is hauling this woman here and then carting her away again, she's doing it all on her own.

He wonders what the hell he did with the butcher knife, finally clearing his throat and preparing to speak to her, realizing he hasn't done that yet. He's stared at her, fantasized about her, fondled her, carried her in his arms, worried over her—but he hasn't *said* anything to the woman.

"I locked everything, how'd you get in?"

No response.

"You've been faking it all along, haven't you? You weren't dead, you weren't in a coma, and now you walked right in here and got in bed with me. *Why?*"

No answer.

He rests his head on his hand, elbow up on the pillow, close to the woman but not touching her. "What's the point, what're you trying to prove?"

Nothing.

"You're awake now, you're just pretending. You were awake when I touched you before too, when you were in that crate. Now you're lying here waiting for me to start it all over again, aren't you?"

He feels stupid talking to her like this, thinking maybe he should take her by the shoulders and shake her until he gets a response. He pulls the sheet down a little. Lyon has a hard-on.

He scoots close enough under that sheet for his erection to touch her. He smells soap and perspiration —hers and his both—as he moves his face against her long neck, kissing her there.

"Why are you pretending to be asleep?" he asks, whispering into her ear.

He leans back from the woman and pulls the sheet completely away, exposing her naked body, seeing the butcher knife lying across the top of her thighs, right over her sex.

He mutters a curse. Then tells her, "That's supposed to be a message?"

Tired of this shit, being jerked around by everyone. "I know you're awake!" he hollers into her placid face.

Lyon throws the knife onto the floor, climbs on top of the woman, reaches down to pull her legs apart, and positions himself until his penis is against her.

"Okay, *now* tell me to stop."

But she tells him nothing. Going by her face, she could indeed be sleeping or in a coma—or dead.

"Damn you."

Pressuring his cock hard against her, breathing heavily, intrigued by it all, he lowers himself until his face is against hers, his lips full on the woman's, feeling weirdly erotic to be kissing a mouth that does not respond, using his tongue to part those lips and then play across her teeth, the tip of his tongue working those teeth until a space is opened, and then his tongue is in her mouth, her mouth as wet and warm as she has become between her legs.

Suspending all good judgment—*rape*—and in fact no longer caring, Lyon realizes now that it's going to happen, unless she comes suddenly awake and demands that he stop, screaming at him and beating upon him with her hands . . . or maybe it's gone too far now to stop even if she awakens and tries to resist, Lyon reaching down between them to move his cock, trying to help it find entry.

Feeling how wet she is down there excites him, Lyon pushing against her, then withdrawing and feeling her wetness cool upon the head of his cock, pushing again, his hands up around her slender shoulders to hold her so he can push harder, farther in this time, farther.

He pauses, knowing this is his absolute last opportunity to stop, that if he pushes against her one more time that'll be it, no stopping him then.

"Yes or no—tell me!"

But she says nothing, she's like a doll in his arms, and Lyon knows he can't put the decision off on her anyway, he knows this is wrong, knows he should roll off of her and . . .

. . . fuck it, Lyon crushing his mouth upon hers, moving his left hand to cover her right breast, pinching that fat nipple, wanting to say something really crude, *You like that, huh, you like that, don't you, bitch!*

When she parts her teeth and slips her tongue into his mouth, Lyon thrills, her chest pushing upward to press that breast all the harder into his hand, the woman's legs spreading so that he drops lower between them, both Lyon and the woman pressing and pushing now, nothing spoken as she snakes a hand down to where they are joined, arranging something there and then withdrawing her hand, Lyon raising up to see her face, the eyes closed but her mouth wide, as open to him as her legs.

They're fucking each other, holding on, not speaking, just grunting and fucking, Lyon feeling like a goddamn freight train, that's what he feels like, hot and hard and on tracks, the woman squeezing her ass muscles and raising it up off the bed, placing a hand under her ass so she can grasp his cock from below, encircling it with thumb and forefinger, tightening that ring so he has to push even harder to enter her, pushing himself through that finger-thumb circle for burial deep into a vagina that has become soft, wet, lush, then immediately pulling out of her vagina, back out through that hard, tight ring made by her thumb and finger, then back through it again and into her easy flesh, like screwing the tightest of virgins and the most willing of whores rolled into one, back and forth, hard ring and plush cunt, his blood pressure testing artery walls for weaknesses, holding his breath, grinding his teeth, fucking and animal-grunting, investing this act of intercourse with every frustration and embarrassment of the last eight days, every ruinous event, all of his humiliation getting fucked away inside this silent, pliable woman.

And when she detects its impending arrival she grabs his cock with her entire hand, squeezing it *hard* . . . then releases him and moves her hand away, making John Lyon feel as if he's been dropped from a height, both falling and spilling, the woman breaking her silence by laughing, not a ridiculing laughter but a laughter so *happy* that Lyon joins in, laughing and climaxing simultaneously, hugging her and holding on, still grinding against her, still pumping into her, putting his head down and digging his toes into the sheet, still laughing, still coming.

"Are you going to talk to me now?" he asks after they have uncoupled, both of them on their backs, both of them bright with sweat, Lyon and the woman both looking straight up at a skylight filled with stars.

"Yes," she says.

"Who are you?"

"Claire. My name is Claire Cept."

22

ON TOWARD DAWN OF THAT TUESDAY, JULY 3, RANdolph Welby walks out of his shack, down a hill, and to the edge of a thirty-foot cliff. The multiflora rosebushes and the berry briars that are growing on the face of the cliff have already begun to straighten, to repair the damage that's been done to them. And at the foot of the cliff, where the patrol car ended up, it's such a jungle of brush down there that you can barely see the car's roof. To keep the smell in, Randolph made sure all the windows were up. The car's interior will reach one-twenty in this July heat. Randolph too easily imagines how the sheriff's body will look—what's left of his body—in a few days. It'll swell up and burst and splatter all over the insides of that car. Even if you could winch the car back up the cliff and repair the damage to its engine and frame, you couldn't drive it—never be able to get the smell out. Don't think about such things, he tells himself. In ten days' time the roses and briars will obliterate the patrol car from sight, which is how it will remain until come autumn.

Not that Randolph thinks he's gotten away with anything. Oh, he knows they'll be coming for him. Whole bunch of 'em, Carl too. Fat Carl.

Got to go see that TV man now, even if he does do nasty things to a black woman he keeps in a box. There's too much in the outside world that Randolph doesn't understand, can't explain, and now it's going to have to be up to the TV man to explain everything.

Randolph returns to his shack and prepares for the hike.

23

MASON QUINNDELL IS ONLY VAGUELY AWARE THAT somewhere outside a child is crying. The doctor is sitting at his desk this Tuesday morning, his mind's eye roaming over the office, seeing-remembering in exact detail. He hasn't permitted anything to be changed since he departed for the hospital five years ago, returning here to his house ten days later, blinded. Quinndell always thinks of it that way, not that he lost his sight or became blind but that he was *blinded*.

Impeccably dressed as always in suit, tie, and crisp white shirt, Dr. Quinndell sits tapping his long clean fingers on the desk.

He can see his office the way a master chess player sees the board while playing a game in his mind, Quinndell sitting there silently listing the titles of the books on the top shelf in that glassed-front oak bookcase on the north wall. Was that all of them? He does it again, counting this time. Twenty-three. He smiles.

Nothing touches him. If I get struck deaf next, Quinndell thinks, and then struck mute after that, I'll simply find a place to reside more deeply and more vividly within my mind, taking every insult in stride, howling for more.

He sits there tapping, thinking. But then stops tapping, that child's incessant crying having finally intruded upon the doctor's thoughts. It's the kid from across the street, an eighteen-month-old boy regularly left in the care of a teenage sister. Quinndell has twice sent Mary to warn the family about the sister yakking on the telephone while the little boy is left alone out in the yard, getting stung by bees or playing with dog turds. Unforgivable, Quinndell thinks. The way some people treat their children.

Then Quinndell puts the child out of his mind and considers what should be done about John Lyon. There's always the possibility that he's not quite as crazy as he's acting. Maybe that story he told the sheriff—finding a black woman in a coffin—was carefully constructed to unhinge me. Then Lyon comes here pretending he hasn't done any research into Claire's charges, feigning incompetence, carrying a concrete frog (Mary confirmed that), laughing at me. Perhaps trying to spook me into doing something rash. Like coming after him with Mr. Spoon when he broke into that hyena laughter. Yes, that was rash. I wonder if he saw me. More to the point, I wonder what I would've done had I reached him before he got out of the office.

Quinndell clears his throat and raises his chin as he takes a linen handkerchief from his pocket and dabs at the moisture collecting around the beautiful blue eyes he commissioned from an old-world craftsman in Oslo, Norway.

He recalls making that decisive telephone call to Claire, "confessing" to her that not only did he murder those infants but he butchered them as well, Quinndell convinced now that it was that telephone call which nudged Claire over the edge and prompted her suicide—but apparently not before she infected Lyon.

I know what I *could* do, I could introduce Mr. Lyon to Mr. Gigli. I could . . . but once again Quinndell's thoughts are derailed by the child's crying. He angrily presses the buzzer that quickly brings Mary to his office.

"Yes, doctor?"

"Can you hear a child crying?"

"Yes."

"And?"

She doesn't know what he means. "It's that little boy from across the street, his sister—"

"I *know* the story. What I want is for that child to be silenced."

"I'll go over and get his sister off the phone."

But the doctor abruptly smiles his yellow smile. "No, I have a better idea. Bring him here."

"What?"

"Bring me that crying child."

"You mean—"

"I mean walk across the street and yank the little bastard out of his yard and bring him here. I'm sure his sluttish sister won't miss him, she's undoubtedly on the telephone arranging to have sexual intercourse with a squad of football players, a team sport with which you're familiar, I'm sure."

She doesn't know what to do, doesn't know if he is serious.

"Mary, if you defy me one more time before your year is up—"

"All right."

Five minutes later Mary is back in the doctor's office holding a plump toddler in her arms. "He was on the porch trying to get the door open but he couldn't reach the handle."

"Did his sister see you take him?"

"No, I don't think so. But—"

"Bring him here."

Mary carries the boy, dirty-faced and wide-eyed, to Quinndell's desk.

"I'm surprised he came with you," the doctor says, reaching out to touch the child's face.

"I play with him sometimes."

Quinndell grins. "So the aging slut has some maternal instincts after all. You'll be needing those soon, won't you, Mary?"

She says nothing.

"Put him here on the desk."

But the child's fat arms cling tenaciously around Mary's neck.

"He won't let go," she tells Quinndell, who reaches out and takes the boy under his armpits, pulling him away from Mary and sitting him hard on the desk.

The child whimpers and reaches for Mary, but Quinndell holds him firmly by the shoulders. "I know how to stop his crying."

Mary doesn't like where this is going.

"I could show you."

"Show me what?" Mary asks.

"Show you how to operate on him."

"What?"

"Yes, one small incision, two tiny snips . . ." The doctor's fingers toy with the boy's dirty neck. ". . . and we'd have his vocal cords disabled, never to be disturbed by the little bastard's crying ever again."

Mary knows he's capable of doing it.

"His parents and his sister would be grateful to us."

The boy is reaching for Mary, who takes his hands and presses them in hers.

"Come on, Mary, you've helped me with more difficult procedures. Why just this past March—"

"No!"

Quinndell chuckles. He finds the boy's round cheek and pinches it, not hard enough to bruise the child but hard enough to make him start crying again. "Do you think his parents *value* him?"

"Of course they do!" Mary says sharply, taking the boy out from under Quinndell's grip, holding him in her arms, rocking the child back and forth until he stops crying.

The doctor pauses, considering something. "Yes, but how *much* do they value him, how much would they take for him, how much could I get for him?"

Patting the boy gently on his back, Mary doesn't reply.

"I *like* children," Quinndell tells her.

She snorts in contempt, immediately regretting it, then is surprised when the doctor insists, "I *do* like children, it's after they grow up to be adults that I find them wanting. When toddlers like this one were brought to me in my examining room, they held me in awe. I often thought a child's reaction to me in the examining room was exactly how a man would act when ushered into the presence of God: awestruck and trembling with fear."

The little boy has begun to cry again, reaching out over Mary's shoulder, reaching toward the door, wanting to go home.

"Oh, yes, Mary, in my examining room I was God to these people and their children. Then as soon as they departed my presence, I was out of their minds. Never paying their bills on time or in full. Never thinking about me. Do you know how that upsets God? Mary, if you don't quiet that child, I swear I'll cut out his vocal cords, right here on this desk."

She desperately rocks and bounces the boy in her arms but he cries all the harder.

"Early in my practice here a woman came in and offered a dozen jars of jelly as partial payment on her bill. I said, 'Madam, I do not operate on the barter system.' Then I dropped her jars of jelly—blackberry, I believe—one by one on the floor. *Then* I sued her for nonpayment. The only asset she had was a cheap little shack of a house but I took it, I—" Quinndell's face suddenly twists in anger. *"Shut him up.* I can not tolerate the sound of a child crying, not since I was blinded, that goddamn crying is an abomination, it's—" He opens a drawer and takes out a scalpel. "Mary, put him down on the desk." He waits a moment and then screams at her. "Goddamn you, Mary, put him down here, I'm going to slice his vocal cords and you're going to help me do it!"

"No."

Getting control of his anger, Quinndell manages a rough laugh. "Tell me dear, do you think I'm a tad too theatrical?"

"I—"

"Oh, he's cute now, Mary, but what about in fifteen years when he's raping girls in the backseats of cars, drinking himself stupid on cheap beer, another piece of useless, violent debris. Let's save the world the trouble and slit his fat little throat right now."

She is shaking her head, moving away from Quinndell, the child howling in her arms.

"I'll stop that crying," the doctor says, coming around the side of his desk, smiling broadly as if this might all be a joke, "I'll stop it once and for all. Bring him here."

But Mary has stepped quietly to the double doors.

"No one cares about children, thirty-five years doctoring them proved that to me. Parents starve their children, abuse them, abandon them. Why do you think that happens? *Because no one cares. I* cared, I tried to correct the inequities, and look what it got me, got me blinded!" He's shouting now. "But I found out how to make people care, didn't I, Mary, I found out how to make them pay—" He stops when he realizes he's alone.

Quinndell stands there a moment before returning the scalpel to the drawer. Then sits at his desk, the doctor once again seeing-remembering his office, gazing over the photographs, lingering on the one taken back when he had his own dark eyes instead of these unnaturally blue ones, a photograph of the doctor surrounded by his pediatric patients, several of whom are holding a homemade banner, Quinndell able to *see* each of those kids and each of the words scrawled on their banner.

An hour later Mary is upstairs in her room, still shaking. From under her bed she takes out a little box she found on the front step yesterday morning. Six inches long, three inches wide, two inches thick, made of wood, painted white, and containing a crude wax figure covered with hair and feathers and the letter *Q*. If she tells Quinndell, he'll go into a rage and then God knows what'll happen. Mary has only twelve days left until she gets her soul back, she doesn't want anything to go wrong. On the calendar by her bed, the days are marked off with big red *X*s, the way a convict counts down to freedom.

She first met Quinndell almost twenty years ago. He was on a business trip to New York, Mary was working as a hostess in a very expensive Manhattan restaurant, and they "dated" (a euphemism Mary clings to tenaciously) all during the week that Quinndell was in New York. They continued a sporadic "affair" for several years, the doctor arranging to meet her in New York or sending her first-class tickets to whatever city he was visiting, paying all of her expenses including a generous allowance for clothing. Mary would be insulted at any suggestion that she ever worked as a prostitute; she simply had occasional affairs with men who paid her way.

She didn't hear from the doctor for a period of fifteen years—until last July when he finally traced her to the restaurant where she was working (as a waitress then) and outlined The Deal.

Quinndell explained that he had been blind for four years and wanted her, someone he knew from the old days, to come and live with him, read to him, chauffeur him, sleep with him. If she would do everything he requested, he would at the end of one year pay her fifty thousand dollars. Mary was forty-two at the time, lived alone, and had three hundred dollars in her checking account. She was in West Virginia the following Monday.

Upon her arrival in Hameln, Mary was relieved to see that Mason Quinndell looked even more handsome, more distinguished, than he had in his forties, although she did find his overly blue eyes a bit unnerving. But it wasn't the blindness that had disfigured Quinndell, he had turned ugly inside. When she knew him fifteen years ago, the doctor had always acted superior, disdainful of people he considered his inferiors—after all, he was a *doctor*. But even when he was making fun of someone's ignorance or obesity or ugliness, he did it in a way that made you laugh. You might feel bad for laughing but, fifteen years ago, Mason Quinndell could be terribly funny and he had a zest for everything he did. He loved taking Mary to museums, recommending books to her. He was full of himself, full of life. But *now,* now something inside of Dr. Quinndell had turned rancid.

Mary tried to be sympathetic and supportive, always keeping in mind the fifty thousand she would receive at the end of the year, but Quinndell took such joy in humiliating her and treated her with such contempt that by the end of the first month Mary had had enough. Dressed to travel, she came down to breakfast one morning and announced she was quitting.

"If you leave now," Quinndell reminded her, "you don't get any money. That was the deal, you get paid at the end of the year. Quitting now means that you endured an entire month with me for absolutely no compensation."

She told him she couldn't tolerate eleven more months of the way he'd been treating her these first four weeks, eleven more months of his snapping his fingers and telling her to get down on her knees and "service" him or to bend over a chair and pull up her dress, eleven more months of belittling her, eleven more months of ridicule. She knew what the deal was but she would just write off the past month to experience. All she wanted from Quinndell was enough money to get back to New York.

He thought for a moment and then announced that he was raising her compensation to seventy-five thousand. "In eleven months, Mary, you'll have more money than you've ever had in your life."

She considered it. "Will you stop treating me so bad?"

"So *badly*," he corrected her. "And the answer is, I will treat you exactly as I choose to treat you—and in exchange for indulging me you get seventy-five thousand dollars. If your answer is no, then you can hitchhike to New York for all I care, I'm not giving you a dime."

"Make it a hundred thousand."

Quinndell laughed. "Let's see now, if I were to request your sexual favors, such as they are, on the average of four times a week for fifty-two weeks, some two hundred sexual contacts in the year covered by our deal . . . at a hundred thousand dollars that comes out to roughly five hundred dollars per session. *Mary.* Not even in your dreams did you aspire to being a five-hundred-dollar whore."

"This is exactly why I'm leaving!" she cried. "The way you're always humiliating me. It's not the sex I'm complaining about, it's the—"

"The *principle*. Yes, yes, I know all about whores and their principles. All right then, a hundred thousand dollars."

That seemed too easy. "Are you serious?"

"Stay with me for a year, do whatever I ask, and I'll give you an envelope containing a cashier's check for one hundred thousand dollars. I've never lied to you, Mary. Is it a deal?"

With a hundred thousand dollars she could buy into a small restaurant and begin a new life.

"Mary?"

"All right."

Smiling, Quinndell reached out and found the quart bottle of maple syrup that was on the table, getting up from his chair and carrying the bottle to where Mary was sitting. He unscrewed the cap.

She asked him what he was doing.

"I'm going to pour this syrup over your head."

"This is my best outfit, I just had my hair done, I—"

"Think of the money, Mary."

And with that he upended the bottle of syrup over her freshly coiffed hair, down the front of her navy blue jacket with the big white buttons, moving the bottle in lazy circles across her shoulders, and finally pouring the last of the sticky, viscous fluid right onto her face. Then he tossed the bottle into her lap and left the room.

She sat there at the breakfast table with both of her hands drawn tightly into fists, crying from anger and humiliation, rigid with her hatred for him.

After that, life with the doctor became even more hellish, the atrocities he performed and forced her to perform so sickening Mary that she awoke each morning convinced she would leave him *today*. But each day became an investment in her year-end payoff. To quit and walk away with no money would mean she had suffered in vain. So Mary endured, chipped away at day after day, using her hatred for the doctor as fuel to keep herself going, just hold on until the year was over.

Then this past March, eight months into her year with Quinndell, he brought a baby girl into the house. He told Mary he was going to deliver the child to her new family and ordered Mary to drive him and the baby deep into the mountains, past a hermit's shack, to a cave with a hidden entrance. Mary waited in the car while Quinndell went inside. He came out alone.

Mary lies back on the bed.

She tried to quit after that of course but Quinndell got her to stay by offering Mary an enticement she was unable to refuse: at the end of her year with him, Quinndell said, he would give Mary *two* envelopes. In one would be a cashier's check not for a hundred thousand dollars but for *two hundred and fifty thousand*. In the other would be a name, an address, and twelve photographs.

She asked him to explain.

He did—and ever since then Quinndell has owned her soul.

When the buzzer above her bed sounds, Mary gets wearily to her feet, crams the wooden box into her shoulder bag, and takes the bag with her downstairs. What now?

"Yes?"

"Mary? I heard you crying upstairs. Maybe it's *your* vocal cords that need snipping."

She asks him what he wants.

"All business, that's what I like about you, dear. We need to find out if Mr. Lyon is playing games with us."

She glances at her bag containing the little white coffin. If Lyon is the one who put it on the doorstep yesterday then, yes, he's playing games with

Quinndell's mind. Lyon must know how much the doctor hated and feared Claire Cept. Not that Mary is going to mention any of this to Quinndell. She doesn't intend to do anything that'll rock the boat for the next twelve days. Just twelve more days.

"I was thinking perhaps you could seduce John Lyon and find out how vigorously he intends to pursue his inquiry. Do you think you could do that?"

Yes. She saw how Lyon was looking at her legs when they met in the front yard. Going to bed with him would be nice—and Mary hasn't had anything nice happen to her in eleven and a half months. But she knows better than to display any enthusiasm for the assignment.

"I suppose I—"

"Except seduction isn't your forte, is it, dearie?"

Here it comes, she thinks.

"I mean, sexually speaking, you *are* rather Pavlovian, aren't you. I lower my zipper at the cemetery and you're immediately on your knees. You see the color of a man's money and you're on your back with your legs spread before he can count out the fifteen dollars you used to charge for your services—hardly what one would call *seduction,* is it?"

Twelve more days of this, then I get my soul back.

"No, I don't think your *servicing* of Mr. Lyon will be required at all."

When the front doorbell rings, Quinndell activates a button that releases the lock. "Here comes the man I want you to seduce."

Mary turns toward the double doors just as they open. Quinndell can't be serious, she thinks. Not *Carl.*

The sheriff's deputy is thirty years old, five feet eleven inches tall, weighing in at four hundred and thirty-five pounds. The fat covers his belt all the way around and hangs from his neck like a lard-filled cowl. His face has been obliterated by bulging flesh; there's a nose in there someplace and a mouth and tiny pig eyes looking out at you. He walks in a lumbering gait, his legs forced apart by massive thighs, his arms pushed out to the sides of his body—a crudely mechanized and grotesquely overinflated doll that's about to burst.

"Hiya, Doc. Got your message."

"Carl, my boy, we were just talking about you."

"Huh?"

He's stupid too. Double-digit IQ. Ludicrous for him to be a sheriff's deputy, he can barely get in and out of a car, but Quinndell arranged the job for him as a way of showing his contempt for the locals—and because Carl is dog-loyal to the doctor.

"The thing is, Carl, Mary wants . . . well this is kind of embarrassing, I've never played cupid before, but Mary would like to go to bed with you. Only she's afraid if she suggests it you'll think she's too forward so she asked me if I would find out if you were interested."

Horrified, Mary looks from the doctor to Carl, whose mouth is open as he dully tries to comprehend what he is being told. Christ, there's drool starting to drip from the corner of his lips.

"Sure," Carl says—and then finally closes his mouth.

"There you go, Mary, your dream come true."

She's standing well away from the deputy, her arms crossed tightly over her chest. "What're you doing?" she asks Quinndell.

"I'm arranging for you to have sexual intercourse

with Carl, that's what I'm doing. What do you weigh these days, Carl?"

The deputy is red-faced (either from embarrassment or from sexual excitement, Mary can't tell), stammering his reply, "Don't . . . don't know, Doc."

"Come now, Carl, no reason for shyness among friends. Have you topped five hundred yet?"

"Don't . . . don't think so."

"Mary likes 'em big, don't you, Mary?"

She gives the doctor a murderous look.

"Carl, you *will* have to promise to let her stay on top—all right?"

"Whatever you say, Doc." Now the deputy is leering at Mary, who feels nauseated because she realizes maybe this isn't a joke, maybe this is just the sort of thing Quinndell would force her to do during these last twelve days.

"I think he's warming to the prospect, what do you think, Mary?"

"I'm not going to bed with him."

"Fine, then you can pack up and get out of my house. Just saved me a quarter of a million dollars."

Against her will, Mary begins crying. This is what she hates the most about Quinndell, that he can still get to her, still make her cry.

"Here come the tears, Carl. Next it'll be nagging. She has a voice that would put a fishwife to shame. Nag, bitch, shrill, shrill—but in the end, Mary always spreads 'em on demand, don't you, Mary?"

He's really serious, he's really going to make me go to bed with that monster. No, Quinndell's the monster; Carl's just fat and stupid.

"Something I should warn you about, Carl, before you let your fantasies get the best of you. Mary is . . . how shall I put this delicately . . . somewhat *worn*. Widely worn you might say. In fact, I've been meaning to ask you, Mary, did you ever perform on the stage? I'm thinking Tijuana. Donkeys."

Carl glances over at Mary and sees how miserable she looks. The deputy feels vaguely sorry for her—but if the Doc makes Mary go to bed with him, Carl ain't saying no.

"Another thing, she has a certain odor problem—"

"Stop it!" Mary screams.

Quinndell laughs.

When Mary is getting a Kleenex out of her shoulder bag, she sees the wooden box. Biting her lower lip, she takes the box in hand.

"I'll have to be in the room of course," the doctor is saying. "When you and Carl 'do it.' The boy may need some pointers, although with an old pro like you—"

Mary walks quickly to Quinndell and slaps the box down on the desk, right in front of him. "I found it by the front door yesterday morning."

Still smiling, he runs his hands over the box's exterior, picks it up, puts it back down, gets the lid open, then touches what's inside.

"I would describe it as a little white coffin," Mary says. "What you're feeling now is a wax figure with hair and feathers on it. Wrapped in string. Someone has cut out a bunch of *Q*s—the letter *Q*—and stuck them all over the figure."

Then Mary stands there enjoying the doctor lose his smile.

"Lyon gave you this."

"No, I found it by the front door yesterday morning before he got here."

"Why didn't you tell me then?"

Mary doesn't answer.

"If I thought you were in this with Lyon I'd take you to Mr. Gigli right now."

"Mr. Gigli!" Carl shouts with a laugh.

Mary insists that she's had nothing to do with John Lyon. "I never even talked to him until he showed up here yesterday. I'm sorry, I should've brought it to you right away but I didn't want to upset you."

"Didn't want to upset me." Quinndell pushes the box away with the tips of his fingers. "Take this and *do* something with it."

Mary grabs the box, closes it, and stuffs it back in her shoulder bag.

Now it is Quinndell who is suddenly all business. "Carl!"

"Right here, Doc."

"I called you because our ambitious sheriff has turned up missing. The sudden appearance of John Lyon may have given Stone a case of cold feet, I want you to go to his place and see if he's packed up."

"You got it, Doc."

"Then go out to that rental cabin and sneak up on John Lyon—if such a thing is possible for you—and find out if anyone is staying with him. Specifically a black woman. Maybe she's not dead after all, Claire and Lyon in this together, cooking up some kind of . . ." Quinndell loses his thought. Mary can't help smiling.

Carl finally says, "Still here, Doc."

"Yes." The doctor is distracted. "After you find out who's staying at the cabin, drive over to Randolph Welby's place and bring the little idiot back here, I'll talk to him myself."

"That's where the sheriff was heading last time he reported."

"I *know* that, Carl."

"I don't like them dogs of his."

"Carl, I don't *care* what you like, you will do precisely as I say—understand?"

"Yeah," the deputy responds like a chastised child, a four-hundred-and-thirty-five-pound chastised child.

"And your assignment, Mary . . ." Quinndell is sweating, which worries Mary because she's not sure she's ever seen him sweat before. "Your assignment is to take off your clothes and get down on all fours and bark, crawl around on the floor barking *like the BITCH YOU ARE!*"

Mary stands there frozen. He's scary enough when he's methodical in his humiliations, but his rages are terrifying.

"Are you taking off your clothes?"

"She's just standing there," Carl says.

Quinndell swivels in his chair, bends to open a safe, and comes up with two white business envelopes. "Here they are, Mary! Just as I promised. You know I always keep my word." Then he opens the desk's center drawer and finds a lighter. "I'll burn them!" he tells her. "Swear to God I'll burn them!" He flicks the lighter three times before he gets a flame—and then plays that flame close to the corners of the envelopes.

"Please don't make me do this," she begs.

"Do it! I want Carl to see what he's getting. That's right, Carl, if you complete your tasks successfully, when you return here, Mary will be waiting in all her glory, naked and on all fours, you can take her like you were fucking a sheep. Now *do it,* Mary!"

She is trembling, crying, slowly working the buttons of her blouse.

"Goddamn you!" Quinndell shouts, lighting the corner of one envelope.

"I'm doing it!" she screams.

"Yeah, she is, Doc!" Carl adds.

Quinndell snuffs out the flame and waits a moment before asking, "Well?"

"She's got her blouse undone but she ain't took it off yet," Carl informs him.

"Come on, Mary, we're on a tight schedule."

She slips the blouse off and then steps out of her shorts before making the mistake of looking at Carl, who has pushed the tip of his tongue between his teeth, causing him to appear as if he had three lips, the center one pink, fat, and wet.

"I think she's going to throw up, Doc."

Quinndell laughs.

Closing her eyes, Mary removes her bra and panties before dropping to the floor on her hands and knees.

"She's doing it, Doc!" Carl crows. "Buck naked and down on all fours like a dog!"

Quinndell returns the envelopes to the safe and then stands, pulling down his suitcoat and adjusting his cuffs. He has regained control, his voice once again smoothly modulated. "I don't hear any barking," he says quietly.

"Yeah," Carl shouts, well into the spirit of things, "go on and bark! And she ain't supposed to be staying there in one spot, she's supposed to be moving around, *ain't* she, Doc?"

"Indeed she is." The doctor takes out his handkerchief again, wiping his brow and then dabbing delicately at the moisture beneath his glass eyes. "Mary?"

Sobbing now, hating herself as much as she does Dr. Quinndell, Mary begins her crawl about the room, sobbing and barking.

"Louder," Quinndell says softly. "Bark *louder,* dear."

24

John Lyon awakens alone in bed that Tuesday morning, taking a moment to lie there and recall the events of last night, feeling a dull but not altogether unpleasant ache in his pubic bone. She wouldn't answer his questions last night, promising to tell him whatever he wanted to know in the morning—but now Lyon assumes the woman is once again gone. Then he smells breakfast.

He uses the bathroom, pulls on a pair of slacks and a shirt, hurrying into the kitchen to see her standing at the stove with her back to him. She's wearing one of his teeshirts, which strikes her just below the ass, bare-legged and barefooted and nothing on under that white cotton teeshirt. When she stirs whatever it is she's cooking in that frying pan, her ass shakes tautly.

"Good morning," he says, the woman turning and smiling at him. He can see her large, dark nipples beneath the teeshirt.

"Sit down, John. I didn't have much to work with but it'll pass for breakfast."

"Smells good."

She serves him and pours two cups of coffee, taking hers to the opposite end of the table.

"Aren't you eating?" he asks.

"No, you go ahead."

Lyon looks at the plateful of food—corned beef hash from one of the cans he brought, combined with onions and salsa (he doesn't know where they came from). He picks up the fork but then hesitates, wondering why she isn't having any.

"According to some hoodoo beliefs," she tells him, "if a woman mixes in her menstrual blood with a man's food and then watches him eat it, he will forever be powerless to betray her." She has her hand on her chin, watching Lyon.

He chuckles nervously. "Hoodoo?"

"It's an African-American reference to voodoo."

"Oh."

She smiles over the cup of coffee she's bringing to her mouth, waiting to see if he's going to eat.

"Menstrual blood, huh?" Lyon asks, using his fork to move the hash around. "You certainly are a strange young woman." Then he figures, what the hell, he's famished. Forking in the food, he tells her how good it tastes.

She keeps watching him.

"I have a million questions," he says between bites.

"I told you I would answer all your questions this morning."

"What're you doing here? How did you *get* here? Where do you keep disappearing to?"

"Whoa."

"Okay, what's your name?"

"Claire Cept."

Lyon puts down his fork and looks away.

"The Claire Cept you met in New York, John, was my grandmother—my mother's mother, after whom I was named."

"Oh."

"And the reason I'm here is to help you prove Claire's accusations against Quinndell—because I promised my grandmother I would."

"Why the crate or coffin or whatever it was, and what happened to it?"

"Yes, well, that takes a bit of explanation."

"You were awake the entire time, weren't you?"

She doesn't reply but he can tell by her expression that she was.

"God, what you must think of me."

"It *was* an unusual evening."

Lyon is embarrassed as he stares into her dark eyes, marveling at how small she seems in his big white teeshirt. "How old are you?"

"Fourteen," she answers without hesitation.

Lyon stops breathing.

And it isn't until she laughs that he resumes breathing. Then he asks, "How old—really?"

"Of all the things I thought you'd be worried about, my age isn't one of them. I'm twenty-six, a professor of American folklore at NYU."

He wonders if this is another joke. "Really?"

"Yes. My mother was the youngest of Claire's four daughters and I'm one of eleven grandchildren. I have two older sisters. I was orphaned by my parents' divorce, I went to live with Claire. I took her last name. She raised me from age eight until I went to college. And she's been living with me in New York for the past year or so. I watched her deteriorate, getting worse every day because of Mason Quinndell, her crusade against him, and I promised her I would come here to help you."

"But why the crate?"

"Do I get to ask questions about you too?"

"I'm afraid my story is not very interesting."

"I want to hear it anyway. Are your parents living?"

"No. My father was a corporate executive and my mother was devoted to playing the piano. I have one sister, Millie. The rule in our family was, *Don't talk about it.* So that's how I grew up, learning to keep a lid on what I was feeling. It was safer that way." He doesn't tell her about his mother's queer behavior. Neither does he tell Claire about his father's nightly routine, closing himself up in his study, drinking until he passed out, spending the night there instead of in bed with his wife. What Lyon does tell Claire is that his parents were nice. "Not particularly demonstrative but *nice.* They were always sort of . . . I don't know, *distracted,* I guess you'd say. My sister has two sons and a daughter but I haven't seen any of them in years. I've always been a loner. When I'm around people too long they begin to . . . *bother* me."

"Bother you?"

"Irritate me. Their tics and habits, the way they misuse certain words or keep repeating a favorite phrase, certain physical flaws—"

"That's awful."

Lyon feels as if he's been caught at something embarrassing.

"No close friends?"

"Tommy Door," he answers quickly. "But he's dead."

"Dead?"

Lyon nods.

"Wait a second," he says, "we're off the point here."

"The point?"

"You and the crate, that point."

"Yes, we keep coming back to that, don't we?" Her slender fingers toy with the tightly curled hair above her left ear. "Claire was a nurse, a pediatric nurse. Her interest in hoodoo was purely on the level of a hobby, collecting books and paraphernalia; she was interested in her heritage. She was born in New Orleans and was fascinated with how the powerless try to gain some element of control over their lives. Witchcraft, the supernatural, voodoo-hoodoo, even religion. I studied American folklore because Claire passed her fascination along to me. She never really became serious about hoodoo practices—never *believed* in them—until after she found out about the children Quinndell had killed, then he got her fired from the local hospital here, and my grandfather died—and Claire became obsessed. Seeing her lose control of her life, it was heartbreaking."

Claire looks up at the ceiling. She is softly biting the inside of her cheek.

"My grandmother took a special interest in me because I've always been overly quiet. One of my older sisters is an actress, the other is a fashion model. They're both much lighter than I am, more flamboyant. The whole reason I stayed in the academic world is that I could succeed there simply by moving from grade to grade, degree to degree, just doing the work. I received my bachelor's degree at age twenty-one, master's at twenty-three, a year's fieldwork, Ph.D., teaching for the past two years.

"But you didn't ask for a biography, you asked why

I was in that crate." Her tongue comes pinkly from her mouth, touching her upper lip briefly before withdrawing. "I believe in the power of the *unexpected*. And I was afraid that if I simply showed up here, introduced myself, and offered to help . . . I was afraid you would tell me that I'd be in the way, that you preferred to conduct the investigation on your own. I needed some method for *affecting* you just as Claire affected you by committing suicide in your presence."

"You know about that."

She nods.

"Before Claire . . . before your grandmother died, she gave me a small white box that was very similar to the crate you were in. I left it here in the kitchen somewhere. It had a wax figure in it, representing Quinndell, I guess."

While Lyon is looking for the little white box, Claire tells him, "Sticking pins in dolls is not a primary practice of hoodoo, in spite of the movies you've seen. The point is to get something into the hands of the person you're trying to affect, an enemy you want to hurt or a lover you're hoping to win back. When they receive something that demonstrates you're working your magic on them, they keep thinking about it, and if they're believers, it has an effect on them. Psychology. Sitting somewhere in private and sticking pins in a doll wouldn't work unless the person *knew* you were doing it."

He returns to the table. "I can't find it. Do you know what I'm talking about, that little white box your grandmother gave me—have you seen it?"

Claire shakes her head.

He watches her a moment and then asks, "What

about the *big* box, the one you were in—what did you do with it?"

"My grandfather, Stuart, was quite a bit older than Claire. He came here to retire. They owned a house right in Hameln and then this cabin, which they used as a getaway. They brought me out here when I was having troubles."

Lyon realizes she's not answering his question. "And the crate you were in?"

"I got that from Claire's house in town. That's where she kept her hoodoo collection, except everything in that house has been thoroughly trashed. Claire doesn't own the house anymore anyway, lost it in the bankruptcy. Same with this cabin."

He's trying not to lose his patience. "But what did you *do* with the crate?"

"Claire was buried in the Hameln cemetery this past Saturday."

Lyon nods. "Oh. And that's why you came here from New York, for her funeral."

"Yes."

"And then hearing that I was here, you decided—"

"I knew where you were staying, I didn't have to hear about it."

"How long have you been plotting—"

"John, I had to find a way to *insert* myself in your life."

"You certainly did that."

She makes a sound of exasperation. "I get sick to my stomach when I have to face a roomful of people at a cocktail party, no way could I have forced myself on the famous John Lyon. If I had just shown up here and knocked on the door, offered my help, you would've dismissed me."

"You weren't dismissable last night."

She covers her face with both hands, laughing—John Lyon finding this enormously attractive.

He asks her, "How do you manage to lie there so *still?*"

Even when Claire lowers her hands, she still won't look him in the eye. "It's a form of self-hypnosis. I've done a lot of meditation and . . . I've never been very successful with men, they find my silences off-putting. I have difficulty expressing my emotions. People think I'm a cold fish. I'm too black."

Lyon keeps watching her as she speaks.

"What I did with you, in the box the first night and then in your bed last night, just lying there, hypnotizing myself into a trance—it's what I do best."

"Did you . . ." And now it is Lyon who is hesitant. "Did you want to make love to me, I mean from the beginning, from when you first got into bed with me and I was still asleep, is that where you thought it would lead—to our making love?"

She thinks about it for a moment before speaking. "I don't know. Sometimes I just put myself into certain situations and then let events unfold."

"Let events unfold?"

She finally looks him in the eye. "I guess neither one of us should analyze it too deeply. I know I certainly don't want to defend my need to be that passive."

Yeah, Lyon thinks, and he doesn't want to explain his untoward interest in her that first night either—back when he was still assuming she was a corpse but touched her anyway.

They sit awhile longer and then Lyon asks, "Where were you yesterday, when I brought the sheriff here?"

"I hid. I didn't want to put you in an awkward position."

"Awkward position? Like telling the sheriff there was a comatose woman here and then—"

"I'm sorry. I know I've botched everything."

"I didn't have much credibility to start with—because of what happened on the air a week ago Sunday. You know about that?"

"Of course."

"Of course," he repeats. "Anyway, I'm sure the sheriff has reported me to the network, I'm sure I'm unemployed, I still get these crying and laughing spells—"

"Laughing?"

"Yes, a new development since the one everybody saw on television. Your grandmother picked the wrong person to be her champion."

"You can still use a shovel."

He looks at her.

"Claire always said that the way to prove the case against Quinndell was to dig up one of the graves."

"Why didn't your grandmother do it then?"

"She was always watched when she was in town."

"Are you going to dig up the graves?"

"Yes—and you're going to help."

"No," Lyon replies with what he hopes is ironlike conviction. He raises the cup to his lips but finds that the coffee has cooled.

"I'll pour you a fresh cup."

As Claire goes from table to sink to stove, then back to the table, Lyon keeps his eyes on her. The sudden lust he feels disorients him, and twice Lyon has to stop himself from getting out of his chair and going to her. He keeps catching glimpses of the way her ass moves beneath the hem of his teeshirt.

She puts his coffee cup in front of him and then,

before Claire has a chance to step away, Lyon runs his hand under the teeshirt, onto her bare ass. All he's waiting for is one hint of encouragement—a smile, a soft word—and then Lyon will have her down on the kitchen floor. But as soon as his hand touches her ass, Claire simply halts and looks off into the middle distance, neither encouraging nor discouraging him. And when he withdraws his hand, she proceeds to her chair at the other end of the table as if overlooking some social gaffe he has made.

Lyon sips at the coffee, waits for her to say something, and then asks Claire to tell him about her grandmother.

"She was one of those remarkable black women who holds everything and everyone together. Her marriage to Stuart was beautiful, they doted on each other. It was a combination of Stuart dying and Quinndell harassing her that drove Claire crazy."

"Was she actually . . . Yesterday when I met Quinndell he gave me a file on your—"

"You met the beast?"

"Yes. You knew he was blind."

"Claire always said that his blindness proves that God still answers prayers. He had a brain tumor. I hope I never see him again."

"He scares you."

"He's evil. If it weren't for his being isolated in a small town where he controls the authorities, Mason Quinndell would've been committed to a hospital for the criminally insane a long time ago. He's murdered babies, raped women, tortured men—"

"Come on, Claire, no one gets away with stuff like that."

"Really? How did John Wayne Gacy go on for all

those years, killing young men and burying them under his house? How did Jeffrey Dahmer keep on without getting caught, chopping up victims in his *apartment* for godssake? These were not master criminals. They got away with it because no one *cared* about their victims. And that's how Quinndell operates, that's how he gets away with it, he hurts people who are powerless."

"Did your grandmother know about these other victims?"

"Claire kept in contact with people here, people who hated Quinndell and have been hurt by him but can't do anything about it except feed information to Claire."

"The file he gave me contains some damaging information."

"I'm sure it does. The vampire accusation, right?"

"For one."

"It was a setup. He got one of his doctor friends to pretend he was drinking blood so Claire would see him and report it and cast doubt on her accusations against Quinndell. Very effective."

"Your grandmother gave me a file too, but in it she never mentions *why* Quinndell killed those babies."

"We talked about that a lot of course. In her last months, Claire really went off the deep end and began speculating about Quinndell harvesting body parts or performing Satanic rituals, but she was grasping at straws by then. The fact of the matter is I don't know *why* he did it. That's what we have to find out. All I know for sure is, evil *exists.*"

Lyon thinks that, after all he's gone through since he's been here, if he's still having trouble believing Quinndell is a babykiller, then how in the hell is he going to convince the network or anyone else that an investigation should be launched?

"When I was with him in his office yesterday," Lyon tells her, "and Quinndell was defending himself, I . . . well, don't get mad at me, Claire, but I believed him. Do you think there's any possibility that your grandmother was mistaken?"

Claire surprises him by saying, "Sure. Anything's possible. But I gave her my word, John—I promised I would come down here and help you."

She stands and walks to the kitchen window. "She left me a full account of what she intended to do. Contacting you because of the way you cried on television when you reported that story about murdered children, knowing she would never be able to arrange an appointment to meet you, knowing she had to do something dramatic to get your attention. Of course by the time I found her note it was too late, Claire had already met you and killed herself. And it worked, didn't it—you're here. I guess I was hoping my dramatic appearance in that crate would have a similar effect on you."

He laughs bitterly. "Everyone's certainly been dramatic. I was such a dramatic idiot with Quinndell that right before I left he turned out all the lights and I had this feeling he was coming after me, or maybe I was just being scared of the dark. What I do know is when I was out in the hallway I saw him standing there pointing something at me."

"A spoon?"

Lyon jerks his head. "Yes!"

"Was Carl with him, the deputy?"

"No, but Sheriff Stone mentioned Carl."

"Carl brings Quinndell his victims."

"His victims?"

She turns to face Lyon. "It's not just babies that Quinndell has killed. People disappear around here, people whose disappearance won't be too closely investigated. Claire was told that Quinndell gouges their eyes out with a spoon."

"Jesus."

"If we dig up one of the graves, we can put an end to it."

"Claire, I'm not digging up any graves, okay? So far I've made a fool of myself on national network television and I've gotten myself fired, that's enough for this summer."

She gives him a look that's both angry and disappointed, then departs the kitchen, leaving Lyon to rub the left side of his forehead, feeling the pain unfold there and behind both eyes.

When he finally goes into the bedroom, he finds Claire dressed in jeans and a light blue blouse.

He asks her where the clothes came from. "And you never did tell me where you've been hiding or how you got in here last night either. I had everything locked. And what did you do with the crate?"

She's sitting on the bed.

"Claire?"

"I'll hire a private detective."

He sits next to her. "A detective will happily take your money, investigate anything you tell him to investigate as long as you keep paying—but he won't nail Quinndell. And a private detective won't dig up a grave for you."

"Neither will you."

"But at least I'm not charging anything."

"Just taking it out in trade?"

"You're the one who crawled into bed with me last night." He stands and walks to the window, finally turning to Claire and telling her, "You're manipulating me."

She laughs. *"Of course* I'm manipulating you. I'm manipulating you the way women used hoodoo to manipulate their men—and for the same reason too. Women resort to intrigue because they have no other power. Manipulation is a reasonable response to a woman's reality, just as guerrilla warfare is a weaker force's reasonable response to a stronger, better equipped force. Just the way Claire manipulated you into coming here by killing herself in your presence. It's hardly a news flash, John, for you suddenly to announce that I'm manipulating you. The only news is that my manipulation obviously hasn't been successful."

He returns to her, gently pushing Claire down on the bed. "Try again."

"You won't like it. I'm not good at sex."

"Are you kidding?"

"Not unless I'm playing a role, the way I was last night. Otherwise I'm clumsy and self-conscious. . . . I told you I wasn't very good with men."

"You were good with me last night."

"You're not listening!"

He starts undoing the buttons of her blue blouse, intrigued by the white bra she's wearing. It has a tiny rose on—

"John!"

"Yeah?"

Claire takes a moment to organize what she's going to say. "I was in love or thought I was in love only once in my life and that was with an older man who was married. I got pregnant, he paid for the abortion, and since then I've been living very nicely, thank you, without a male presence in my life."

"Until last night." He has her blouse completely open, trying to figure out the mechanics of opening the bra. It's been a long time.

"Shall I pretend I'm dead again?"

That stops him. Lyon gets off the bed and stands. From behind him, however, he can hear her removing clothing.

"Don't turn around," she warns. "Not until I'm under the sheet."

He waits.

Claire tells him okay. "Now you take off *your* clothes."

Lyon turns. "I don't want you to watch me undress either."

"Of course I'm going to watch you undress, I didn't get to see anything last night."

He removes his shirt but then stops, holding the shirt in front of his chest and feeling terribly self-conscious—feeling, in fact, like a teenager doing this for the first time. "Please, I'm serious. Turn over until I get in bed."

"You're being silly." She has tears in her eyes, just enough to make them glisten. "Cute but silly—now drop that shirt and take off your pants."

"No."

"Why?"

"I don't want you to see how fat I am, how old and fat I am."

"And white. You're very white, John."

He doesn't know how to answer that.

"Okay, okay." Claire turns over.

Lyon drops the shirt and slips off his pants, trying to get in bed quickly—but not quickly enough, Claire turning back toward him and staring at his body as she opens her mouth and eyes in cartoon exaggeration, Lyon cursing her and laughing as he grabs for the sheet, Claire holding it so he can't get under, both of them laughing, and John Lyon for the first time in his life feeling self-conscious about the color of his skin.

"I told you it wasn't going to be any good."

"Don't be silly," he says. "You were fine, you were great."

"Which? Fine or great?"

"Great."

"Liar."

"I feel . . . Claire, anything I say is going to sound like a cliché."

"Let me hear your clichés, John."

He takes her wrist and turns it so he can see the inside of her forearm. "Where did you get these scratches, you didn't have them last night." They look like scrape marks, a half dozen long parallel lines where something has gouged into Claire's flesh. Distracted by the wounds, Lyon doesn't catch what Claire has just said. "What?"

"I said I want to hear the clichés, John."

He puts her arm down. "Okay. You make me feel . . . *whole*. I feel like a new man. Nothing's worrying me anymore, not losing my job, not the embarrassment of breaking down on camera, not these stupid laughing-crying spells I've been having, nothing. I want to take you back to New York, I want us to move in together, I want . . ."

"You want to have my babies?"

"Sure! Scientists talk of a procedure where they could implant an embryo in the lining of a man's intestines, I'll stay home and have babies, cook your meals, go to your faculty parties and flirt with the chairman of your department."

"The chairman of *my* department would love that."

"Let's pack up and leave right now."

She has her head on his chest, listening to his heartbeat. "I can't. I have to keep my promise to Claire."

"When we get back to New York I'll talk to some people, I still have contacts. We'll get Quinndell investigated, I promise. In fact, it'll be better if it's done by an impartial third party."

"An impartial third party won't do what's necessary. Claire tried impartial third parties."

"You can't let your life be ruled by a promise—"

"He raped me."

Lyon says nothing.

Claire can hear his heartbeat quickening as she speaks. "I was fourteen. I went to him for something routine, a school check-up or an inoculation, I don't remember. A lot of this I've blocked out completely."

"Why in God's name would your grandmother let you go to Quinndell?"

"John, this was years before she suspected him of doing anything to those babies. I'm not even sure she had worked with him at that point. And Claire never knew this happened, I've never told anyone until now, until you."

But Lyon isn't sure he wants to be the one to hear it.

"There wasn't a nurse with us in the examining room, I knew that was wrong but I didn't have the nerve to question a doctor. I was only fourteen. He

had my feet up in the stirrups with a sheet covering
. . . covering what he was doing."

"Jesus."

"He never even acknowledged what he was doing,
like it was all part of the examination or like I
wouldn't know what was happening down there under
that sheet. He kept looking off into the distance, I was
watching his eyes, he had dark eyes and . . . It hurt."

"God, I'm sorry."

"I'm sorry too. I'm sorry I let him get away with it
and I'm sorry he messed up my life. I was shy to begin
with but what Quinndell did to me, that's when I first
learned how to go dead inside." Claire is crying. "Do
you understand now why I believe Claire's accusations against him? He ruined my childhood, John, and
he killed my grandmother—I'm not leaving here until
he's dead or in jail."

They are quiet for a long time—then Claire bolts up
in bed.

"What's wrong?"

"Shh."

"What is it?" he asks.

"Do you hear a baby crying?"

Lyon listens. "No."

"I heard a baby crying."

"Come on, Claire, don't start on—"

"I'm not starting on anything!" She looks terrified.
"I heard a baby crying!"

Lyon gets out of bed, slips on his trousers, and
walks to the window. "Jesus Christ!"

"What?"

"It's that little . . . *man* who peeked in the window!
He's standing out in the woods, just standing there
watching the cabin."

"Does he have a baby with him?"

"I don't know." Lyon grabs his clothes. "You stay here." He runs barefoot through the cabin, to the front door, opening it and rushing out into the arms of the fattest man he's ever seen in his life.

25

LYON IS BEING PRESSED AGAINST AN EXPANSE OF UNIFORM that looks as if it was manufactured by a tent and awning company. Above the left pocket is stitched the word *Deputy*. Above the right pocket, in the same bowling shirt stitching, is *Carl*.

After struggling out of those massive arms, Lyon staggers back to see how many people are stuffed in that uniform.

"In a hurry, asshole?" the fat man asks, even his speech seemingly garbled by an excess of flesh.

Lyon tries to look around him. "Did you see someone out in the woods there?"

Carl turns ponderously toward the forest and then back to Lyon. The deputy says nothing.

"And where's *your* car? I have to drive an hour from town to get up into these mountains, but everyone else keeps showing up here without a vehicle."

Carl doesn't comment on that either.

Lyon steps back for another look. "So I finally get to

meet *Le Grand Carl* I've heard so much about—and there's so much of you to hear about too." Lyon isn't sure why he's acting so jocular. Nerves—or maybe it's because of Claire. "What can I do for you, Deputy?"

"Come to see that nigger woman you got."

When Carl takes a step toward the door, however, Lyon puts himself—shoeless, pants unzipped, shirt unbuttoned and hanging out—in the way. Feeling small and frail next to Carl, Lyon is surprised when the deputy retreats.

"Sorry, Deputy, but you can't enter my residence without a warrant or probable cause, in pursuit of a felony suspect with reason to believe he might destroy evidence or endanger someone—it's a constitutional thing." Why am I being such a smartass?

But Lyon's comments seem not to register with Carl, who removes a foil pouch from his pants pocket, takes out a plum-size handful of black tobacco, which he stuffs with some difficulty into his surprisingly small mouth.

"Nice touch."

Carl offers an incomprehensible reply, working the plug to his cheek and then spitting. "Come to see that nigger woman you got."

"So I gather." Then Lyon connects with Carl's sunken eyes, like something feral in there, staring out from a cave—Lyon realizing that this man, fat and stupid though he be, is not someone to be treated frivolously.

Carl spits over the porch railing and then reaches out to grab Lyon's shoulder, the deputy grunting either from the effort or with contempt. "Move, asshole."

"Take your hand—"

Carl moves him out of the way as easily as you would a child.

Lyon follows him into the kitchen. "Listen to me, Deputy—"

"Where's the bitch?" he asks in a grim voice.

"To whom are you referring?"

Another grunt as Carl turns his bulk and heads for the living room like a sumo wrestler in a hurry. Lyon catches up with him in the middle of the room, grabbing his elbow, Carl swinging around to put one hand at Lyon's neck, the other grasping the front of Lyon's trousers, Carl suddenly—breathtakingly—lifting Lyon into the air, lifting him so high his head actually touches the ceiling, then carrying Lyon like that—head bumping along the ceiling—across the room to slam him against a wall.

Lyon has no breath left.

"Touch me again and I will fuck you." He says this with surprising clarity. Then he drops Lyon to the floor.

By the time Lyon recovers his composure, Carl is moving—fitting himself—through the bedroom doorway.

Lyon is desperate now. "Claire!"

But when he enters the bedroom he sees only Carl there—opening a closet, looking into the bathroom, and finally turning to face him.

"Where's the bitch?"

Lyon shakes his head.

"Going to *fuck* you, man," Carl announces as he resumes searching, pulling aside the shower curtain and then with considerable effort actually getting down on his knees to check under the bed.

After finally struggling back to his feet he walks out

of the bedroom without acknowledging Lyon, searching through the rest of the cabin, finding nothing that
interests him.

In the kitchen he asks Lyon, "Who you calling to?
Claire?"

"I didn't call to anyone."

"*Claire,*" Carl repeats. "*Heard* you. That nigger
nurse?"

"Fuck if I know."

Carl steps out onto the porch and spits over the
railing, Lyon following, excited, on an adrenaline
high. Wherever Claire has hidden, she's safe for now,
and Lyon wishes he had the nerve to pick up some
kind of club and hit this fucking fat man right across
his jack-o'-lantern head.

Instead, he settles for this: "On second thought,
Carl, I *don't* think you're the *fattest* man I ever met.
When I was a young reporter I was sent out on one of
those weird-character stories that newspapers sometimes do, this was decades ago when I worked for the
Tribune, and I went to interview a guy who hadn't left
his house for eight years, mostly just staying in bed,
relatives coming over to feed him. He was too fat to fit
on a toilet so he had to shit in the bathtub, sitting over
the edge of the bathtub, and then when he finished he
had to turn on the shower to wash the mess down the
drain. My editor wouldn't let me use that part, of
course. I was wondering, Carl—can you still fit on a
toilet?"

The deputy has listened to this without reaction,
unless you count the rolling of that tobacco plug in his
cheek. When he realizes Lyon is done, Carl sucks to
gather a mouthful and then spits a thick brown stream
right into Lyon's face.

"Jesus! *Damn* you!" Lyon wipes at his eyes, getting

what feels like warm, sticky snot all over his hands, trying to wipe it on his shirt but it won't come off.

"Har . . . har . . . asshole."

"You *son* of a bitch!" Lyon takes a swing which Carl catches in his hand, twisting Lyon's arm, stepping one boot—a surprisingly small boot—on Lyon's bare foot, knocking him to the floor of the porch. Then Carl puts that boot on the side of Lyon's face.

Lyon is cursing, trying to wriggle free.

Carl eases a hundred or so of his pounds behind that boot, Lyon afraid now that the deputy is going to press down until Lyon's head splits open like an overly ripe cantaloupe.

"Har . . . har . . . asshole," Carl says again, spitting another brown-snot tobacco stream into Lyon's face.

He can't get away, Carl's foot on him the way a circus elephant places a foot on the beautiful trapeze artist—and to crush her, all the beast has to do is step down.

"Going to fuck you," Carl says, jamming that boot on Lyon's face—once, hard—before pulling back and then just standing there to see what Lyon is going to do about it.

He's crying. Lying in a mess of tobacco spit, a reddened imprint of a boot tread on the side of his face, Lyon doesn't move, remaining on the porch exactly the way he was when Carl had that boot on him, staying there, crying.

Carl laughs before lumbering away toward his patrol car, parked a hundred yards down the road.

In the cabin's tiny bathroom Lyon is washing his face for the third time, the tobacco juice already cleaned away, Lyon trying without success to obliterate the *idea* of it—and he can't seem to stop this goddamn crying either. It's not a sobbing breakdown this time, just a constant womanlike weeping.

"Claire."

Where is she, he needs her. Lyon leaves the bathroom to stumble through the rest of the cabin, calling her name, going to windows and looking out, assuming that's how she escaped, through a window, and now she's hiding in the forest somewhere, maybe that freakish little hermit caught up with her.

"CLAIRE!" Lyon bleats at each window he opens, still weeping, still needing her.

He ends up scrounging for some proof that she ever existed, but the evidence is sketchy: a second cup among the breakfast dishes, that dull ache in his pubic bone, the way his heart hurts.

He's back on the bed, begging her to come out from wherever she's hiding, calling her name, unable to stop crying.

26

RANDOLPH WALKS AS A MULE WALKS, TAKING MINCING steps that carry him up and down these hills with surprising efficiency. And as long as he's walking, the baby on his back is quiet. Randolph is heading home, never going to try to talk to that TV man again, it's too confusing what's happening over at that cabin.

It's also confusing what happened to the sheriff now that Randolph, walking, thinks about it. He didn't exactly *mean* for his dogs to kill the man, though Randolph did indeed give them that instruction, but mainly he just didn't want the sheriff to leave before understanding why it was that Randolph was keeping a baby girl in the back room. Except Randolph couldn't explain it no matter how long the sheriff stayed. Confusing.

He gets so confused sometimes, it hurts—hurts worse than . . . than what? It's difficult to rank his pain, he's had such an abundance of it in his life. Confusion hurts worse than that molar that went bad on him somewhere back in the 1960s, Randolph working the molar to and fro with his tongue and then his fingers, placing in the side of his mouth a small rag-knot soaked in hard cider, biting and pushing and pressuring over two weeks' time until that molar became sufficiently loose in its socket that he was able finally to wrench it free with a cloth-covered pair of Klein No. 9 pliers. The pain caused by that bad molar during those fourteen days of self-dentistry became so exquisite that at times the little man could do nothing but sit in his shack, stunned.

Randolph keeps walking. She ain't heavy. And that molar didn't hurt him anywhere near as much as the confusion caused by these troubles with babies.

The troubles started some five years ago when that big deputy Carl drove up to the shack and sat in his patrol car honking the horn until Randolph came out and tied up the dogs, Carl explaining he was looking for a cave, any cave that nobody else knew about, said he was going to start shooting Randolph's dogs unless the hermit showed him a cave. Randolph led him to the one you get into through a limestone cleft behind a big white oak tree, the little man not mentioning that the cave could also be entered by following a sinking creek just below his shack.

A week later this fancy four-wheel-drive truck—all black and chrome—went past Randolph's place and stopped up at that white oak, the hermit taking off along the sinking creek to get to the cave's other entrance. Once inside he hid in a niche, snuffed out his carbide lamp, and just sat there and listened. Someone had been left in the cave without a light, someone who was mad at God, cursing God for what God had done to him—but howling for more too. Randolph had never heard such *anger*.

The little hermit loves the burrowlike security of caves but in spite of rumors to the contrary, Randolph can't maneuver around in underground blackness minus a light. Randolph was confused about what this man had done that was so bad he had to be left in a cave without a lamp, convinced finally that the deputy had caught the Devil and put him blind in that cave for safekeeping.

Went on for a month, Randolph sneaking in there every day to listen to the Devil rail, cursing God, the Devil claiming he could take whatever punishment God could hand out, howling for more.

Carl would drive past Randolph's shack each morning and leave the Devil's food and water by the white oak entrance. More confusion—because if you had gone to the trouble of sticking the Devil in a cave without a light, why would you bother feeding and watering him?

Then one day Randolph went to the cave and found that the Devil was gone.

Came back though.

Two seasons later, in the dead of winter, that fancy black and chrome truck drove past the shack, heading up to the white oak, Randolph making his way to the cave's other entrance to find out who or what was being put in there this time.

By the time Randolph got in position, it was all over. Later on, he explored the cave's lower reaches, finding the baby's body on the shore of a cold black underground lake.

Mother always said curiosity killed the cat.

When she died the lawyer who sold her house came to the institution looking for Randolph, telling him that he had money coming and that he also had the legal right to be set free. The lawyer even sold Randolph some land. It just so happened that the land cost exactly what was left in mother's estate.

But once he had the land, Randolph didn't need much money, discovering that self-sufficient independence was largely a matter of doing without *things*, doing without a telephone, electricity, plumbing, vehicles. Growing his own food. Keeping a few random dogs that had wandered away from the rich men who once hunted in this area, Randolph breeding his own line and selling them for enough cash to buy books. He considered himself happy, an island—until he found that baby on the shore of a cold underground lake.

The little boy was less than a year old, the baby's head showing some kind of defect that Randolph didn't understand, though he understood enough to realize the child was discarded for the same reason Randolph himself had been banished and institutionalized: because of defects.

It happened again the following spring and then once more the next summer.

The first baby went in a grove of sycamores down by the creek, the second went on a ridge covered with wild roses, the third was buried between two walnut trees.

What could Randolph do about it, couldn't tell the law because Carl *was* the law. Shouldn't get involved at all, Randolph's lack of involvement with people was what kept him safe, but the more he thought about it, the more he realized he couldn't just let babies keep piling up on the shores of that black lake.

So the next time the fancy truck went by his shack, Randolph *ran* along the sinking creek and got positioned in that cavernous room well before the Devil made his way underground. Sitting in the dark, Randolph listened to the Devil curse God, saying, "Here's another one for you, Old Man, what're you going to do with this one!" Then waiting for a response. Then howling. "Nothing," is what the Devil kept howling. *"Nothing!"*

Waiting until the Devil was gone—but *barely* gone—Randolph lighted his carbide lamp and hurried over to a crevice, seeing that the child had been left out on a round-topped boulder in the middle of a narrow limestone bridge that crossed this crevice, which dropped a hundred feet down to that underground lake.

Randolph scurried onto the bridge and got to the child just before it—he—rolled off the boulder. The hermit brought him home but the little boy died the next week and Randolph put him among the roots of a Virginia pine, a tree known to flourish in poor soil.

As soon as he reaches his shack he takes the little girl into the back room and washes her, changes her clothes, getting ready to feed her—or at least try. He's had this one since March, the fifth baby Devil-delivered to that cave in five years, the second one Randolph was able to save, the only one who's lived.

And for almost four months now Randolph has been confused about what he should do with her. Also confused about who the Devil is or what the Devil will do to him when it comes out what Randolph has been up to. And he's confused about what people will do to him—something bad but *what?*—when they come looking for Sheriff Stone and find his exploded body in that brush-covered patrol car.

It hurts, being this confused and being this scared —there's no other way for Randolph to explain it except that it hurts.

What Randolph likes remembering best about mother is the part where she used to come in his room at night when he was a child, constantly crying from the pain, and mother smelled of soap and her skin was cool, coming into his room to tell him stories of heroes—books about heroes are the kind Randolph likes to read—and how these heroes endured great pain to rescue the innocent, Mother kissing his eyes and nuzzling along his neck, telling Randolph she was eating up all his pain, eating where it hurts, eating his "ows."

Randolph is surprised when the baby girl finishes her entire bottle and then howls for more. Maybe she's getting better. He's confused about whether he has any right to keep her.

In fact, about the only thing that doesn't confuse him is the knowledge, the certainty, that some kind of trouble—Devil trouble or people trouble—is coming his way. Or as he puts it, carrying the little girl about the shack, feeding her a second bottle, whispering into her pink pearl ear: "Twouble's comin' and we got no hewo."

27

LYON'S NOT GOING TO LET HER CATCH HIM ASLEEP THIS time, here he is in the middle of the night, lying on his side, under the sheet, but by God he is *watching* that bedroom doorway, absolutely sure she's going to appear there any minute now . . . and then not so sure, convinced one moment that Claire is an apparition, the creation of his inflamed insane mind, but telling himself the next moment that of course she is real, that *she's* the one who is unbalanced, as voodoo-hoodoo crazy as her grandmother was . . . he loves her, he loves her not, that kind of Ping-Pong bullshit, and it goes on and on as night deepens—until there in the doorway Claire appears, small, black and naked.

When she sees his eyes, sees that they are open, Claire immediately looks down in embarrassment, then she pads, bare feet dry-kissing the hardwood floor, over to the bed to slip under the sheet with him.

Thrilled that she's here, Lyon now tries as hard as he can to be angry with her. He turns his back and refuses to speak for the longest time. Why doesn't *she* say something? Then, still not facing her, he finally asks, "Where did you go?"

"I disappeared."

"I *know* you disappeared, what I'm asking is where did you disappear *to?*"

Claire takes so long to answer that Lyon begins to wonder if she's fallen asleep.

"When I'm forced to attend one of our departmental dinners," she finally says, "and the person on my left turns away from me, ignores me during the entire dinner, and the person on my right is doing the same thing, both of them having found someone more interesting to talk to, and I'm forced to sit there for an hour, rearranging food on my plate and feeling smaller and smaller—for all intents and purposes I have disappeared from that dinner table, haven't I? So you tell me, John—where did I disappear *to?*"

Lyon doesn't want to hear this shit, he wants to know where the hell Claire has been hiding.

"Or when my sisters drag me to one of their parties and they assign some man to talk to me but then the entire time he's standing there his eyes are working the party and I'm hating myself for going through the motions of making conversation with him and then he interrupts me in mid-sentence to leave and go talk to someone more interesting and *the way* he leaves, a quick nod, a false smile, touching me on the shoulder when he says 'excuse me,' patronizing and dismissing me at the same time, then *fleeing* with this sense of relief, and for the rest of the time I'm at that party he makes sure he never sees me. I was invisible when he and I were standing together and as soon as he got away from me I disappeared from his sight. So you tell *me,* John, where do I keep disappearing *to?*"

"I understand what you're saying but—"

"Do you have an answer?"

He doesn't. "All right, forget where you were hiding this afternoon. Why didn't you come back after Carl left? Didn't you hear me calling you?"

"You shouldn't have let that man come in here. This was Claire's cabin. She and Stuart used to bring me out here, we had great times at this place, and even if Claire did lose this cabin in the bankruptcy, letting Carl come in here is like defiling—"

"Wait!" Lyon turns toward her. "I didn't *let* him come in. I didn't invite him in, I didn't say, 'Hey, let's go in the bedroom and see if we can find Claire.' Have you *seen* Carl? Carl is immense. Carl came very close to crushing my—"

"I can make other people disappear too."

Lyon sighs dramatically. "You know, what I really need in my life right now is a stabilizing influence, someone who—"

"My sisters are always trying to fix me up with guys, it's probably a running joke among their men friends, how you have to be careful or you'll get stuck with the ugly sister, the one who just sits there and doesn't say anything."

"Why are you always running yourself down? You're the most exciting, the sexiest woman I've ever met in my life."

"Yes, John, but you found me in a coffin."

Lyon can't think of a comeback.

"These 'dates' are always disastrous," Claire continues, "and usually they end after a very quick dinner, I'm dropped off at my apartment before eleven. But on a rare occasion my escort will figure, well, if he got stuck with the weird sister maybe at least he can knock off a quick piece of ass. I may be invisible but men are transparent. So after our quick dinner he takes me home and asks if he can come up for a drink and as soon as we're in the door he has his hands on me and you know what I tell him? I say let's hurry up and get to bed because it's been a long time since I've screwed anyone, what with my herpes always acting up and then that darn old positive HIV test—got a rubber?"

This strikes Lyon as funny but his laugh suddenly dies when he remembers that the sex he and Claire have had has been decidedly unsafe.

Claire tells him he has nothing to worry about. "I'm one of the few twenty-six-year-old women you'll ever meet who can count on the fingers of one hand the number of sexual partners she's had."

"Does that include the thumb?"

"You're number four, John—do you want to hear about the first three?"

"No."

"Back to my date then. After my little announcement he of course changes his mind about having sex with me and begins making his way toward the door, suddenly remembering work he was supposed to do that night, appointments he has for very early the next morning, remembering he had promised he would call his mother before midnight, remembering he forgot to feed his dog. You wouldn't believe the excuses they come up with. But, see, I won't let him leave. I keep talking, long rambling stories about my students, dragging out a photo album from my fieldwork, suggesting we listen to a ninety-minute audio tape I made of an old hoodoo woman living just outside of New Orleans, telling him about my eleventh birthday party, listing all the guests who attended, describing the presents I got."

Claire is smiling, enjoying the memory of this. "I call it the ruby slipper syndrome. The poor guy is so desperate to leave, to disappear from my presence, that he wishes he was wearing ruby slippers he could tap together three times for immediate transportation home. And then finally when I tire of tormenting him I say well it's getting kind of late, maybe you should leave now—and he *runs* for the door. And guess what? I never see or hear from him again. Ever. I have made him disappear."

Lyon can believe it, can easily imagine Claire tormenting her dates. "Tomorrow morning," he tells her, "I'm tapping *my* ruby slippers three times and transporting myself back to New York."

She doesn't comment.

"Will you come back with me?"

"I wish I had kept my baby," she says softly, speaking more to herself than to Lyon. "At the time it seemed like such a disaster being pregnant by a man I loved but who was married to someone else, I *had* to get an abortion. Now I wonder if I'll ever have a baby. What I hadn't counted on, I just never dreamed I would end up *alone."*

This hits Lyon hard. *"End up?* For chrissakes, Claire, you're only twenty-six, you haven't *ended up* in any way yet. You want to talk about ending up, try being fifty years old and having no one, no family of your own, no real friends, no . . ." And here he has to fight against crying. How can it be you go all your life being hard and dry inside and *end up* like this, weeping at the slightest provocation?

She turns to him. "John?"

"I could've gotten married but I always kept women at a distance, kept everyone at a distance because I . . . I don't know. Because I was selfish, I had my well-ordered, well-financed life organized just the way I wanted it—why mess things up, why take a chance on getting hurt or altering my schedule to accommodate someone else, eating because someone else is hungry or going out when I wanted to stay in or . . . I had one friend, one good, close friend, and when Tommy died this spring, that's when *I* ended up alone."

Claire doesn't say anything.

"I'm sorry, I don't mean to play one-upmanship on which one of us is the more miserable but, really, Claire, you're only twenty-six, you have plenty of time to get married and have babies."

"Men don't want to marry invisible women."

I'd marry you, Lyon thinks—but he doesn't tell this to Claire. Instead he lies there feeling sorry for himself and then feeling like an asshole for engaging in self-pity when in fact his life has been easy, charmed, and any trouble he's had, any heartache, has been of his own making. "You should've known me before the breakdown," he tells Claire. "I never whimpered back then. I was never a whiner. I never . . ." He turns and sees that she has closed her eyes.

"Claire?"

He nudges her shoulder but gets no response.

"Claire!"

She's not sleeping, she's doing *it* again, feigning that deathlike state, on her back, arms at her sides, breathing so shallowly that her chest doesn't move, face placid. Waiting—and implicit in that waiting is an offer.

"Grinding this little self-hypnotic trance routine into the ground, aren't you?" he asks, getting no answer and then turning away from Claire, pulling the sheet to the top of his shoulder, absolutely determined not to respond to her implicit offer, not this time.

And as Lyon lies there he wonders what Claire is thinking, that he gets off on having intercourse with comatose women? Is this how she's going to prevent him from returning to New York, offering to feed his perversity—lying there right now thinking that soon he will be parting her legs with his hands, touching tentatively to reach that place high between her black soft thighs, thinking that this supine offer is irresistible, waiting in blank repose for the perversion to be played out one more time, thinking that Lyon will soon be lowering the sheet to expose her breasts, sucking at them and then at her mouth until she comes alive *hungry,* Claire making sounds deep in her long black throat, a kind of growled warning, warning that once aroused her appetites are enormous, offering herself up, thinking that he has no choice now except to go after what is being offered?

No.

Not this time.

He turns onto his back and looks up at the skylight where stars are fading in favor of the moon's rising.

"Claire?"

No answer.

"Can I just talk to you, please?"

Nothing.

This maddening act of hers so twists Lyon with frustration that he could strangle Claire, he really could—and what's even more frustrating, damning, is that he's got another massive hard-on.

Lyon waits, time passes, and with one hand choking his erection instead of Claire, Lyon continues waiting until he is finally borne reluctantly away by sleep.

* * *

"Tomorrow," she whispers at some point in the dead of that night, her lips touching his ear, "I will make you invisible. Tomorrow at two in the afternoon."

"Huh?" Lyon not quite awake, sensing that she has been talking into his ear for some time.

"Do you believe I can make you invisible, John Lyon, John Lyon?"

She is speaking in a singsong voice that to Lyon's still half-asleep mind sounds Jamaican or vaguely French. "Tomorrow you will believe me, John Lyon, John Lyon, because tomorrow you will be invisible. Sweeter though for you to believe Claire tonight. Jesus said, 'Blessed are those who have not seen but still believe.'"

He remains disoriented, lying on his back with Claire sitting up and leaning over him, the whites of her eyes in that black face striking him as ominous, somehow dangerous.

"I am the spirit conjured by Claire, created by the sacrifice of her life, sent here to help you do what you must do—dig up a child's grave, John Lyon, John Lyon. Dig it up at night and no one will see us. I'll be black, you'll be invisible."

"Why are you talking in an accent?" he asks her simply.

Her face still hovering over him, those big eyes staring.

"Kill him," she whispers.

"What?"

"Kill the monster Quinndell and we won't have to disturb those babies in their graves."

"Jesus," he says, trying to roll out from under her—but Claire won't let him escape.

"Kill him."

"You're not serious."

"Serious? He raped that little girl in his examining room, fourteen years old, she wasn't even wearing a bra yet, and he put her legs up in those stirrups—"

"I'm sorry that happened to you Claire but I'm not capable of killing anyone."

"Not capable? You're capable of fondling a dead woman in her coffin, *quelle horreur,* John Lyon, John Lyon—surely you can deliver justice to the monster Quinndell."

"I'm not even sure he's guilty of what your grand-mother—"

Her eyes flash. *"Kill him!"*

"Jesus."

"Kill him and I'll be waiting in your bed every night the rest of your life."

He wants to make a joke of it, asking her if that's a threat or a promise.

But Claire won't let up. "Kill him."

"I can't even successfully investigate him, much less—"

"Tomorrow I will make you invisible, then we will talk of what you can or cannot do."

"Right," he says, trying to dismiss her. "Until tomorrow then." Lyon finally rolls out from beneath her, swinging his legs over the side of the bed, sitting there with elbows on knees, his hands rubbing his puffy face.

She comes close behind him, breasts cool on his warm, sweaty back. "How much do you love me?"

He looks around the room realizing he can see colors, so bright has the room become in that skylight. He *does* love her. Lyon tells Claire that he does.

"Of course you love me, it's hoodoo love, you had no choice in the matter, what I'm asking is *how much?*"

"A lot."

She laughs. "Such a small answer from so large a man."

With surprising strength Claire pulls him back into the bed, forcing Lyon onto his back and then clambering atop him, her arms and legs long and strong, giving Lyon the impression that she is a woman built for holding on, some kind of black squid, black spider—long limbed but voluptuous too, his hand reaching for one of her fat plum nipples, Claire knocking that hand away, laughing deep in her throat.

"Ask me how much I love *you*," she demands.

"How much do you love me?"

"I'll show you," Claire says, grinning white teeth.

Yes, he thinks—*show me*.

"I love you enough to keep you from the grave," she says, still speaking in her island accent, "because when your death is near I will take you away to a place like this where we can be alone, unmolested, and there I will lay you out on my kitchen table. Like this." Claire arranges his arms by his side, pushing both of his knees flat to the bed, her long fingers brushing hair off his forehead.

"Oh I see, this time *I* get to play the corpse."

"If after your death you are to be eaten, then better by me than the worms. I will begin while you're still warm from life, eating each square inch of your pale skin, chewing patiently each white finger . . ." She bends over and takes the fingers of his right hand into her mouth, gnawing on them not as gently as Lyon had hoped.

"I will drink down all the blood from your vessels, draining your heart, chewing its fibrous tissue, a hard heart but it will soften in my mouth, I'll put your bones in a grinder and sprinkle their bone dust over steaks cut from your thighs."

Lyon watches as she turns to place her hand on one of his thighs, testing it as if for tenderness, Claire still straddling him, surprising Lyon with her impossible lightness.

"I'll eat your eyes." She leans down slowly, breasts hanging over his chest, touching and then flattening against him as she puts her mouth on his left eye, kissing it softly at first but then sucking and then sucking harder, Lyon actually able to feel his eyeball being suctioned, scaring him enough that he twists his head violently away from her.

But before he can protest, Claire continues her singsong litany. "Kidney pie and brain sausage and John Lyon's sweet sweetbreads, I will eat everything until nothing is left of you, not even an eyelash, eating John Lyon until my stomach is as heavy with his meat as my womb is with his child."

What?

"And each day during this consumption of John Lyon, rescuing you from the grave, each day I will collect what passes from my body, what remains of you after I have sucked your nourishment, and I will spread it on my garden, wasting nothing of what was once John Lyon, who is too precious to waste, spreading you on my vegetables which I also will eat until every essence of what once was you will be absorbed totally into what is me, John Lyon living on after death, residing in my cells until I die and return *both of us* to the ground where we will lie mouldering together forever. That's the answer—how much I love you, John Lyon, John Lyon. More than your mother did, more than any woman ever has."

He waits a moment and then laughs. "Well you're right about one thing, Claire—no woman has ever said she wanted to eat me, shit me, spread me on her garden."

She slides slowly snakelike down his body until her face is at his navel. "Like this I will eat you," she tells him.

And he thinks, *yes.*

Claire sucks into her mouth a fold of his stomach flesh, biting gently at first but with an increasing pressure that soon takes away his breath, Claire clamping down until she is hurting him, then biting even *harder,* Lyon bolting upright and shrieking in pain, demanding for her to stop, Claire biting so hard now that her teeth actually penetrate his skin, Lyon cursing her again and again, jerking around in the bed, grabbing the sides of her head but unable to dislodge her even as he bucks his hips and yanks desperately on her hair.

He slaps her. Then he rears back to get better leverage and slaps her again as hard as he can on the side of her head, Claire releasing him from her teeth and looking at him with fear flashing in her eyes, Lyon slapping her a third time, full strength right across her face, knocking her away from him with such jarring violence that it looks as if he could have broken her neck.

He doesn't care if he did, both of his hands pressed over his bloody belly wound. "What the *fuck* were you trying to do!"

She's crying, holding an arm across her eyes. "Eat you."

"That's supposed to be a figure of speech, you spooky bitch."

She keeps her arm up, crying as she talks. "African warriors honor enemies by eating their hearts, that's no figure of speech, John—should lovers do any less?"

He's never struck a woman in his life. He grasps her wrist to take her arm from her face, again seeing the deep scratches along her forearm. "I'm sorry but for chrissakes, Claire . . ."

"I *would* eat you to save you from the grave."

"Yeah, well . . ." He lifts his hand from the bite wound, blood everywhere.

"If I could make you invisible tomorrow—"

"Fuck that, Claire, okay?"

She is speaking in her normal voice, the accent apparently slapped out of her, asking Lyon to humor her. "If by some miracle I *could* make you invisible, let's say just for the sake of argument that in my research I discovered an ancient voodoo rite that would make you invisible, if I could do that, could really make you invisible at two tomorrow afternoon, would you dig up one of those graves for me then?"

He's not going to respond to this kind of nonsense.

"John? If I proved I had that kind of power, the power to make you invisible, would you—"

"You just don't know when to stop, do you?"

She begs him to answer her.

"Okay, yes, if you were really able to make me invisible I would be so goddamn impressed I'd dig up the whole fucking cemetery—happy now?"

She's wiping her eyes with the base of her palm, smiling, telling him, "Yes, I'm happy now," Claire kneeling beside him, lowering her face toward his genitals.

"Hey!" he warns.

Claire smiling up at him. *"Mon petit chou,"* she says, flicking out that pink tongue for him to see.

Quickly reviewing his high school French, Lyon vaguely recalls some froggy endearment—my little cabbage. Oh fuck. "Now, Claire, goddamn it." Another mindless hard-on.

She moves over to get between his legs, burrowing down low to reach it.

"I swear to God, Claire, if you . . ."

With both black hands she holds that demanding hardness directly in front of her face, each wide eye looking up at him from either side of Lyon's moon-white tremulous shaft.

"So much do I love you," she says slyly, that singsong accent returned, tongue tip tasting him, laughing as she catches Lyon's frightened expression, her mouth opening to accommodate that first tender round inch.

"Jesus," he says, more prayer than blasphemy. *"Jesus,* Claire."

Her mouth is warm and her tongue is wet but what truly electrifies Lyon is the lingering possibility of what she *might* do, what the still fiery, bloody wound on his stomach proves Claire is capable of doing, Lyon watching carefully that woman crouched animal-like and black between his legs, thinking he should stop her but not stopping her, Claire a small dark bundle down there, capable of such a wicked bite.

With her fingers interlaced along his length, Claire's mouth works the top of him as her eyes keep watching him watching her.

Then, breathtakingly, she ingests it deep into the pink-tinged blackness of her jungly mouth.

"Claire?"

He's staying up on his elbows, the pleasure every bit as extreme as the fear, waiting for teeth.

"Claire!"

Too busy to answer, sucking him hard, making wet sloppy sounds, tongue sliding fatly up and down against his underside.

But he can't get his mind off of her teeth. *"Claire,"* he says, less of a warning now than a pleading.

She slowly raises her mouth away, one thin web-strand of saliva still joining them, Claire asking Lyon how much does he love her, punctuating the pauses between words with long languid licks of tongue, with up and down movements of her black fist, which slides wet but holds tight, tongue and fist up between the first two words, "How . . . much," down between the next two, "do . . . you," keeping her eyes on his the entire time, "love . . . me," up and, "John . . . Lyon," down.

She's actually got him trembling.

"You'd better answer," Claire warns, putting it in her mouth again, taking it out, drawing back her lips to show him those teeth he continues to worry about, bringing them together with the distinctive click-clinck of enamel on enamel. "How . . . much . . . do—"

"Damn you," he groans, can't take being teased like this anymore, grabbing the back of her head and forcing himself deep into that dangerous mouth. "You want children? Make me invisible . . ." holding her head with both hands now so he can thrust in and out of her mouth. "Make me invisible tomorrow . . ." rolling on his side and taking her with him, the better to buck his hips against her, both white legs locked around her black shoulders, "I'll do it, goddamn you, Claire, I'll dig 'em up and pile them at your feet!"

fucking that mouth which shields its teeth from him as it sucks back hungry to be fucked.

Lyon soon ejaculating in great clenching spasms that seem to be draining his spinal cord in gulps, Claire going after it with the eager grateful sounds of someone who moments before had been starving.

Because if African warriors honor enemies by eating their hearts, who are we to argue lovers should do any less?

28

On that Wednesday morning, July 4, John Lyon wakes up still sore from Claire—his stomach bruised ugly, *his* blood on the bedclothes—but feeling *good*. He wants to marry her. Crazy? A fifty-year-old white man, a white bread white man, marrying a twenty-six-year-old black woman, he suffers from crying spells and she believes in magic, of course it's crazy, but no more so than anything else that's happened to him in the past ten days, Lyon whistling in the shower, which is something he hasn't done since he can't remember when.

By 8 A.M. he's showered, shaved, dressed, and packing his suitcases when Claire comes in from the kitchen where she has been cooking another breakfast. She hands Lyon a cup of coffee and leans against the wall, crossing her arms.

"Thanks," he says, sipping from the cup and looking at Claire's outfit. "Where do you keep coming up with these different clothes?"

She glances down at the sleeveless white dress she's wearing but says nothing.

Putting the coffee cup on a bedside table, Lyon leans back from the waist to unkink his muscles. He winces because of the stomach wound and is aware that she is watching him closely. "Breakfast smells good."

"Where're you going?" Claire finally asks.

"I thought we could get an early start. I have to close up this place and then stop in town to turn in the keys."

"An early start to *where?*"

"Back to New York."

She thinks about it a moment. Then: "Last night you promised—"

Claire is cut off when Lyon shoots a look that warns her not to start in on any more of her nonsense. She leaves the bedroom and Lyon finishes packing.

When he comes into the kitchen he can still smell the food—after last night, Lyon is voracious—but breakfast has disappeared. Two frying pans are soaking in a sinkful of water.

"Couldn't wait for me, huh?" he asks jokingly.

She says nothing.

"Ate everything yourself, did you?"

She's leaning against a counter, her arms still crossed.

Lyon steps over to the garbage pail, opens the lid, and sees his breakfast.

"All right," he says with a show of exasperation, "here's what I'm doing. I'm going back to New York and getting an appointment with a doctor, a psychiatrist, try to find out why I keep losing control. Then I'm going to the network brass and say that I'm under a doctor's care, my breakdown is behind me, please take me back. They'll ask about these strange reports they received regarding my behavior in West Virginia and I'll tell them it was all a big mistake, a misunderstanding."

"A mistake," Claire says as if experimenting with that explanation, to see how it plays, to see if it works. "A misunderstanding."

"Yes. Nearly thirty years working as a newsman, that's got to be worth something. They won't let me go back on camera but I can produce or write, something, anything, I don't care. I'm going to put my life back together. That's it, that's my plan. And I want you to come with me."

"To come with you."

"Yes." Then he almost asks her to marry him.

"Last night you promised that if I made you invisible today, you'd dig up one of those graves."

"Don't start in on that shit again."

"You didn't think it was shit last night."

"All right. Okay. Make me invisible, *do it.*"

"I will. At two this afternoon, just as I said I would."

"I plan to be halfway to New York by then."

"Either you're going to keep your promise to me or you're not."

Lyon rubs his eyes with the fingertips of both hands. "Try to be patient with me, Claire," he says wearily. "I don't understand the *point.* Okay. You're going to make me invisible. Now is that like a metaphor for something, for example what you were talking about last night, how you become invisible at dinner parties when people ignore you? Do you understand what I'm asking? Invisible as in what?"

"As in people can't see you."

He steps to the counter and embraces her, but Claire keeps her arms crossed between them.

"Sometimes you seem so small."

"Black diminishes size."

"So perfectly black," he says running his hands over her slim shoulders and down her bare arms.

"Were you lying to me last night?" she asks stubbornly. "And if you were lying, were you lying about everything? Lying about loving me too?"

Lyon turns away from her and sits on the edge of the kitchen table. "All right. *All right.* I'll stay. I'll stay and let you play out this game—okay?"

"Okay." She gives him a big smile. "Time for your bath," Claire says, coming to Lyon and unfastening his belt.

"I already took a shower."

"But I have to wash you again, use unscented soap this time. You should brush your teeth with baking soda and salt too, because I can smell the toothpaste. You must have no scent, nothing anyone can detect. Just because you're invisible doesn't mean people can't smell you."

"Of course."

By this time Claire has his belt unbuckled and his zipper down, pulling up Lyon's shirt and gasping. "My God, did I do that to you?"

He joins her in looking at the multicolored wound on his lower belly. "Yes."

"I'm sorry." Claire sinks to her knees, tugging down his trousers and underpants. She takes his limp dick in her hand and wiggles it back and forth. "John? There seems to be something wrong with it, John."

"All right, all right," he says, hauling Claire to her feet.

She surprises him with a tender kiss.

"Whatever little experiment or performance you have planned for two this afternoon," he tells her, "I'll go along with it. But if I *don't* become invisible, then you have to promise *me* something. You'll come back to New York with me." And marry me. "And stay at my place at least until after I see a doctor, until I find out if I'm crazy or have some kind of weird crying-laughing disease, okay?"

"Okay."

"Claire."

"I *promise.*"

Claire makes him another breakfast but continues evading questions about where she hides when other people show up and what she did with that crate and how she got to Hameln from New York City.

They go back to bed and make love. Then Claire does indeed bathe Lyon with unscented soap, careful with his belly wound.

Around one that afternoon Lyon asks·about lunch —he's been so constantly hungry since he met her— but Claire says she doesn't want the odor of food to be on his person. Besides, it's time to leave. "I'll drive," she tells him.

"Where is this invisibility trick supposed to take place?" Lyon asks as he follows her out to his rental car.

"You'll see."

They drive off the mountain and to a state highway, which they travel for half an hour before turning onto a blacktopped road, then a dusty, rutted lane, Lyon still asking questions about where they're going and how his invisibility is going to be accomplished, Claire still refusing to explain.

Then she stops the car. "Get down."

Lyon looks out the window. Pastures on both sides of the road, no houses in sight.

"Get down and lie across the seat here, you can put your head in my lap."

"Why?"

"Just do it."

"But if I'm invisible," he says, thinking himself clever, "why are you worried about anyone seeing me?"

She grabs him by the hair and pulls him down.

"That hurt damn it, you're always hurting me," he complains.

She tells him to stop being such a baby. Claire moves the car forward as Lyon turns facedown in her lap and finds a space between the buttons of her dress, a space large enough for him to get his tongue through. She starts to slap the back of his head but then reconsiders it, easing her legs apart and humming tunelessly as she drives.

Ten minutes later Claire stops the car and tells Lyon he can get up. They are parked in the driveway of a simple one-story house in need of paint. No other houses in sight. The yard is overgrown.

"Who lives here?" he asks.

Claire is acting nervous, telling Lyon, "You must promise not to embarrass me."

"Me embarrass you?"

"I'm serious, John. In that house you're going to be invisible, you have to keep that in mind at all times. You can't suddenly clear your throat."

"Claire—"

"Please! You agreed to this, you promised."

"I'm not going to walk into someone's house and pretend I'm invisible."

She tells him he won't have to pretend, he *will* be invisible.

Claire gets out of the car, goes around to his side, opens the door, takes his hand. "Come on."

Shaking his head, Lyon goes with her.

After leading him to the house and knocking on the front door, Claire turns to Lyon and points a finger right in his face as she raises both eyebrows meaningfully, warning him one last time.

A pleasant woman in her early fifties answers the door. She seems overdressed for the country, a string of pearls around her neck, long teardrop pearl earrings, two brooches on the bodice of her dress, makeup applied with a heavy hand. "Claire?"

"Yes! How are you, Barbara?"

"Fine, we're both doing just fine, come in, please."

Lyon smiles and is about to bring up his hand and introduce himself when he realizes the woman can't see him.

After Barbara turns and walks into the house, Claire grabs Lyon by the front of his shirt and pulls him in after her. Once they are over the threshold, Claire shuts the door behind them and then positions Lyon in the center of the living room. All the windows are heavily curtained, the interior of the house as dark and cool as a movie theater.

Lyon can't make his mind work.

Another woman walks in from the kitchen. In her early sixties, wearing a housedress with an apron over it, she also is decked out in a surplus of jewelry. "Who is it, Barbara?"

"It's Claire Cept. Remember I told you she was coming over."

"Claire Cept?"

"Not the nurse, honey, her granddaughter."

"Oh."

Claire goes over to the older woman and takes her hand.

Lyon is rigid in the middle of the living room, measuring his breathing, wondering if either of these women can hear him shift his weight or smell him or somehow detect his presence. Neither one of them can *see* him, that much is obvious. He tries to signal Claire—get me the hell out of here—but she refuses to look at him.

Claire is chatting with the two women while Lyon, standing no more than ten feet away from them, becomes increasingly agitated—until, like some character from a screwball comedy, he begins tiptoeing toward the door. Except how's he going to get it open without their hearing him? Lyon tries turning the knob slowly, grimacing with each click it makes.

Claire finally catches Lyon's eye, seeing such anguish that her heart feels suddenly weighted, as if someone has put a brick on it. None of this is working the way she thought it would.

Lyon starts to cry.

"Oh," Claire says softly, in pain.

The woman who met them at the door—Barbara—asks Claire if she's okay as the woman in the apron reaches out to touch Claire's face, asking, "What is it, dear?"

"I'm sorry," Claire tells them. "I have to leave."

"I thought you were going to have lunch with us," Barbara says.

But Claire has already gone to the front door and is turning the knob for Lyon, who is trying his best to remain silent, trying not to make any crying sounds even though the tears have already arrived and his belly is quivering with muffled sobs, the migraine summoned by the crying and by Lyon's efforts to suppress the crying. He bends over a little, becoming crippled with pain.

I'm sorry, he mouths to Claire.

She gets the door open and ushers him out onto the front step, Lyon immediately breaking away from her and running crouched over to the car.

Before Claire can follow, Barbara's hand finds her shoulder. "What's wrong with your friend?"

Claire's mind is scrambling. "He's got a mental problem, some kind of breakdown, strange delusions."

"Really?"

Claire says, "Yes."

"Why didn't you introduce him?"

"I couldn't. Poor man thinks he's invisible."

"I see," Barbara says, smiling—but as soon as Claire leaves, the smile fades and the woman's face sets hard. She marches into the house and makes her way to the telephone where she angrily punches in a number.

29

"BARBARA, CALM DOWN. WHAT? NO, I DIDN'T—
Barbara, if you don't lower your voice I'll hang up. No
one harangues me, *no one*. All right then. Start over,
calmly."

As Mason Quinndell listens on the telephone, asking the occasional question to encourage his caller to
greater detail, the massive Carl waits in a chair in
front of the doctor's desk. Quinndell is tapping his
fingertips but Carl remains unmoving, tapping nothing, neither his fingers nor his toes, sitting there large
and ugly like something badly carved.

After Quinndell hangs up he pauses a moment,
fingertips still tapping, finally telling Carl, "Our Mr.
Lyon apparently was *not* lying about a woman being
at the cabin."

Carl grunts and tries to cross his arms, a surplus of
fat making the maneuver impossible. "Wasn't no
woman there." Still struggling for position in the

chair, the deputy settles for rather daintily grasping his fingertips together, both hands resting on one of the upper belly rolls. "He called to her, called her name, but he's crazy, wasn't no woman there."

"Yes, well, you obviously missed her. And what's more, this woman is passing herself off as Claire Cept's granddaughter."

"The nigger nurse?"

Quinndell allows himself a small sigh. "Yes, Carl, the one and the same."

"But she's dead."

"Lyon is with her *granddaughter*." Quinndell is forced to take conscious control of his temper. "Or with a woman claiming to be the granddaughter. I remember that little girl, she came to live here in Hameln when she was only eight or so." Quinndell smiles, showing his small yellow teeth. *"Of course. I examined her once."*

With the doctor lost in some memory, Carl does what he does best: sitting and waiting.

"Well. *Well.* I see it all now, see it clearly. This . . . *conspiracy* arrayed against me. Carl, my boy, the center will not hold much longer."

Carl doesn't have a clue.

Quinndell takes out a handkerchief and wipes at the moisture collecting around his beautiful glass eyes. *"Of course."* He's curiously delighted with what he takes to be the ingenuity of his enemies. "Except where does the hermit fit into this scheme? You said he wasn't home, is it possible he left with Sheriff Stone?"

Carl tries to think of an answer.

"You did search the hermit's shack, didn't you?"

"Yeah!" Carl lies enthusiastically. No way was he

going to get out of the patrol car at Randolph's shack, then have them dogs come tearing ass around the corner and catch him out in the open, no way.

"Yes, well you *have* been a disappointment, Carl," Quinndell says as he stands, straightening his suitcoat and adjusting his red tie. He walks around and leans against the front edge of the desk, the doctor's posture casual but perfectly correct. "I suppose we should have disposed of the hermit five years ago but I was hoping that the rather bizarre reputation he enjoys among the locals would keep people from wandering around out there. Do you suppose he somehow got *in* the cave?"

"Don't see how, Doc. You had me build that door 'cross the opening, padlocked it and all."

"Hmm. And Sheriff Stone still hasn't checked in?" The deputy shakes his head.

"CARL!" Quinndell thunders.

"No." The deputy releases his fingertips and tries to straighten up in the chair. "Nobody's heard from him, his house looks same as always, nothing missing from what I could tell, his pickup still in the driveway."

"If he's gone over to them, that will be troublesome indeed." Quinndell leans away from the desk, standing erect now, turning one way and then the other, almost as if he's posing. "All right, Carl, let's try this again. You will drive out to the rental cabin and you will bring Mr. Lyon and the granddaughter back to me."

"Told you," Carl whines, "ain't no woman there, just Lyon and he's crazy."

Quinndell steps to the deputy's chair, places his fine clean hands on its arms, and moves his handsome face to within an inch of Carl's. "Listen to me, you imbecile," the doctor says in a shockingly coarse voice, "if you don't do exactly as I tell you, I will slit your fat throat."

Carl's face turns red.

Quinndell straightens up but when he speaks now his voice is once again honey soft. "If the granddaughter does manage to evade you again, then simply bring Mr. Lyon here. I'm sure Mr. Gigli can convince him to cooperate with us."

Carl coughs out a nervous laugh. "Yeah, good old Mr. Gigli."

"Then when we have the two of them safely in our possession, Lyon and the granddaughter, we'll take them to Randolph's shack. It will be easy for people to believe that the little deviant has been killing children, that when the television star and his black helpmate got too close to the truth, Randolph murdered them too and in a suicidal rage set his own house on fire. Do you like that scenario, Carl?"

The deputy grunts an affirmative, though he has no idea what *scenario* means.

"Good. Because I don't intend to leave behind any loose ends, none at all," Quinndell says with a sense of the ominous that Carl misses completely.

Now the doctor is walking about his office, touching a vase, moving a finger along a picture frame—Carl watching, amazed.

"After bringing Mr. Lyon here, you will drive out to the hermit's place one more time and wait for him. He has nowhere to go, he'll eventually show up. And when he does, kill him."

"Kill him?"

"Take one of his own guns, place the barrel under his chin, and pull the trigger."

Carl's underarms step up their already heavy production of sweat.

"Do you understand?"

"I ain't never *killed* anyone."

"You've assisted me and Mr. Gigli often enough."

"But I never did it on my own, that's different."

"Suddenly everyone around me is revealing his *principles.*"

"Ain't that, Doc, it's just—"

"Do you have any idea what they're going to do to a fat boy like you in prison?"

"Prison?"

"God, I hate your whining voice." Quinndell steps behind the deputy's chair and places a hand at the back of his neck. "You're clammy." Quinndell takes out the handkerchief and meticulously wipes his hands dry. "You wouldn't try to run away from me the way our sheriff has apparently done, would you, Carl?"

"Not me, Doc."

"Because believe me, Carl, my bite is worse than any of those dogs out at the hermit's place."

Carl struggles to rise from the chair. He doesn't like the doctor standing behind him, gives Carl the willies.

"Kill the hermit for me," Quinndell announces, "I'll pay you the princely sum of twenty-five thousand dollars."

"No shit?"

The doctor returns to his desk. "You'll get your payment this evening."

Carl is considering it.

"Give me your answer *now.*"

"If you wanted to, Doc, you could throw something in to sweeten the pot."

"I'm listening."

"You know, what you said before, about me and Mary."

The doctor smiles his yellow smile. "Faint heart never won fair hand, Carl."

"Huh?"

"You keep failing in your tasks, that's why you haven't sampled Mary's favors yet."

"But I mean if I do it, if I bring Lyon back here and then go out and *do* Randolph, then . . ."

"Then what?"

"Then could me and Mary . . ."

"Yes?"

"You know."

"Say it."

"Then could me and Mary . . . *make love?*"

Quinndell laughs. "Make love?" The doctor is laughing harder now, genuinely amused. "Oh, Carl, by all means, *by all means.*"

After the deputy leaves, Quinndell spends the next hour on the telephone. Making airplane reservations. Calling the local bank president at home and arranging for certain funds to be transferred first thing in the morning. Telephoning foreign countries. During his final call he gives elaborate directions to a man who has worked for Quinndell before, telling the man that once he gets within a mile or so of the hermit's shack he'll have no trouble finding it, flames will light his way.

Then Quinndell sits at his desk for a long time, going over in precise detail what has to be done. Finally he presses the button to summon Mary.

The doctor is bending over getting something from the safe, his back to the double doors, when Mary enters the office, one of the doors slipping from her grasp and knocking back against the wall, so startling Quinndell that he turns too quickly, hitting an elbow

on the edge of his desk and dropping the envelope he
had in his hand.

"Don't you EVER sneak up on me."

"I'm sorry, I thought—"

"That's your first mistake, thinking."

She begins chewing on her lips. "I thought . . . I
assumed you heard me coming."

"No, I usually *smell* you coming. I mean, you really
should do something about the odor. A woman in
your line of work? I would have thought you'd have
learned by now how to keep it clean."

Mary's insides knot up.

Once he has picked up the envelope, Quinndell
orders Mary to take a seat.

But she remains standing. "I saw Carl leaving
earlier. If this is about me going to bed with him, I told
you before, I'm not letting that man touch me."

"Pity. Carl so has his heart set on making love to
you. And the truth of the matter is that you would
have sexual congress with an orangutan if the money
was right, isn't that correct?"

"No."

He laughs. "Speaking of money." Holding out the
envelope. "Go on, open it."

She does, finding inside a transfer of funds that
Quinndell has signed, authorizing Mary to withdraw
in her name a sum of two hundred and fifty thousand
dollars from the local bank.

"I'm sorry it's not a cashier's check, no time for that
now, there's been a change of plans. I'm not going to
make you wait until your one year anniversary with
me, I'm paying off my debt to you *tonight.*"

She doesn't know if she should allow herself to
believe it. The bank transfer, which Mary keeps
staring at, *seems* authentic.

"Mary?"

"Yes."

"Don't you have anything to say?"

She isn't sure if she should press her luck.

"Mary?"

"What about the other envelope, the one with her address, the pictures of her on her birthdays."

"Of course. I haven't forgotten *that*. She's more important to you than the money, isn't she?"

"Yes!" Mary gushes.

"You'll be reunited with your daughter as soon as you complete one last task for me."

She feels giddy.

"You will complete one final task for me, won't you?"

"Yes!"

"Don't even want to know what it is?"

"It doesn't matter."

"You're right, dear. At this late stage, nothing matters except freedom. My freedom from persistent enemies, your freedom from me." Quinndell is speaking to her in a voice of surprising kindness. "And oddly enough, Mary, I do think I'm going to miss you."

She responds quickly, without thinking. "I'll miss you too."

Quinndell puts his head back, opens his mouth, and moves his shoulders up and down in that obscene parody of his, laughter without sound.

30

NOT WITHOUT REASON ARE THESE HEADACHES CALLED blinding. Lyon rides all the way back to the cabin with his face turned to the passenger door, his back turtle-humped toward Claire, his eyes tightly closed, both hands over his face—like a man who's been shot inconclusively in the head. If he were given a red button that would end his life, ceasing pain, Lyon would press it gladly. And he can't stop this goddamn crying either, though by now the sobbing has turned to a muffled and shamed weeping. Lyon keeps wanting to apologize to Claire.

She meanwhile says nothing, shaken not only by Lyon's condition but also by what happened at the house, so deeply ashamed of herself that she wishes she could be the one slumped in the seat with her eyes closed and her face hidden.

When they finally reach the cabin, she sits with Lyon for a long time in the car, wanting to say the right thing but unable to find the words, wanting to touch him but unable to find the opportunity to do that either.

Lyon finally takes one hand away from his face. Getting the door open, he manages to put his right foot out and then the left but can't straighten up, so heavy is that engine of pain housed in his skull, Lyon walking bent over to the cabin, reaching out for a porch column, supporting himself there. At least he's stopped weeping. And now instead of wanting to apologize to Claire, he'd like to crucify her.

Claire comes behind him and puts a hand on his shoulder, but when Lyon looks up at her from that hunchbacked position, his expression is so bitter that Claire has no choice but to withdraw. "I'm sorry," she whispers.

He staggers into the cabin and through the living room, into the bedroom, opening a suitcase and finding a bottle of aspirin in his shaving kit, lurching into the bathroom where he takes four of the tablets, each washed down with a handful of water, standing there bracing himself against the sink, head down, eyes closed, the rag-knotted pain exquisite within his skull.

"I'm sorry," she whispers from the bedroom doorway.

Ignoring her, he tries lying on the bed with a damp washcloth across his eyes but the skylight makes the room too bright, Lyon sweating and hurting and remembering back to the night he arrived here, a lifetime ago when he first entered this cabin and couldn't get the lights to work, stumbling over that crate-coffin in the middle of the kitchen, kneeling on the floor next to it, opening the lid—and now, lying in bed recalling the scene, he remembers the warning he wanted to shout, *Don't do it, don't open it*—but now it is too late for warnings, Claire is out of her crate and Lyon's head hurts too much for shouting.

Sometime later he rises from the horizontal at great cost, sick to his stomach as he lamely closes one suitcase and picks it up along with the other one, carrying them both into the living room and past Claire, who is sitting in a big easy chair looking stunned.

"I'm sorry," she whispers.

He continues on out of the room, leaving her in that oversized chair, all balled up and watching his exit with the eyes of a frightened animal—*prey,* not predator, not now, not the way she was last night when she had eyes and teeth to terrify him.

The pain has hardened him, he says nothing more to her and does not wait by the car for Claire to join him.

Back in the living room she whispers, "I'm sorry."

Lyon drives the mountain road, each pothole and rut ratcheting the head pain a notch or two tighter, unable to think things through—whether he should spend the night at some motel rather than trying to drive in his current state, whether he should have told Claire he *intended* to ask her to marry him but not now, not after she pulled that obscene prank with those two blind women, or whether saying such things would be too petty, whether he wasn't somehow nobler leaving her without saying anything—or whether he should turn around right here and go back to get her.

A few miles from the cabin he brakes the car to a stop. Lyon hurts too much to keep driving. He lies down across the front seat, curling into a fetal ball. He feels like Job, his soul weary of his life.

By the time Lyon awakens, night is just arriving in the hollow and he knows what he must do, go back and get Claire, taking her by the wrists if that becomes necessary—just drag her into the car and force her to come home with him.

He turns around, driving slowly and with his lights off, trying to do nothing that might disturb the iron bolt of pain still lodged in his head.

The cabin is dark.

As soon as Lyon steps through the front doorway he looks into the kitchen wondering if the coffin-box will be there—it isn't. Neither is Claire. Lyon doesn't call out for her, however, or turn on any of the lights, his migraine more manageable in the darkness, quietly checking the living room, the bedroom, and then the bathroom. She's gone.

Then, still standing in the bathroom, he hears a faint tinkling of bells, then someone crying, someone speaking softly and crying at the same time, the sound eerie because it doesn't seem to be coming from a single source, instead the entire cabin has seemingly been wired with that soft weeping, that whispering voice, Lyon thinking, she's done it again, Claire has found another brand-new way to terrify me.

But just as he is about to leave the bathroom he notices a narrow slit of light in the corner of the ceiling. Lyon steps up on the edge of the tub, getting right under that faint line of light and seeing that it comes from one side of a trapdoor that has been so ingeniously fitted into the pattern of the ceiling that it would remain unnoticeable if not for that faint light in the attic.

Moving stealthily—and as yet unaware that the excitement of this discovery is rather magically eliminating his head pain—Lyon spreads his fingers on the trapdoor and quietly pushes up one side, just a few inches, enough to see what's in that crawl space which runs above the entire cabin.

Claire is naked except for a blue cord around her waist and a blue ribbon, hung with bells, around one ankle. She is sitting on a large suitcase balanced across three floor joists, leaning forward working on something, whispering and crying at the same time. She has placed candles on floor joists all around her, their flickering yellow light making Claire appear more apparition than real.

Although her crying is soft, containing none of the hoarse sobs and body wracks that have afflicted Lyon, hers seems the more wretched.

He sees her in profile, wondering what she is working on up there. Over in the shadows behind Claire is the coffin-crate, Lyon trying to imagine the effort it must have taken Claire to haul that heavy crate up through the trapdoor and into the attic. No wonder her forearms were scratched.

There is probably another trapdoor over the kitchen or back room, giving Claire access to all parts of the cabin.

He finally makes out what she's whispering. "I'm sorry, I'm sorry."

She's up here crying, Lyon thinks, because she's

convinced I've left her. She's sorry for making me angry, for losing me. And his heart is breaking because no one has ever cried for him like this, not to his knowledge, never.

But then Claire raises up and he sees what she's been working on: a foot-tall plaster statue of the Virgin Mary. Except Claire has carefully chipped out Baby Jesus from the larger statue, leaving the Virgin's arms empty.

Claire cradles the three-inch plaster Jesus in one hand, holding Him to an upright post and gently wrapping colored string around Baby Jesus to keep Him against that post, tying Him there. She arranges the empty-armed Virgin Mary on a floor joist eighteen inches away, the Virgin facing her Baby but unable to hold Him—Claire crying and constantly apologizing for what she's doing.

Rattled, Lyon eases the trapdoor shut and steps off the bathtub.

What the hell is she doing? Holding Baby Jesus hostage? And threatening the Virgin: You get your Baby back when I get what I want. Good God, what else is she capable of?

Only just now appreciating that his head has stopped hurting, Lyon creeps out of the bedroom, through the living room, and into the kitchen. He wonders if she'll hear him run some water, needing a drink, needing to wash his face. He is just reaching for the tap when he notices something in the sink, jerking his hand back and immediately retreating a step. Something black, an animal, *rat*.

He steps again to the sink, carefully up on tiptoes, to peek in. Not a rat, it's a wax figure of a man lying there in the sink.

In a kitchen drawer Lyon finds a box of matches. He strikes one and holds it over the sink. A photograph of his face has been cut out of a newspaper, a photograph taken from a television monitor, one of those news photos that appeared in Monday editions following his Sunday afternoon on-camera weeping. This cutout face, barely an inch across, has been affixed to the wax figure.

Lyon nervously strikes another match to search the figure carefully for wounds. It seems to be intact but on the cutting board next to the sink are items—a variety of needles with colored thread through their eyes, for example—that turn Lyon ice-cold inside.

He's outside by the rental car now, reaching in the window and sounding the horn, hitting it repeatedly and calling for Claire.

In a few minutes lights come on, then Claire steps out the front door. She's wearing the white dress she had on before, Claire barefoot and waving to Lyon, then running to him.

"I knew you'd come back," she says.

They're embracing.

"Let's go."

She is suspicious. Does he still want her to return to New York with him? "Go where, John?"

Lyon thinks carefully about his answer. He sees Baby Jesus tied to a post, he sees that wax figure in the sink, and he hears again Claire's soft and wretched weeping. Then he answers. "Dig up that grave."

Claire is nodding. But before she gets into the car she tells Lyon she's forgotten something. "You wait here."

When she's halfway to the cabin, he calls, "What're you going to do?"

"Put on some shoes," she tells him without turning around.

Yes, he thinks, but you're also going to untie Jesus and put Him back in His Mother's arms.

31

DURING HIS FIRST YEAR ON THIS ISOLATED PROPERTY, Randolph Welby nearly starved to death. He knew nothing about living off the land and after running through a supply of store-bought food the lawyer had helped him assemble, Randolph was reduced to wandering the forest, eating berries and roots he selected on a random, uninformed basis, some of it making him ill, the little man frequently hallucinating either from near-starvation or from the plants he was eating or both. He became adept at catching field mice with his hands. No wonder people thought he was mystical, an occasional hunter spotting Randolph in the woods, the old gnome wearing rags and pulling up roots or scurrying through the undergrowth, occasionally pouncing like a fox, this hollow-eyed man speaking to creatures no one else could see, calling for Mother and owl eaters.

Books saved him—books he'd brought with him

from the institution and then later books that the lawyer showed him how to order, books arriving at his shack via the almighty United Parcel Service, books through which Randolph learned what forest products could be safely collected and eaten and which ones should be avoided. Back-to-the-land, self-sufficient, independent-living books. Books that taught him to garden and how to care for the dogs that came wandering up to his shack.

And just as important as these practical manuals were the books that nourished his soul, the stories Mother once read to him, books about heroes.

On this evening, July 4, he is walking along all those running feet of bookcases that line the walls of his shack, the little hermit looking for answers. Except he's too agitated to read anything beyond the titles. All day long his three dogs have been restless, given to bursts of sad howling that begin suddenly and end just as abruptly, caused by what Randolph can only guess. Caused by premonition. They know what's coming too.

He feeds the baby girl for the fifth time since noon. Why has she turned so voracious? What does all this *mean?*

With the infant balanced on one cocked hip, Randolph carrying her like an experienced wet nurse, he searches with increasing worry among the titles of his books. Here at the bottom of one row of shelves are six juvenile westerns that Mother used to read to him, books starring the Wyoming Kid, an authentic hero.

Of course.

Carefully holding the infant's head, just the way it said to do in that baby-care book, Randolph rushes to the back room where he keeps the trunks that he inherited when Mother died. Stored away in one of them is a gift she handed him on the very day he was driven to the institution a lifetime ago.

Finding it too awkward to search through trunks with a baby on his hip, Randolph places her in the crib, where the infant girl turns on her side to watch the gnome open various of those old trunks, then close them, pulling out another one, opening its lid. . . .

Here.

Triumphant, Randolph reaches in and brings out a real leather bandolier holding a dozen cartridges, carefully placing it over his right shoulder and across his chest. Although it was given to him at age twelve, it still fits. Then he brings out a second bandolier, placing it over his other shoulder, crossing the first bandolier at his heart.

Stepping to a mirror, he straightens up to assume an approximation of cowboy bearing. And from her crib the baby girl watches with total absorption.

Next he takes from the trunk a real leather belt with double holsters, the rig closing around Randolph's tiny waist with a big buckle, silver plating flaking off to reveal the tin beneath. Randolph bends down to tie the bottoms of the holsters to his thighs with real leather thongs.

In the mirror he likes the way he looks.

Then two six-shooters come from the trunk, Randolph dropping them into their holsters, the weight of those silver-plated pistols making him feel potent.

The real leather chaps are red, a bright, shiny, cowboy-inappropriate red, but when Randolph ties them on and walks around the room he enjoys the way they flap, especially the real leather fringes.

The baby girl grips one tiny pink-fleshed hand on a

bar of her crib, the better to keep herself turned over on her side to continue watching this spectacle.

Now the crown, kept in its own box within the trunk: a real cowboy hat with a colored string that goes around your neck, the string able to be tightened or loosened by pulling it through the hole in a red wooden bead the size of a marble.

He puts it on.

Unfortunately, his head size hasn't improved since he was twelve, and although the cowboy hat is child-sized, it is still too big for Randolph. In fact it rests down on his ears, making them bend out even more than they do naturally, the hat nearly covering his eyes, the effect so comical that even the baby girl is prompted to laugh from her crib.

But when Randolph steps to the mirror and pushes up the brim of the hat, pushes it all the way up and over so that the cowboy hat falls onto his back, held there by the colored string around his neck, then, yes, Randolph—at least in his own eyes—could pass for a miniature and ancient Wyoming Kid.

When Mother presented him with this outfit—the big black car was already waiting at the curb to take him away—she emphasized that it was very expensive, all real leather, and was a precise duplicate of the outfit worn by the hero in those westerns Randolph loved.

He goes up on his tiptoes in front of the mirror.

The Wyoming Kid. Shy with women but h—l on leather. Randolph rests the palm of each small hand on the butt of each silver pistol. Cocks his hip a little. The Wyoming Kid, steely-eyed and good with a gun. Never a better friend, never a worse enemy. He squints off into the middle distance, wondering where the cowboy boots ended up. And spurs. Which reminds him, that's what the Wyoming Kid's sidekick was called, Spurs.

Randolph turns to the baby and draws both pistols, absolutely delighting her.

"Stands before you, a hewo," he insists. "A big two-hawted hewo."

She gurgles happily.

"What's tat you say, wittle wady? Am I weddy? *Weddy?*" In a gunman's crouch, he swivels ominously toward the mirror, getting the drop on himself before straightening up and reholstering the twin hoglegs. Telling the baby, "Shoot, ma'am, ta Kid was *bawn* weddy."

32

IN SILENCE THEY DRIVE TO THE OUTSKIRTS OF HAMELN, past trailers with vegetable gardens in the side yards, with chained dogs lying on the tops of homemade plywood doghouses that during the day are protected from the sun by scraggly trees trying to survive the dogshit.

"Why did you take me to that house where those two blind women live?" Lyon finally asks her.

Claire makes a sound, a sighing groan, that indicates she has been dreading this question.

"What was the point?"

She speaks reluctantly. "When I was a teenager, my grandparents would occasionally visit those women, bring them things from town, and whenever I was in a room with them, with those two women . . . it's when I first felt invisible, felt the power of being invisible. I was hoping . . ." Claire shakes her head. "It was stupid. It was embarrassing for you, for me, for the women, just totally inexcusable."

"But you started to say you were hoping. Hoping for what?"

Claire doesn't answer.

"I'm not criticizing, I'm trying to understand."

"I was hoping to show you what it felt like, being invisible. I was hoping you'd think I was, that I was different from any woman you've ever met, that I—"

"You *are* different from any woman I've ever met, there's no doubt—"

"I was hoping to stop you from leaving me."

They are just driving into Hameln proper when it occurs to Lyon that he and Claire have no tools with which to disinter a coffin. No stores open either, not on the Fourth of July. He is jolted by hope, because without tools they'll have no choice except to call off tonight's adventure.

But when he mentions this to Claire, she says they'll simply steal some shovels out of a garage.

Lyon mutters a curse.

"What's wrong?"

"It's just one thing after another, isn't it? I mean, now we're going to precede the obscenity of grave robbing with a little breaking and entering, theft— what else?" His famous face is twisted with worry.

Claire is worried too. She doesn't want to lose Lyon over this, especially not after the way he stormed out on her following the debacle at that house where the two blind women live. "We could try going through official channels," Claire suggests. "Maybe petition a judge to issue a disinterment order."

"Based on what?" he snaps back. "Your grandmother's accusations have been thoroughly discredited, I'd break down crying in the judge's chambers, you would disappear before—"

"All right, John."

Driving the side streets of Hameln, he realizes he doesn't know where he's going, what he's looking for. The town is deserted, Lyon passing no cars, seeing no one walking. Most of the houses and trailers are dark; there are no streetlights.

Then in the middle of one quiet residential block, Claire orders him to stop.

Lyon does, asking her what's wrong.

"See the garage to the side of that house?"

He turns around in his seat.

"Just pop in there and grab a couple shovels. The house is dark, no one's home. We'll bring the stuff back after we're done. Not stealing, John, *borrowing.*"

But he makes no move to get out of the car.

Claire nudges him. "Taking a shovel from a garage is not the worst of what we'll be doing tonight."

"I know. God, I should've had a drink back at the cabin. Several." He settles for taking deep breaths. "When I was a little boy I was attacked by a dog. Got put in the hospital." His mouth is dry. In the past few days Lyon has thought a lot about that episode. "Did you notice those trailers we passed on the way in, all the dogs? Everyone in this town has dogs. There's probably two or three in that garage. Waiting for me."

"You stay here," Claire says, opening her door.

"No." He gets out, closes his door, and then turns around to talk to Claire through the open window. "Slide over here so you can drive, make a quick getaway if it comes to that. And if you see anyone near that garage, anyone at all, give the horn two short honks. Make sure that passenger door stays unlatched so I can get in fast if I have to."

Claire reaches up to the window and takes his hand. "You'll be in and out of there in thirty seconds."

He nods, looking up over the car's roof to watch the

garage for a moment, then bending down to speak to Claire again. Except he can't think of anything else to tell her.

Finally Claire says, "Why don't I just dash in there and—"

"No, no. I'll do it."

Lyon has on his face a little boy's expression—*I'm trying to be brave about this*—as he nods a farewell to Claire and pushes off from the car, walking around the back of it and heading for the garage, blowing air through pursed lips as if to whistle.

At the driveway leading to the garage, Lyon pauses. Still no cars, no pedestrians, all the houses on this street dark. Where has everyone gone? Maybe people are afraid to be out at night because that's when Quinndell roams the town, finding his way through these yards by memory or being guided by Carl, the two of them looking for victims. Lyon actually shudders—fifty years old and still scaring himself the way he did when he was a kid. Doesn't this ever change?

He reaches the side door to the garage and looks in one of the four panes of glass. No car there but Lyon can see a long row of tools hanging along one wall: shovels, axes, hoes, everything you could possibly need to dig up a grave. Turning the handle, he finds that the door is unlocked.

Two steps into the garage, however, and Lyon is attacked by a dog.

It has him by the pants leg, this fiercely yapping little fur ball clamped down on Lyon's cuff, shaking its head and ripping the material as Lyon bounces backward on one leg, dragging the creature with him, reaching the door and hopping out on that one leg,

closing the door on his leg so the dog can't escape,
finally able to retrieve his leg and then shut the door
between him and the Pomeranian.

Looking through the glass, Lyon sees the fluffy red
bastard sitting on the other side of the door staring up
at him with a malevolent grin, a strip of trouser
material hanging from the dog's pointy mouth.

If it were a real dog in there, a German shepherd,
for example, Lyon would simply return to the car and
tell Claire to forget this particular garage—but he can
hardly admit to her that he was held at bay by a
Pomeranian.

He opens the door a crack and yells, "Sit!"

The dog does.

Opening the door a little wider, Lyon orders,
"Stay!"

And the creature acts as if it's going to obey that
too.

When Lyon finally screws up enough courage to
step into the garage he draws out a warning,
"Staaayyy," the Pomeranian opening his mouth to
pant, dropping the swatch of material and keeping his
eyes on Lyon—but the dog stays.

Moving gingerly, Lyon makes his way to where the
tools are hanging, selecting two shovels, a pick, an axe,
and a crowbar. Bundling these tools under his left
arm, Lyon turns now for the open door, reminding the
dog, "Staaayyy."

He is halfway to the exit when the Pomeranian bolts
from the sitting position and runs to the doorway, the
dog's red fur bristling, the animal suddenly *angry* at
Lyon, growling and then yapping, the Pomeranian in
the doorway obviously prepared to make a Horatius-
like stand.

Lyon tries out a variety of commands on the dog—*Sit, Stay, Get outta here, Go home, Fetch*—but nothing works. He tries feinting in one direction and then the other, only infuriating the dog all the more. Lyon is worried that someone is going to hear the barking and come out here to the garage with a gun. He tries speaking softly to the dog, *asking* him to be quiet, using babytalk—nothing works.

Lyon takes out the shovel. He's going to have to brain the little mutt. But can he do it?

Raising the shovel overhead, he approaches the Pomeranian, which continues that maddening yapping, Lyon hefting the shovel to gauge its weight, its deadliness. He'll probably only wound the little beast with the first blow, have to keep hitting and hitting, maybe use the axe to cut off its head. Ghastly business. Can he *do* it?

Within shovel range now, lifting it high with his right hand, the other tools still tucked under his left arm, the dog ignoring the overhead weapon, staring boldly into the man's eyes, Lyon assuming a firm grip on the shovel's handle, about to strike when a shadow —black and white—moves in from the side of the doorway.

It's Claire, bending over to scoop the Pomeranian into her arms, petting the dog's head and then when the creature continues barking at Lyon, she puts her hand over its snout and holds its mouth closed. "Oh, John, what were you going to do?"

He looks up at the raised shovel, guilty.

The tools are in the trunk, Lyon is in the front passenger seat. When Claire, who is driving, starts to speak, he stops her by holding up one finger, "Not a word."

Fighting to contain her laughter, she says, "At least you got the shovels."

"Yeah, so far it's going like fucking clockwork."

The entrance to Cemetery Road is blocked by a single steel pipe hinged on one end, chained and padlocked at the other. To the middle of that pipe is taped a hand-lettered sign: CLOSED ON THE FOURTH.

"I guess that pretty much kills the plan for tonight," he says hopefully.

"Don't be silly. This is *good*. Now we know no one else will be up there to bother us, to see what we're doing, this is perfect."

"Except how do *we* get in?"

She answers him by slipping the car into gear, depressing the accelerator, and bumping into the pipe—making a terrific racket but not breaking the chain. Claire backs up and hits the pipe a second time, harder, snapping the chain and causing the pipe to fly open and then bounce back against the car, shattering a headlight.

"Damn!"

But Claire is unconcerned, driving forward to push the pipe out of the way and then calmly telling Lyon, "Go back and close it, wrap the chain around the end so no one can tell it's been broken."

He obeys, wondering, if Claire is so goddamn resourceful dealing with dogs and chained gates, then why the hell does she need him to dig up the grave?

Cemetery Road continues on up the side of a ridge, Claire driving the steep incline slowly but without using the single headlight she has available to her. When Lyon suggests she should at least turn on the parking lights, Claire tells him, "We don't want anyone to know we're up here."

"Right," he replies, gripping the armrest and seat edge, waiting tensely for Claire to drive off the side of the shadowy road and plunge them into the darkness below.

The cemetery itself is on four sloping acres just down from the crest of a hill high over the town of Hameln. Claire and Lyon walk one of the paths to the edge of the cemetery, seeing there at the base of Cemetery Hill a hundred cars and perhaps five hundred people around an open field so far below the cemetery that Claire and John Lyon feel as if they're looking down from an airplane.

"Fireworks," Claire informs him. "That's why no one was in town, they're all waiting for the fireworks to begin."

"Good, I hope they stay down there. I'll go get the tools. I assume you've already selected a grave for desecretion."

She flashes him her big eyes.

"Now listen to me, Claire, if we open the coffin and find that the body . . . I can't believe I'm really going to do this. If the body is intact, if there's no indication that the baby was butchered by Quinndell, then we put everything back and go home—yes?"

"That's the plan." Except Claire sounds as if she's keeping her options open.

"You don't have any *alternative* plan in mind, do you?"

"Of course not."

He doesn't believe her.

She takes his hand. "Claire always said that the babies themselves would bring Quinndell down, that his victims are waiting to indict him. I'm trusting that she knew what she was talking about."

"I'm not doing this for your grandmother, I'm doing it for you."

"I know," she says softly. Then more businesslike, "Go get the tools and the flashlight, I'll find the grave. I know all those children's names by heart, Claire drilled them into me."

A few minutes later they are standing by the grave of Nancy Masters, who died six years ago at two months of age.

"What's going to be left after six years?" Lyon asks.

"Well, we can continue talking the rest of the night about what we might find, what it'll mean, whether we should even be here, what our alternatives are—or we can *simply do it.*"

"Right. I guess I just start digging, huh?"

"Yes."

The project turns out to be nothing at all like it is shown in the movies, where graves are dug up in the middle of the night with seemingly little effort, the dirt loose and sandy, in one scene the digging is started and then in the next scene the gravedigger is at the bottom of a neatly rectangular six-foot hole, his shovel blade hitting dramatically against the coffin.

Lyon soon discovers that the reality of opening a grave is brutally hard work, jumping on the shovel to get the blade in and then struggling to wrest free a clump of dry clay soil. After a half an hour of it Lyon is exhausted, totally soaked through with sweat, and discouraged by what he has created, a roughly oblong hole about the size of a bathtub and barely a foot deep. Now he knows why he was needed for this project.

The flashlight Claire is holding for him is going yellow. Lyon rests there in his modest hole as the sounds of a school band drift up from the field far below. He looks around, the large trees and well-kept grounds striking him as peaceful rather than scary.

Claire suggests that he had better start digging again, he still has a long way to go.

Muttering, Lyon shovels, using the pick when that becomes necessary, coming across tree roots that he has to cut out with the axe, shoveling some more, discovering at one point that he has piled the dirt too close to the hole, disheartened when a bushel of that dirt falls into the hole and he has to take it out a second time. He digs and sweats and rests and digs. Claire takes over for a while but Lyon is frustrated watching her bring out only a handful or two of dirt with each trip of the shovel. He gets back in the hole and digs some more.

Lyon is waist deep into the ground when he tells Claire that at this rate it's going to take him all night to reach the coffin. "And speaking of coffins, I never did find that little white one your grandmother gave me. She said as long as I kept it in my possession, Quinndell couldn't hurt me."

"I took care of it."

"How so?"

"Just *dig,* John—this town has eyes."

He somehow knows what she means by that, Lyon resuming the digging, grumbling and digging, expanding the hole's perimeter, throwing dirt up and over the pile that threatens to slide again into the hole, shoveling and picking, back muscles tightening, going deeper, finding rocks that have to be dug around and then pried loose with the crowbar and lifted up over the edge, Lyon unaccustomed to prolonged physical labor, digging and finally resting in a hole that is now chest deep.

Claire is sitting on the ground, leaning back against the infant's headstone, occasionally hitting the flashlight in an attempt to jar some life into its failing beam.

Leaning on the shovel, Lyon says, "You always read that murder victims are found in 'shallow graves.' I know why that is now—because the murderers get too goddamn tired to dig a deep grave, that's why. I mean, if we were burying someone tonight instead of digging someone up, I would've stopped a long time ago. Push the body in, kick some dirt over it, go home and have a drink. Enough of this shit."

"More digging, less talk, John."

He goes back to it, eventually finding himself in a hole over his head. When the shovel hits against something hard, Lyon thinks it's another rock, but as he digs away more dirt he realizes he has uncovered the domed top of a small brass coffin.

"Claire!"

She peers in over the top of the hole.

"Give me the flashlight."

"You found it?" she asks.

"Yes! It's set in some kind of form, I'll need the crowbar too."

She passes down the crowbar and the flashlight, telling Lyon that the batteries are almost shot.

He continues digging and prying, handing debris up to Claire, finally exposing enough of the coffin that he should be able to pry it open.

"I'll have to smash off the latches."

When she realizes he's hesitating, Claire tells him, "Go on, John, you can't hurt that baby anymore."

"Yeah." He pounds the latches until they break, working the edge of the crowbar under the lid, prying and grunting and straining until he feels something like a sigh: the lid giving. "This will be the second coffin I've opened in the past three days, I don't know if I want to—" Hearing a brief commotion overhead, Lyon grabs the flashlight and shines its yellow beam upward, seeing nothing. "Claire?" No answer. She couldn't have left him again, not *now*.

Finish this business with the coffin first, he tells himself, getting his fingers under the edge of the lid and lifting slowly, holding his face back, excited and curious and scared all at the same time, Lyon's heart bass-drumming as he opens the lid enough to shine some light in.

"Claire! Do you see this? *Claire!*"

Still holding the coffin lid open with one hand, Lyon is looking up when a brilliant light fills the grave, blinding him. He thinks Claire has found another flashlight somewhere—but why is she shining it right in his eyes?

"Claire?"

And why doesn't she answer him? Damn her anyway.

"CLAIRE!"

Then something reaches down into that grave and grabs Lyon by the collar of his shirt.

33

HE IS HAULED UP OUT OF THE HOLE, DRAGGED OVER PILES of dirt, and deposited facedown on the grass with his shirt ripped open and half the buttons torn off.

Held to the ground with a boot on his back, Lyon is staring at Claire's bare black feet. She's on tiptoes.

"Har . . . har . . . asshole."

Then Carl removes the boot from Lyon's back and kicks him in the ribs, getting him to turn over. The deputy is holding a huge flashlight in one hand, his other fat arm tight across Claire's neck, keeping her up on her toes, Claire's eyes white with fear.

When Lyon asks her if she's all right, Carl tells him to shut up, shining the light in his eyes, blinding him.

"Goddamn it, Carl, you have no idea the trouble you're causing for yourself. I got that coffin opened! Tomorrow morning this place is going to be crawling with reporters, I'll have lawyers all over your fat ass—"

Carl kicks him hard in the stomach and then sniggers.

Lyon is back over on his hands and knees, trying to get his breath, waiting to find out if he's going to vomit. He feels impotent, threatening Carl with reporters and lawyers. He should stand up and knock the fat man on his ass, that's what he should do.

"Doc was right all along about this nigger girl being with you. Doc's always right," Carl says, shaking Claire back and forth like a rag doll. "Now I'm taking the two of you over to his place. Start walking to my car, asshole." He nudges Lyon with the toe of his boot.

Lyon finally struggles to his feet and puts one hand in front of his eyes, trying to shade them from the blinding beam of Carl's flashlight.

"John," Claire says with a strangled voice, "don't let him take me there, please."

"All right, Carl, let her go."

The deputy backhands him, delivering the blow casually, the way he might strike a woman. Blinded by the light, however, Lyon didn't see the blow coming and the *surprise* of it causes him to drop back to his knees.

"Get up, pussy boy!" Then Carl increases the pressure on Claire's neck, causing her to choke.

Remembering the Pomeranian's attack, Lyon grabs for one of Carl's legs, hugging it with both arms, Carl trying to kick free as Lyon starts biting the man's massive calf muscle.

"Son of a *bitch!*" Keeping Claire in that choke hold, Carl begins beating on Lyon with the flashlight.

But Lyon holds on, still biting even though the heavy flashlight has opened wounds on his head, Lyon feeling the blood warm and sticky as it flows over his scalp.

Claire manages to slip out from under Carl's arm but he immediately grabs her by the hair. He keeps beating on Lyon until the flashlight's lense shatters, extinguishing the light. He tosses it away and draws his revolver.

"No!" Claire screams.

Lyon turns loose of Carl's leg and looks up. Even in this darkness, he can make out the tiny black *O* of the muzzle's mouth.

"If it wasn't for Doc wanting the both of you," Carl grunts, "I'd blow you away right here. And I might do it anyway, asshole, so get moving."

The deputy's pudgy fingers are buried in Claire's hair, keeping her well away from Lyon.

"Move!"

Not seeing that he has a choice, Lyon stands and begins walking up the hill toward the cemetery's entrance.

Claire is trailing the deputy at arm's length, being pulled along by her hair. "My God," she says, "it's my grandmother!"

Carl and Lyon both stop.

"My grandmother! Over there by her grave, she's wearing her nurse's uniform—can't you see her?"

Lyon looks where Claire is pointing. "There *is* someone!" he says, trying to reinforce what he takes to be Claire's effort to distract and frighten the deputy.

But Carl just laughs. "Doc believes in that voodoo shit, not me." Then he jerks violently on Claire while keeping the revolver pointed in Lyon's direction.

Still looking toward the grave, Lyon sees what appears to be a shooting star traveling the wrong way, shooting from the ground into the sky. "Jesus," he whispers.

Just then a massive explosion high over their heads

lights up the cemetery in a brilliant red. All three of them duck. Then another explosion, this one blue, followed by a series of white-bright detonations so loud that the three of them bend instinctively into crouches as all around them rain sparks and then burning chunks of paper and cardboard and wood.

Before anyone can speak, there's another explosion, a blinding white light just ahead of a concussion that causes a piercing pain in their eardrums.

Carl tries to order Lyon to run for the patrol car but a quick series of overhead detonations leaves all three of them disoriented, blue and green and red sparks hitting the ground around them, one flaming chunk landing just a few feet in front of Lyon and then burning there like a small campfire.

This is why the cemetery was closed off. The town of Hameln is surrounded by high hills well-populated with houses and trailers. When fireworks are launched from the valley floor they are aimed up at the cemetery where the burning debris can fall without endangering anyone's property.

After a brief pause the explosions resume, more than they can keep track of, rockets and starbursts and those white-bright detonations that hurt their ears and shake their flesh, each explosion producing the relatively harmless shower of sparks and then the more dangerous debris, some of it aflame and some of it merely charred, falling with heavy thuds all over the cemetery.

Although Carl is no longer pointing his pistol at Lyon, the deputy still has Claire by the hair, jerking her around with him as he steps back and forth in a futile effort to keep away from what's raining on both of them.

Lyon jumps Carl. He hasn't planned this attack,

operating on instinct as he puts his arms around that fat neck, trying to bulldog the deputy to the ground, but of course Lyon weighs half of what Carl does and the two of them end up dancing in a tight circle, Lyon holding on to Carl the way a child might, flaming pieces of cardboard landing on both of them, the deputy finally falling backward on his ass but then managing to roll over on Lyon, trapping him beneath his suffocating bulk.

"Told you I was going to fuck you!" Carl screams, pressing more of his weight onto Lyon, who can't breathe, who can't even get enough air to speak, to surrender.

But then the deputy realizes that in the confusion of Lyon's attack, Claire has escaped. Carl raises up in time to see her running away, Claire's flight across the cemetery illuminated by a brilliant overhead display of red and blue starbursts.

Driving through the streets of Hameln, Carl is grim. "Doc is going to be pissed I ain't bringing in your girlfriend, and it's all your fault. I hope he kills you real slow."

Bruised and burned, exhausted, his clothes torn, handcuffed, Lyon is behind the wire mesh in the backseat of the patrol car. "What you should do, Carl, is just keep driving. Take me to the nearest state police office. Turn yourself in. If you agree to testify against Quinndell they'll go easy on you. I opened that coffin. Do you know what I found—or is Quinndell keeping you in the dark about that?"

But Carl's not listening. "He was going to pay me twenty-five thousand dollars to bring the two of you in, now what am I getting, jack-shit, that's what."

Lyon can't resist the cliché: "You won't get away with this."

"Doc's been getting away with it for years." He pulls into the driveway to the side of Quinndell's house. "And now you got an appointment with Mr. Gigli."

"Who?"

The deputy laughs.

34

"YOU SMELL OF DIRT, MR. LYON. OF THE GRAVE."

Still handcuffed, Lyon is standing in Dr. Quinndell's darkened office. Carl has been sent out on another assignment, something to do with that hermit, Randolph Welby, and Lyon feels oddly confident, being left here alone with the doctor. Even if those double doors are locked, Lyon thinks he can probably kick them open or go through a window. How difficult can it be, escaping from a blind man?

"Where's your friend?" Quinndell asks casually. "Her name is also Claire, right? Named after her grandmother."

"Yes."

"I knew the family. It's been a while since I've seen Claire, though—your Claire. On this visit she's been terribly elusive, hasn't she? Sheriff Stone couldn't find her and now he's turned up missing. Carl couldn't find her when he first went out to the cabin and then tonight, when he finally met up with the two of you, she escaped. The deputy has his uses but he *is* a bumbler. I'm hoping you can tell me where Claire escaped *to,* Mr. Lyon."

"It's all over, Quinndell. We dug up one of those graves tonight. I got the coffin open."

The doctor waits a moment in the darkness before speaking, his voice smoothly unperturbed. "And found it empty."

"What did you do with the bodies?" Lyon asks quickly.

Quinndell chuckles. "Sent them to a far, far better place, Mr. Lyon—I promise you. I'll tell you all about it, but in exchange you must tell me where Claire is hiding."

"Go to hell."

"Undoubtedly. By the way, that grave will be filled in by morning. No one the wiser."

"Bullshit! I'll have the network down here tomorrow, the FBI, the fucking National Guard if it comes to that. We'll have all eighteen of those graves opened."

"Twenty."

"What?"

"There are *twenty* empty coffins in that cemetery, not eighteen. Nurse Cept's investigation missed two."

In the darkness Lyon finds an overstuffed chair and collapses into it, groaning.

"Rough night?"

"I don't care if you tell me what you did with those children, Quinndell, because it's all going to come out in the morning."

"I think not."

When the lights in the office come on, Lyon sees the doctor standing behind his big desk, Quinndell again dressed in a dark and expensively cut suit, wearing a brilliantly white shirt, a hundred-dollar tie—looking like a Wall Street investor. No, more elegant than that, more like a handsome English lord with a superior sense of himself. Lyon, meanwhile, looks nothing at all like someone who once had the nickname *His Lordship,* because now his shirt is completely unbuttoned, torn and charred, his belly exposed, shoes caked with dirt, pants filthy, his mouth swollen and painful from where Carl backhanded him, both hands blistered, dried blood all over his head from the beating he received with that flashlight.

"Do you have your frog with you this time?" Quinndell asks, speaking softly.

"I'll fucking walk out of here anytime I want." He looks down at his hands in his lap. "If you think these cuffs are going to stop me—"

"How do you plan on reporting this story? Aren't you worried about sobbing on camera again? You really should have your doctor run some tests, John. Inexplicable and uncontrollable bursts of emotion could be indicative of parkinsonism dementia. How old are you?"

"Fuck you, Quinndell."

"Such language." The doctor takes a handkerchief from his suitcoat pocket and dabs at the tears weeping from around his glass eyes. "Let's begin, shall we? I'll tell you my story and then, in return, you tell me where Claire is hiding."

"Go to hell."

"Yes . . . well then." The doctor straightens up. "I began arranging adoptions about twenty-five years ago. As I explained to you, I'd always had certain patients I handled on a gratis basis, girls who were pregnant and unmarried, some of them as young as fourteen. If they chose to give up their babies, I helped make the arrangements and in the course of this I became associated with certain attorneys who specialized in private adoptions.

"It wasn't until fifteen years ago, however, that I was contacted by attorneys who arranged private adoptions for *very* wealthy clients. Suddenly I was being offered fees of fifteen or twenty thousand dollars for healthy, white babies. Naturally I put the word out, not only among my patients but to anyone who was pregnant but who couldn't care for her child or anyone who knew of such a person. *Bring me children,* that became my motto."

Lyon laughs.

"You laugh in ignorance, Mr. Lyon. Are you married? Do you have children?" Quinndell waits a moment before realizing that Lyon isn't going to answer his questions. "Have you ever wanted children? Have you ever had a child you *didn't* want, couldn't afford to care for? Have you ever done any research into this field? And yet you laugh because I say *Bring me children* was my motto?" The doctor is shaking his head. Then he points toward a photograph on the wall, a framed photograph showing Quinndell surrounded by his pediatric patients holding a home-made banner. "Do you see the photograph I'm pointing to, Mr. Lyon. See what it says on that banner. *Bring Me Children.* Mothers were happy to bring me their children as patients. And do you know something else? The women who brought me their children so I could arrange for their adoptions, they were *grateful.* Mothers on welfare burdened with one more unwanted pregnancy, teenage girls facing the prospect of quitting school and embarking on wretched lives, they would *thank* me for taking their babies out of poverty and delivering them instead to loving couples who wanted children on whom to lavish love and material wealth.

"Everyone came out a winner. The birth mothers were relieved of a responsibility they could ill afford and at the same time received cash payments they desperately needed. The adopting parents rejoiced because I was providing what nature had refused them. I made money, the lawyers made money. But the biggest winners of all were the babies. They had been born in jeopardy but *I*, Mr. Lyon, *I* delivered those babies from their fate and arranged for their arrival in the land of milk and honey. Just as West Virginia exports its other natural resources, coal and timber, I was exporting babies. And making everyone happy in the bargain. There was only one problem— can you guess what that was?"

"Not enough supply to meet the demand."

"Precisely!" Quinndell exclaims, offering his small-toothed smile. "Twenty-five years ago, sixty-five percent of all babies born to single, white mothers were given up for adoption. Now it's down to less than five percent. Prices for newborn white babies kept escalating but I couldn't exploit the market because the supply had dried up. No babies! I found this maddening. Instead of everyone winning, everyone was losing —the birth mothers had another mouth to feed, the wealthy couples had to continue waiting for children to adopt, I was losing out on fees, but most important of all, the infants themselves were being sentenced to unfortunate lives, ill-fed, ill-clothed, poorly educated, when they could just as easily have been placed in homes where they would have wanted for nothing."

"So you started playing God."

"Yes!" Quinndell puts both hands on his desk, leaning eagerly in Lyon's direction. "I say this with *pride,* Mr. Lyon. I began playing God—a benevolent God, however. A wise God. A God who removed babies from households where they would have suffered and delivered them to households where they could prosper."

"I can guess then how you solved the supply problem."

He smiles widely, showing more of his little yellow teeth. "Whenever I needed a baby to place with a wealthy couple, I would wait until some at-risk mother brought her infant to the hospital, some woman on welfare, abandoned by her husband, four or five other children at home, or perhaps some girl who had dropped out of high school to care for her baby, the father having already left the area, and I would inform this woman or this girl that, alas, her baby had died. The mother would be distraught, of course, but I told her it was God's will. In fact, it was *my* will."

Lyon has been watching Quinndell carefully as he speaks, realizing that not only is the doctor telling him the truth, but he believes in what he has done, is proud of it.

"Those twenty children whose coffins lie empty in the cemetery are currently living lives of great privilege—which they owe to me."

"And you owe your wealth to them."

"Of course! Capitalism is the religion of our time, Mr. Lyon, and I am one of its greatest apostles. People in India sell their kidneys for transplanting into rich Americans. Wealthy couples pay poor women to have their babies. Americans are roaming the globe snatching up available children, ten thousand a year for the last ten years—a hundred thousand foreign-born children adopted by American couples in the last decade, at a cost of twenty thousand dollars each in travel, legal fees, and other expenses. Two billion dollars in foreign adoptions alone. Good Lord, man, you don't understand any of this, do you? There is a screaming desire out there for *babies*. Each year fifty thousand children who were born in this country are placed with adoptive parents. But guess how many couples are waiting in line for those children—*a million*. And if you're one of the lucky couples to get a white newborn, you probably waited in line five years. My wealthy clients don't wait in lines. Their money puts them at the head of the line, where I'm waiting to sell them a baby."

"Except the mothers of those twenty babies weren't selling anything. They thought their babies had died."

"Yes, yes," Quinndell says, annoyed. "But that's only because they were too stupid to do what would have been best for them *and* their babies. I had to make the decision for them because they were thinking with their uteruses. It's all hormones anyway, we have shots for that."

"Jesus."

Quinndell sits in the chair behind his desk, extending his arm so he can tap those long fingers on the desktop. "Have you ever heard of Georgia Tann?"

"No."

"During the 1940s she became wealthy by arranging adoptions, selling babies. She paid the medical expenses for unwed women and then charged prosperous couples adoption fees. But Georgia ran into the same problem I did—supply and demand. So she arranged with a judge to have children taken by court order from poor families. She accumulated a fortune equivalent to five million dollars in today's money. Would you care to guess how many children she placed?"

"No."

"Five thousand children, Mr. Lyon. Why, I'm an amateur compared to Georgia Tann. Still, my philosophy is that if you work the upper end of the market—"

"Claire Cept said your blindness is evidence that God still answers prayers."

Quinndell pauses a moment and then smiles. "There are some matters on which Claire and I find ourselves in complete agreement."

"What was the point of calling her and claiming you had murdered and butchered those babies?"

"Why, to drive her mad of course. And it worked too, didn't it? She was so crazy, no *legitimate* journalist would've listened to her. She was so crazy she killed herself."

"If I arranged for a camera crew to come here, would you repeat everything you've just told me?"

Quinndell puts his head back, opens his mouth, and shakes his shoulders up and down—an eerily silent laughter that Lyon is watching carefully and with a growing sense of dread when the lights in the office are extinguished.

He quickly gets out of the overstuffed chair.

"It wasn't until I heard that the granddaughter was in the area," Quinndell says from the darkness, "that I even remembered having her in my examining room when she was a teenager. Oh, I've sampled these young girls before, but Claire had the strangest reaction. There I was having intercourse with her, hiding what I was doing behind the examining sheet, but of course she *knew* what I was doing and yet she remained so totally placid, grimacing occasionally because of the pain, but otherwise showing no emotion at all, not even fear." He pauses a moment. "I was wondering, John, has she become more animated or does she still just lie there and—?"

"I'm going to enjoy doing this story on you, going to enjoy watching you squirm, Quinndell."

"Doctor Quinndell."

"Yeah, well I'm leaving now, *Quinndell.*"

"And there's no way a blind man can possibly stop you, correct?"

Turning away from the monster, Lyon is just reaching for the double doors when they open, flooding the office with light from the hallway, Mary Aurora standing there with the saddest expression on her face. "I'm sorry," she tells Lyon, embracing him.

He hears a sound behind him, turning to see in the shaft of light from the hallway that Quinndell is approaching from the depths of the office, gliding quickly toward Lyon and holding something in his hand. But it's not a spoon this time.

Lyon tries to get out of Mary's arms but she continues embracing him, the handcuffs making it difficult for him to escape.

She keeps telling him she's sorry, Lyon just breaking her hold when his right buttock is jabbed hard with a needle, Lyon twisting around in pain, swinging with both handcuffed hands but missing Quinndell, who has eased now back into one of the office's dark corners.

Lyon turns toward Mary, who has tears in her eyes. Before he can speak, his mind begins to float upward, Lyon suddenly overcome with a feeling of intoxication, trying to turn back around to say something to Quinndell but getting tangled up in his own feet.

"Don't fight it, John," comes the doctor's kindly voice. "Just ease on down to the floor."

"What're you going to do to me?" he asks, surprised

by how dreamy his voice sounds, how it floats the way his body is floating. In fact, Lyon isn't even sure he said those words, he might only have been thinking them. "What was in that shot?"

Then he lurches out into the light of the hallway, Mary trying to catch him before he falls, no longer floating, he's sinking now, gliding downward toward a dark and seamless depth, John Lyon going to black.

35

CARL STOPS THE PATROL CAR AT THE BOTTOM OF THE gentle slope leading up to Randolph Welby's shack, which is dark. The deputy has a bad feeling about this. For five years, ever since Carl forced Randolph to find a cave Doc could use, Carl has had this premonition that the weird little hermit has been biding his time, waiting for revenge.

Carl was surprised that Doc renewed his offer tonight, that even though the nigger woman escaped in the cemetery, Doc said he would still pay Carl twenty-five thousand dollars to kill Welby. Carl keeps watching the dark shack, not sure if he wants Randolph to be home or not. There's a lot of money at stake, but the question is, can Carl do it?

Ever since he was in junior high school, outweighing even the largest of his classmates by a good fifty pounds, Carl has been beating up on people, striking back at them for making fun of his size, striking out from the confusion caused by his low-wattage mental powers. To balance the scales he has bloodied noses, blackened eyes, broken arms; he's even delivered people to Doc for killing and then cleaned up the messes Doc and Mr. Gigli made. But killing someone himself is a line across which Carl has never stepped. He thinks he can do it, however. For twenty-five thousand dollars and the continued blessing of his benefactor, Carl is pretty sure he can kill Randolph Welby.

He exits the patrol car, leaving the door open, and starts what for him is a laborious climb up that slope toward the dark shack. Carl has his pistol out, ready to shoot the first dog that shows itself, but he also has his mind on Mary, wondering if Doc was serious about making her go to bed with him.

He loses the start of a hard-on when he hears ferocious barking coming from behind the door to Randolph's shack. Carl immediately turns to run, pumping his fat legs to get down off the slope, convinced now he's going to need the shotgun.

Two dogs come off the porch just as the deputy is struggling to squeeze in the patrol car, Carl getting the door closed right before the dogs reach the other side of the car, their fury terrifying. Like they hate him. One of the dogs, in fact, has clamped his jaws on a tire, shaking his head and trying to rip the tread loose, the second dog with its front paws up on the passenger window, looking in on Carl, wanting to be in that car with him.

Carl is trembling so much he fumbles getting the shotgun out of its rack, not even checking to make sure the short-barreled, pump-action twelve-gauge is loaded, barely remembering to flip the safety off. The passenger window is rolled down a few inches and the dog there has turned its head sideways to push its jaws into that open space, growling and foaming and snapping.

Anticipating the sound that the shotgun is going to make in the enclosed car, Carl grimaces as he aims the muzzle at the window. But the explosion is even more severe than he expected, deafening Carl, blowing out the entire passenger-side window, those double-ought pellets blasting the hound with such force that it actually does a complete back flip in midair, dead before it hits the ground.

But Randolph bred his dogs for heart, the second one instantly up into that gaping window space, back feet scratching against the car door for traction, halfway into the front seat now with its eyes pinned on Carl's face, the dog eager for that thick neck, Carl repeatedly squeezing the trigger to no effect. In the terror of the moment he has forgotten to pump the next shell into the chamber.

And now that dog is twisting and struggling to get the rest of the way in, still snapping and lunging at Carl, who has braced himself against the driver's door, finally summoning the presence of mind to jack in a new shell, pulling the trigger immediately, the interior of the patrol car once again exploding with flash and sound.

The pellets tear open the dog's chest with a tight pattern no larger than the palm of your hand, the dog screaming as it goes into a violent death spasm, dog's blood all over the car's interior, flung onto Carl's shirt and face, the hound finally dying, lying limply in that window space, half in and half out of the car.

Up on the porch, meanwhile, hidden by the night, Randolph's third dog, the big black, is whining to attack. In some dog way he realizes what has happened to his two companions, also understanding in some sense that the same fate awaits him, but still he is eager for the command, willing to follow his Alpha Master's command into Hell itself.

From behind the front door, Randolph says it with great sadness: "Sic 'em."

And the big black is gone, down the slope and past the dog on the ground, jumping up to the car, clawing over the dead companion who lies half in and half out of that window space, the big black in mortal pursuit now of the object of his fury.

Carl chambers another shell and blows the dog's head off.

Up at his door, Randolph Welby weeps for such valor.

Carl keeps dropping the shells he's trying to load into the shotgun, finally getting three new shells into the magazine and then bracing himself for more dogs.

Ten minutes he waits before carefully, shakily getting out of the patrol car. A lamp has been lighted in Randolph's shack.

Sweeping the shotgun from side to side and occasionally turning completely around, Carl once again climbs that slope.

No more dogs, but Randolph Welby is standing on the porch, half hidden in the shadows.

"How many dogs you got in there, asshole?"

Randolph doesn't reply.

The deputy, meanwhile, is trying to make out

the details of Randolph's getup, some kind of stupid cowboy clothes. "Who you trying to be, Texas
Pete?"

"Ta Wyoming Kid," Randolph replies, pulling
down on the big cowboy hat that is already sitting low
on his head, resting on his protruding ears.

"Yeah, well, Kid, let's go inside, I need to bor-
row one of your rifles." Just like Doc said, shoot him
with his own gun so it can be made to look like suicide.

Randolph steps to the edge of the porch and draws
both pistols from the gunbelt around his tiny waist,
leveling the muzzles at Carl's unmissable girth.

"Those aren't real," the deputy insists.

But when Randolph cocks both hammers, Carl
suddenly isn't sure. The light from the shack is weak,
and maybe those pistols *are* real.

"Dwop it!" Randolph shouts, flicking the barrels to
indicate Carl's shotgun.

With some effort, Carl bends over to put the
shotgun on the ground—but while straightening up,
he draws his own revolver.

Then the two of them wait there, ten feet apart in a
Mexican standoff.

"Did you shoot Sheriff Stone?"

"I tink not."

"Where is he?"

"All bwowed up. You dwop tat hogweg too, mistah,
and get weady to meet you makah."

Carl isn't sure what to do. If the pistols the little
man is holding are real, can Carl get a shot off
before—

Randolph knows what's going to happen when he
pulls both triggers, the hammers clicking into place as

Randolph shouts to supply his own sound effects. "Pow! Pow! Got you!"

Carl twitches when the hammers click and then twitches again with each word Randolph shouts. But after a moment's silence, the deputy grins. "You stupid fuck," he says, already forgetting Doc's instructions about killing Randolph with one of his own guns, the deputy shooting Randolph right there on the porch.

Carl is standing over the little man, picking up one of the toy pistols and seeing that it has been loaded with wooden cartridges. "You stupid fuck," he says again, a trace of regret in his voice, the deputy looking down at the ancient but childlike face, chinless and with a high forehead, a face of old leather, dramatically weathered, the skin around the old man's eyes drooping with the weight of years, that tiny mouth drawn into a small *O*.

"You dead," Randolph whispers without opening his eyes.

Carl grabs one of the bandoliers and drags him inside the shack.

Half an hour later, Carl is sitting in the patrol car making a call on the cellular phone Quinndell gave him last year so they could communicate outside official channels.

Mary answers.

"I have to talk to Doc," Carl demands.

She hesitates. "He's busy right now."

"You better git him 'cause I got trouble out here."

"What kind of trouble?"

"Just git Doc to the phone!"

"He doesn't want to be disturbed. What's wrong, you didn't find Randolph?"

"I found him all right. But there's something in his shack."

"What?"

Carl doesn't know if he should tell her or not.

"Carl?"

36

"COME ON, MR. LYON, WIDE AWAKE NOW."

He comes awake only reluctantly, however, and although he hears Quinndell's voice, Lyon still can't seem to make his eyes open.

"I've already given you an injection that should have you buzzing, but if you're still groggy I'll give you another."

Lyon finds his voice. *"No."*

"Excellent. Have you opened your eyes yet? The lights are on solely for your benefit, Mr. Lyon."

When he does open his eyes he sees that he is in a small room with glass-fronted cabinets around all the walls, stainless steel counters, no windows, and only one door, which is metal and closed.

Trying to move his hands, Lyon discovers he is bound to an examining table that has a wide strip of white paper running down its center. He's naked and on his back with both ankles and both wrists tied to the table, a rope across his neck too—across his neck and then tied around the table, holding his head down.

Lyon is able to move his head enough that he can see his nakedness, shamed by it, by how weak and white he looks, that bruise on his stomach the only element of color on his skin: his body looking like something harmless brought up from the depths of the ocean, beached and vulnerable.

But then Lyon comes suddenly to life and struggles against the restraints, choking himself when he tries to raise his head higher, twisting back and forth on the table, breaking into a heavy sweat but unable to free himself. Finally he turns a panicked eye in the doctor's direction.

Looking freshly showered and shaved, Quinndell is wearing dark suit pants and a white shirt, the sleeves turned up to his elbows, the red tie he's wearing tucked between two buttons of the shirt, his very black hair neatly combed straight back. Those extraordinary blue eyes are glistening with tears, the doctor leaning against one of the stainless steel counters where he has been listening with an amused smile to Lyon's struggles.

"So—back among the living, are we, Mr. Lyon? Have you convinced yourself yet that you can't get loose? Good, good. I've given this considerable thought and I think I'll start off with some burns. Not third-degree of course, which would destroy your nerve endings and blunt some of the effect. No, we'll begin with second-degree burns, similar to a severe sunburn. If necessary, we'll be here for hours. And the *pain* you're going to experience, oh, Mr. Lyon, in this examining room, here where I once cared for children, you and I are going to create a circle of Hell."

Lyon is wide-eyed. He works his tongue, trying to

keep enough spit in his mouth to speak. "What're you talking about?"

"Why, torture of course. Torturing you in the most excruciating manner possible, bringing the full power of my medical knowledge to bear upon the maximum production of pain, keeping you conscious with drugs, breaking your bones and grinding the shattered ends together, hammering probes into your gums, cutting your penis off, and then of course..." Here Quinndell takes a heavy tablespoon from his pocket and bangs it ominously against the stainless steel counter. "Gouging out your eyes with Mr. Spoon— oh, John, the *fun* we're going to have!"

Lyon tries to tell himself that this is all part of an elaborate ruse, that Quinndell can't possibly be serious, he's just trying to scare me, but when the doctor approaches, Lyon begins speaking rapidly. "Wait, wait a second, *wait,* what's the point, I mean none of this is necessary, you don't have to..."

/ Quinndell pauses and then leans back against the counter. "You're blubbering, Mr. Lyon." Now the doctor is tapping the bowl of the spoon against his palm. "Though I can appreciate how terribly exposed you must feel, how vulnerable, knowing that whatever I choose to do to you I can indeed do, it's entirely up to me, for the time we're in this room together, I am your God."

"Doctor, listen to me—"

"Oh, now it's *Doctor,* is it?"

"You *are* a doctor, your life is dedicated to alleviating suffering, not causing it."

This statement seems to astonish Quinndell, who puts his head back, opens his mouth, and shakes his shoulders up and down in that silently derisive laughter. When he finishes, he takes out a handkerchief, wipes his eyes, and asks Lyon, "Would you care to try another tack?"

Lyon answers immediately. "No one's been hurt yet, not physically. I mean whatever the penalties are for faking those babies' deaths, arranging illegal adoptions, at least Claire Cept was wrong about your having killed anyone."

He is still leaning against the counter and when he speaks he does so without any sense of being in a hurry. "The World's Worst Reporter strikes out again."

The implications of this panic Lyon. "What do you *mean?*"

But just then a teakettle whistles, Lyon turning his head as much as the rope across his neck will allow, seeing the kettle on a hot plate just a few feet from where Quinndell is standing.

Slipping the tablespoon back in his pocket, the doctor walks to the hot plate and turns it off, lifting the kettle and approaching the examining table.

Lyon starts twisting back and forth, keeping his eyes on the steaming kettle. "You're not, God, you wouldn't . . ."

"Yes, I am your God and, yes, I would." Quinndell standing there holding the kettle over Lyon's midsection. "When Mary was undressing you, she said you have a nasty wound on your stomach. Love bite?"

Lyon begging. "Please don't do this."

With his left hand Quinndell is reaching out to find Lyon's thigh, the doctor's other hand tipping the kettle.

Lyon arches his back, trying to turn away, seeing the steaming water appear at the kettle's spout, screaming, "DON'T, GODDAMN IT, PLEASE!"

Quinndell pours the water down the inside of one

thigh, instantly blistering the skin, Lyon so shocked by the pain that his body goes into spasms.

Quinndell, meanwhile, speaks in a mocking voice. "I believe this is when you're supposed to say, 'You're mad! Do you hear me, doctor! Mad, I say. *Mad!*'" Then Quinndell, laughing to himself, returns the kettle to the hot plate.

Lyon is groaning through clenched teeth, his scalded thigh on fire with pain. "Oh Jesus," he cries, "what do you want from me?"

As if waiting for this exact question, Quinndell turns from the hot plate and faces Lyon, the doctor's glass eyes wet and bulging. "I want that cunt's granddaughter."

There's a hesitant knock at the steel door and Lyon, thinking that the police have arrived, begins screaming for help. Quinndell takes a two-foot length of pipe from a counter, finds his way to the head of the examining table, and quickly raps the pipe right across Lyon's mouth.

This new injury stuns him into silence, Lyon feeling blood leaking from his front teeth, running down his throat.

"I've always wanted to smash one of you sanctimonious television commentators across the mouth," Quinndell says bitterly, raising the pipe. "Care for another?"

Lyon turns his head to the side and spits blood.

The knocking at the door resumes.

Quinndell unlatches two dead bolts and opens the door to confront Mary. "I know it's you," he says, "because I can smell it. What I don't know is what could possibly convince you to interrupt me in spite of my explicit orders to the contrary. Want to watch, is that it, Mary?"

"Carl called," she replies in a trembling voice, making a point of *not* looking past the doctor to see Lyon on the examining table. "Something's happened out there at that shack but he won't tell me—"

"Call the imbecile back and inform him that whatever he has discovered he can sit on it until I'm finished here."

Lyon shouts from the examining table, "Mary! For godssake help me! He's torturing me!"

Quinndell waits a moment and then asks her, "Would you like to reply to Mr. Lyon?"

She shakes her head, looking down at the floor, whispering a soft "No."

Quinndell slams the door and relocks it.

Lyon begs him for a painkiller.

"Oh, shut up," Quinndell tells him.

Balling his hands into tight fists, Lyon tries to deal with the pain, tries to convert that pain into anger. "You're not very bright, do you know that, doctor— not as intelligent as you'd like to think."

Quinndell is genuinely interested in this. "Why do you say that, Mr. Lyon?"

"Intelligent people don't have men like Carl working for them. He'll betray you out of stupidity if nothing else."

"A keen observation." Quinndell takes out a linen handkerchief and wipes at his eyes. "But let me ask you a question. If this handkerchief is superior to a Kleenex tissue, more durable and more pleasing to the touch—why then are millions of dollars' worth of tissue sold each year?"

"You should leave before the police show up."

"Tissues are useful because they're disposable."

"What are you talking about, I don't understand—"

"Disposability is the key to my entire operation."

"People care about me, people will be looking for me!"

"Really?" Quinndell walks over to one of the cabinets, opens it, and feels around until he finds a box of Brillo pads, still holding the handkerchief in his other hand.

"What're you going to do?"

"I'm going to scour that burn."

Lyon believes him. "Oh Jesus, please don't."

"Then tell me where Claire's granddaughter is hiding. She apparently drove your rental car back to the cabin. I sent Mary out there but she wasn't able to find the woman. No one can ever find her. Your Claire obviously has a hiding place. Where is it?"

"Why are you doing this to me?" Lyon turns his head again to spit out more blood.

"That's always the question people ask God, isn't it? *Why are you doing this to me?*" Quinndell puts the handkerchief away and straightens up. "The key to getting away with murder is to kill people no one cares about. A killer will never be seriously investigated as long as he deals in disposable victims."

"But you said you didn't kill any of those babies. And that coffin I dug up tonight was empty. If all you've done is arrange illegal adoptions—"

"Don't be tedious, Mr. Lyon."

"But I don't *understand.* Please give me something for the pain, please."

Ignoring the request, Quinndell says, "Before I was blinded I was simply interested in accumulating a sufficient amount of money, enough to ensure my comfort, and at the same time I wanted to correct certain imbalances in the way God had distributed children. Does it surprise you that I believe in God? Oh, absolutely, Mr. Lyon. I believe that Claire Cept's prayers led God to blind me. But once blinded I did not turn into a whimpering, defeated man, no, I popped in my blue eyes and *laughed* at Him, howling for more, thumbing God in the eye by giving Him all the babies he could handle."

Lyon groans.

"I arranged twenty illicit adoptions, improving the lives of everyone involved, and my reward was the loss of my eyes. Idiots like Carl are walking around with their eyes but not me, someone who deserves to see the world because I can appreciate it, I can better it. Yet I was the one who was blinded. Why? Because I dared to improve upon God's work."

As Quinndell talks, Lyon quietly struggles against the ropes holding his ankles and wrists, discovering that the rope around his left wrist is looser than the others. By folding his thumb and pulling hard he is able to move his hand within the rope, not getting free yet but making progress in that direction.

Hoping to keep Quinndell talking, keep him distracted, Lyon asks, "Which of those twenty children did you kill?"

"None of those, you idiot, haven't you been listening?" Quinndell tosses the box of Brillo pads back into the cabinet. "I think we'll skip the scouring and move right into bone breaking." He pats around the counter until he finds the steel pipe. Moving to the foot of the examining table, he slaps the pipe menacingly into his opened left hand. "Two percent of all adoptions fail, public agencies reporting that about a thousand children are returned each year by their adoptive parents. Of course I dealt with wealthy people who were willing to pay for—and accustomed to receiving—the very highest quality of merchandise. Designer children, if you will. And thank God none of those twenty babies whose adoptions I arranged ever had anything wrong with them.

"But I learned of a rich couple who had adopted an infant and then discovered she had Rett's syndrome. Her brain simply stopped growing and she slowly entered a vegetative state. Another child adopted by a wealthy couple showed signs of being violently disturbed—strangled a kitten when he was three years old. I was told of a couple in the entertainment business, very rich and very liberal, who adopted a baby whose mother had used crack during the pregnancy. The fetal liver can't metabolize cocaine efficiently and the effect on the fetus in terms of damage to the brain and central nervous system is devastating."

Lyon continues working desperately to free his left wrist, pulling steadily but quietly enough so that Quinndell won't hear him, folding his thumb in and turning his hand back and forth, a panic sweat lubricating his efforts, making progress an eighth of an inch at a time.

"So what do these couples do when they adopt damaged children and then find they can't cope with the consequences? Keep in mind that these are wealthy individuals, people of accomplishment, cultured and pampered, accustomed to getting what they want. They would not tolerate a car that failed to perform properly and yet they were stuck, presumably for the rest of their lives, with these dysfunctional children.

"It occurred to me that in addition to West Virginia supplying the country with natural resources, coal and timber—or in my case before the blinding, with children—West Virginia also accepts what the rest of the country wishes to be rid of, tens of thousands of tons of garbage from Eastern cities entering this state every day, proposals for nuclear waste dumps, our prisons housing out-of-state convicts.

"God blinded me to force me out of the adoption business? Fine, I would simply get into the *disposal* business. What I was surprised to discover was that there is much more money to be made in disposing of unwanted children than in supplying wanted children. Oh, it's true. If you think wealthy couples are desperate to adopt, you should see how they act when they want to get rid of a baby, to be free of any sense of ownership or obligation to a baby that after all isn't *really* theirs, they simply paid to adopt it and now they're stuck with the embarrassment, humiliated each time their friends ask, 'And how is little George, still drooling in the institution?'"

When Quinndell stops talking, Lyon also ceases the struggle to free his left wrist, afraid the doctor will hear him. Got to keep him talking. "I can't believe people really try to return babies."

"Oh, but they *do*, Mr. Lyon, they do. You think children are prized in this country? Don't be naïve. Twelve million American children live in poverty, ten thousand of them dying each year from the effects of that poverty, more than a half a million abused or neglected every year, Mr. Lyon, believe me, I know my market. Children are a *commodity*, prized only if they are in the correct social and economic strata and if they are free of defects. I admit that relatively few adoptive parents are shameless enough to follow through on their desire to be rid of damaged children, but of course to make my point all I needed was a few.

"I fabricated an offer. Religious families living in the hills of West Virginia would readopt dysfunctional children. It was an offer that certain wealthy couples jumped at, willingly paying hundreds of thousands of dollars to sever all connections, moral and legal, to children who were absolutely useless to them. I told the lawyers that these children would live happily with their new parents, these religious families who were serving God by caring for damaged babies. This made the wealthy couples feel good.

"My offer—*Bring me children*—became so popular that I discovered I could charge whatever I wished. After all, even a quarter of a million dollars was a bargain compared to the cost of institutionalizing a child for twenty years, not even counting the shame and heartache these dysfunctional children were creating for their upscale parents.

"But of course there were no religious families, I simply took the five babies and placed each of them on a rock in a cave. Returning them to God, do you understand? He could do whatever He wanted with them. Could strike me dead or lead someone to that cave to rescue the children. But, in fact, He did . . . *nothing.* I thumbed Him in the eye. My soul may burn in Hell, Mr. Lyon, but here on earth I rule—indulging my appetites, consuming life with both hands, unbowed, untouched by guilt, howling for more."

The rope is stuck around the widest part of Lyon's hand and he despairs of ever getting free. He lifts his head a few inches to look at the doctor standing there by his feet. Then Lyon laughs.

Quinndell elevates his chin. "Yes? Something funny, Mr. Lyon?" As he speaks he keeps slapping the pipe in his opened palm.

"No, it's just that . . ." He laughs again and then sobs once before catching himself, putting his head back on the examining table to stare up at the tiled ceiling. What a *perfect* way for me to end up, he thinks—naked and tied to an examining table. All my life I've been insulated, nothing ever touched me, and this is the way the scales are balanced, through this banality, lying here being lectured on the supply-and-demand cycles of a baby-based commerce. He laughs again. "This *is* Hell, being tied down and forced to listen to your stupid fucking ravings."

Quinndell calmly transfers the pipe to his left hand, turning toward the wall and finding a clipboard hanging there, taking from it a sharpened pencil, and then with his right hand he plunges that pencil into Lyon's leg, embedding it two inches into the left calf muscle, Lyon screaming and so violently twisting his body that his left hand is wrenched free.

His other wrist, his neck, and both ankles, however, are still bound, preventing him from reaching either Quinndell, standing there at the end of the table, or the pencil that is puncturing Lyon's flesh, the sudden pain of that new wound making him momentarily forget his scalded thigh and bleeding mouth.

"Any further comments?" Quinndell asks, the pipe back in his right hand, running that pipe along the top of Lyon's left foot and letting it rest finally on his shin.

"Take it out!" Lyon screams, his free hand still reaching pitifully for the pencil.

"I believe the two most excruciating forms of pain are facial," Quinndell lectures, "including the teeth and the eyes, and then of course the bones. Especially this one here." Quinndell taps the pipe up and down on Lyon's shinbone. "No flesh to pad the anterior surface of your tibia, lying as it does so vulnerably subcutaneous."

"Go ahead and kill me, get it over with!"

"Not yet, goodness, not yet," the doctor says, raising the pipe and then bringing it down with a sharp rap on Lyon's shin, again causing him to arch his body as if an electrical jolt has been administered.

Quinndell raises the pipe once more. "And now, where is Claire's granddaughter hiding?"

"I don't know!"

He smashes the pipe against Lyon's shin a second time, Lyon crying and cursing, his free hand opening and closing in Quinndell's direction.

"How about something *truly* painful?" the doctor asks, turning to a counter where he finds a hypodermic. Holding the needle upward, he taps the syringe several times, pushing the plunger until a stream of clear liquid shoots out the needle's point. His glass eyes actually seem to be focusing on the syringe.

"This is naloxone, Mr. Lyon. Would you like to hear the effect it's going to have on you?"

"No—*please.*"

"Your brain produces enkephalins, which are small peptide—" Quinndell chuckles. "But let's not get too technical, hmm? The reason morphine and other painkillers work is that they resemble substances that your brain produces on its own, natural opiatelike substances called opioids. Right now for example your brain is flooding itself with these opioids and although you feel pain, it's nothing compared to the agony you'd be suffering if the opioids weren't present." Quinndell pauses, smiling, enjoying himself. "Do you think I'm overly theatrical?"

A fucking scenery chewer, Lyon thinks—but says nothing as he continues staring at the syringe Quinndell is holding.

"Anyway, naloxone blocks the reception of morphine in the brain. One shot of this and a heroin addict under the influence goes into immediate withdrawal. Naloxone, however, also blocks the effect of the natural painkillers produced by your brain. In other words, John, when I inject this into you, within a few minutes whatever pain you are now experiencing will be so dramatically magnified that . . . well I'm afraid the effect is quite indescribable."

"You're going to kill me whether I tell you where Claire's hiding or not!"

"But if you tell me right now I will immediately give you morphine instead of naloxone. I'll remove the pencil and put salve on that wound and on your burn. Within five minutes you will be largely pain-free. If you don't tell me, I'll spend the next hour or so ruining you. I have a variety of operations in mind, Mr. Lyon, believe me." Preparing to administer the injection, the doctor steps toward Lyon—but not close enough yet that Lyon can reach him.

"It's up to you, John. In fact, I might even be convinced to let you live. I'm leaving the country this evening and if I were simply to walk out of here, by the time you got loose and then managed to get the door opened, I'd be long gone. No matter who you told your story to, no matter who believed you, I'd be out of harm's way."

Lyon is coughing and crying, still reaching for Quinndell but wanting to believe the doctor's offer of life too. "Okay, do that, do it! Leave me here and get out of the country. But give me something for the pain before you go, I was dragged into this investigation, it doesn't mean anything to me, I swear it doesn't, *please.*"

"We're on the right track, John. Killing you is not necessary, honestly it isn't. I could prepare the morphine right now."

"Thank you . . . thank you, Doctor."

"I told you I was an admirer of yours." He's standing less than two feet from Lyon's reaching hand, still holding that syringe, needle pointing upward. "So what's it going to be, a shot of this nasty naloxone or a nice soothing injection of morphine?"

"The morphine!"

"Then tell me where Claire's granddaughter is hiding. You see, she's a zealot. You might go home and eventually try to forget about all of this but she'll spend the rest of her life putting curses on me and praying to God for calamities to befall me, just as her grandmother did. I must have her, John, you understand that, don't you?"

"Claire's crazy, she can't hurt you. She was lying in a coffin, that's how I found her, who's going to believe anything she says?"

"No one believed her grandmother either but look at the trouble *she* caused me. The choice is yours, John."

Lyon wants to grab Quinndell by the throat and choke him to death, but the only way he can do that is if Quinndell comes closer. "We saw her tonight at the cemetery."

"Saw whom?"

Spook him, Lyon thinks. Get him pissed off enough to rush over here so I can get my hand on him. "Claire's grandmother."

The doctor smiles.

"No, we did. It was weird, she was dressed in her nurse's uniform, standing on her grave, she must still be after you."

Quinndell is unable to hold on to that yellow smile, the doctor suddenly angry, stepping toward Lyon and reaching to find his upper arm.

Waiting . . . waiting until Quinndell is well within reach, Lyon keeping the fingers of his left hand outstretched, waiting . . . then striking, grabbing the doctor by the hair and pulling him close, turning him and getting his arm around Quinndell's neck, feeling the gristle of Quinndell's windpipe against his wrist, Lyon squeezing for all he's worth, squeezing and shaking the doctor, determined not to let up or let go until Quinndell is dead.

The surprise of being attacked causes the doctor to squeeze the syringe's plunger, the contents shooting upward in a thread-thin line as Quinndell grabs Lyon's forearm with his free hand, trying desperately to relieve the pressure on his neck.

But Lyon holds on, never more determined than he is now, the muscles of his left arm bulging with the effort, maintaining that death grip, throttling Quinndell.

And it's working, the doctor's handsomely chiseled face blood-red and his glass eyes bulging from their sockets, Quinndell unable to breathe or speak, his tongue protruding between those small and discolored teeth.

Lyon is also red-faced with the effort, shaking Quinndell and squeezing all the harder, the blood lust rising in Lyon as the doctor chokes and gags.

Quinndell is manipulating the syringe, turning it around in his hand until he is grasping the barrel of the syringe the way you would a knife handle, stabbing Lyon in the forearm.

Lyon holds on, screaming with pain and rage as he keeps choking the doctor, who pulls the needle out and stabs Lyon a second time, a third, the needle bending but still going in, through Lyon's flesh and all the way to bone, Quinndell pushing harder and harder, moving the needle around in circles until Lyon is forced to release him, the doctor collapsing to the floor.

Lyon shakes his arm and rubs the hypodermic against the edge of the table until he gets it out, then watches in horror as Quinndell scoots across the floor to sit up against one of the counters, both of his fine hands at his neck, still unable to speak, struggling to take breaths, his beautiful blue eyes leaking blood-tinged tears.

With his left hand Lyon jerks at the rope around his neck, managing to work loose some slack but unable to reach the knot holding that rope. Neither can he free his right hand or either of his ankles. What's Quinndell going to do to him now?

Still stunned, the doctor finally gets around on his knees, one hand up to the counter, pulling himself to a standing position, his back to Lyon, Quinndell breathing with difficulty, coughing and gagging, spitting up blood.

And when the doctor does turn around, Lyon sees a face beyond horror, a mask of monstrous rage.

Quinndell lurches to a cabinet in the corner of the room and pulls it open. Keeping his back to Lyon, he is forced to choke out his words, making a mockery of the civility with which he normally speaks: "Mr. Lyon . . ." More choking. "I'd like you to meet Mr. Gigli."

Then he turns and shows Lyon what he has in his hands.

37

CLAIRE IS HIDING IN THE CABIN'S ATTIC JUST AS SHE DID
when she was a child, when Claire was in her midteens
and her grandparents regularly brought her out here to
this tucked-away hollow because they knew she was
tormented by something. "What is it?" her grandmother would ask. "Nothing you've done or nothing
that anyone has done to you is so bad you can't tell *me*
about it." But on this matter, Claire's grandmother
was wrong—Claire couldn't tell anyone. Maybe if she
had run out of Quinndell's office right after he did it to
her, had run to her grandmother *then* and told her
what the doctor had done, maybe then the words
would've come out. But after waiting a day, a week,
the longer Claire waited, the more impossible it
became to talk about it.

Her grandmother made sure Claire was treated
carefully, handled as you would an object of great
value and fragility, always telling Claire, "Whatever it
is, whenever you want to talk about it, I'll be ready to

listen." But the closest Claire came to talking about what the doctor had done to her was saying to her grandmother, "I just wish I could disappear, I wish I was invisible so nobody could ever see me again."

Then came the day her grandmother took Claire to the house where the two blind women lived, placing the girl in the corner of a room as the grandmother and the two women chatted. Claire never found out if the two women were aware of her presence, if her grandmother had arranged the visit beforehand, but what Claire did know is that her grandmother had briefly granted her the wish: invisibility.

And then it turned out to be a disaster when Claire tried to extend that power to John Lyon.

What's happened to him?

An hour ago someone came out to the cabin looking for her, a woman who walked all around the place, calling Claire's name, saying John had sent her—but Claire knew it was a lie. The woman had been sent by Quinndell, and he'll keep sending people, he'll send Carl out here with five gallons of gasoline to burn the cabin down if that becomes necessary—but he won't give up. He's like Claire's grandmother in that way, neither one of them capable of surrender.

Claire lights a candle and opens an old suitcase. Standing balanced on two floor joists, she removes her dress and underclothing, running her hands over her breasts and down her stomach, marveling at a sense of voluptuousness she has never before experienced. It's because of John, the size of his desire for her making Claire feel powerful for the first time in her life. Even if he *is* white, John Lyon is a man she could marry without disappearing.

But if Carl delivered him to Quinndell, how long is

it going to be before John is forced to tell them where she's hiding?

From the suitcase she takes out a nurse's uniform that belonged to her grandmother, one from the days when her grandmother was just beginning her career as a pediatric nurse, a uniform yellowed with age but that fits Claire exactly. To protect herself from Quinndell's evil, Claire puts the uniform on inside out. She retrieves the nurse's cap, still stiff with starch, and affixes it to her hair with bobby pins. Claire was wearing the uniform and cap several nights ago when she saw the monster defile her grandmother's grave.

And now he has John. I shouldn't have run out on John, I should be in town trying to rescue him, not hiding here playing with hoodoo.

But even as she thinks this, Claire works a piece of white wax. When she has formed it into the shape of a doll she takes a sheet of parchment paper and writes upon it the monster's name. The first step toward controlling evil is to name it.

Claire turns the doll over and with a butcher knife slits open its back. Into that incision she stuffs the folded piece of parchment, sprinkles in some cayenne pepper, and then loosely sews up the slit with black thread. Everything she needs she finds in her grandmother's suitcase.

By teaching Claire about hoodoo, her grandmother had hoped to empower the child: you think you are weak, at the mercy of those stronger than you, but there are ways you can bend people to your will.

She finds two tiny glass marbles, the size of peas, and embeds them in the wax doll's face.

By raping her in that examining room when she was fourteen years old, Quinndell fashioned the rest of Claire's life just as she has fashioned this wax doll in her hands. And Claire never did anything about it. Even when her grandmother was being driven insane trying to bring Quinndell to justice for the murders of those babies, Claire restricted herself to taking care of her grandmother, providing her a place to stay, never really joining the campaign against Quinndell—not until her grandmother killed herself.

And now the monster has John and here I sit playing with hoodoo.

Claire understands the attraction of hoodoo of course, the power it has over believers. Claire, after all, is an expert on the subject, a professor of American folklore, but she doesn't *believe* in it.

"Then why do I keep doing this?" she asks aloud.

Because I don't know what else to do, where to go, who to turn to.

Because the police won't believe her, Quinndell will have the grave filled in, he'll kill John and then get away with that murder too.

Because Quinndell has power—the power of being a doctor, a man, being white, being rich, the power that comes when you can function without a conscience.

And what power do I have? she wonders, looking down at the wax doll that seems now to be mocking her, Claire putting her thumbs on those two pea-sized marble eyes and pushing them deep, out of sight into the doll's head.

38

QUINNDELL IS HOLDING A PIECE OF STAINLESS STEEL wire, not much thicker than string and serrated along its entire twenty-inch length. Into small loops at both ends of this wire, Quinndell affixes stainless steel handles resembling those on the top of corkscrews.

Approaching the foot of the examining table, Quinndell reaches out and feels for Lyon's ankles—to find out if they're still tied.

"Keep the fuck away from me!" Lyon screams.

But Quinndell has already touched the ropes. "You had only one arm around me," the doctor says with a raspy voice, "so I assume you've managed to free just your left wrist." He moves his hand from the ankle ropes down to Lyon's feet, which overhang the end of the examining table. "We'll still be able to operate."

"I'll kill you!"

Ignoring that, Quinndell holds up the steel wire by one of its handles. "Gigli's wire saw, developed in the latter part of the last century by Leonardo Gigli, a

Florentine . . ." He coughs painfully. "A Florentine gynecologist. Signore Gigli developed the wire saw to perform lateral sections of the pubic bone, a nasty bit of business, that."

From one of his pants pockets Quinndell takes the linen handkerchief and holds it against his mouth, coughing into it. The handkerchief comes away bloody.

"Also used for . . ." The doctor coughs again. "Amputations. The wire is inserted in a hole made around the bone so that the bone section, the amputation, causes minimum damage to surrounding muscle and other tissue. Quite effective, still used today." Quinndell opens his mouth and works his jaw back and forth. "In your case, however, I'm going to lay the wire across the lower anterior surface of your tibia—across your shinbone, Mr. Lyon. Then . . ." He clears his throat and coughs into the handkerchief again, the injury caused by Lyon's choking forcing the doctor to speak now in a whisper.

"I will press down on both handles, putting my entire upper body weight onto the wire, sawing the Gigli back and forth, the first stroke slicing through skin and what little subcutaneous tissue lies above the bone, then into the tibia itself. It's the second largest, longest bone in your body, so Mr. Gigli and I have our work cut out for us. Not a lateral section of the pubic bone admittedly, but still . . ." Quinndell pauses, swallowing several times with difficulty before he is able to continue, still whispering. "A few centimeters into your tibia and I'll be tearing through the tibialis anticus—your calf muscle. While Mr. Gigli is wonderfully effective on bone, I'm afraid he does a rather sloppy job on muscle and tissue."

Quinndell puts the handkerchief away and takes the

Gigli saw by both handles, pulling the wire taut. "When we're through, your foot will of course drop off onto the floor." He pauses to let that sink in. "It'll hit the floor like something made of rubber, a heavy rubber thud is how I would describe it. Oh, John, I've done this before and please take my word for it, the effect is extraordinary. There's really no way I can adequately explain the pain, you'll have to experience that for yourself, but the effect of a person seeing his foot drop off onto the floor . . . Goodness. Sometimes I pick it up and try to give it back but the person always refuses it. Strange, don't you think?"

The doctor moves into position at the end of the table, his stomach just touching the bottom of Lyon's right foot, Quinndell placing the Gigli wire across the shinbone, a few inches above the ankle.

"I'll cut the rope before we're finished and along the way I'll be administering certain drugs that should keep you conscious during the entire procedure. Mr. Gigli is so disappointed when they go into shock before he's done, and I know *I* certainly wouldn't want you to miss that dramatic moment when the foot actually drops onto the floor. Then we'll have the other foot to work on. Of course for your genitals I have something quite special in mind."

As Quinndell continues his whispered litany, Lyon thinks this must be what it feels like to face the wrath of God: terrible and inescapable. A sightless God who's going to cut bone and muscle from his body, feet dropping onto the floor, dismembering Lyon piece by piece, reversing creation. And what would you say to such a God, how would you plead your case?

"I'm sorry."

"Oh, too late for weeping regrets now, John,"

Quinndell whispers as he presses down on both handles, the serrated wire across Lyon's shin already hurting even though the sawing hasn't begun yet.

"I'll tell you where she's hiding," he offers.

Quinndell shakes his head. "You'll tell me only reluctantly, with great regret. No, John, when you betray her I want you to do so *eagerly*."

And with that, Quinndell suddenly jerks downward with his right hand, pulling the wire's serrations through Lyon's flesh, touching bone and electrifying Lyon, Quinndell with his weight heavily on the handles as he pulls down now with the other hand, the stainless steel wire making a grating, sawing sound, biting into bone, then down again with his right hand, Lyon scream-shrieking with a pain so severe that his will shatters, becoming as irretrievably lost as water poured out on the ground.

Quinndell pauses here, his glass eyes wet in sockets of red, those gaping horrors looking up in Lyon's direction, waiting, *watching* him.

"Give her to me, John," Quinndell suggests with the seductiveness of the Devil's own whispering.

And Lyon does, eagerly.

39

CLAIRE?"

Standing on the edge of the bathtub and holding the trapdoor open with one hand, Mary Aurora shines a flashlight around the attic space. She doesn't want to be here, not at three in the morning, not knowing as she does what remains to be done before sunup.

The flashlight's beam finds Claire in one of the corners, her skin so easily blending with the attic's darkness that it seems what Mary's flashlight has found is only that nurse's uniform, empty but somehow animated.

"You have to come with me, Claire."

She turns her eyes away from the light.

"John's out in the car waiting for you."

John's alive? "Is he all right?"

"He's fine. Listen, all we're going to do is tie you and John in some shack not too far from here and leave you. By the time you get yourselves free, we'll be long gone."

"*We?* I know who you mean, 'we.' How can you work for that monster? Do you let him *touch* you?"

Mary thinks, it's a long story, honey. "I have a gun."

"You took him to my grandmother's grave, I *saw* you."

Mary puts the flashlight down and pulls a little silver thirty-eight pistol from the back pocket of her jeans. She holds it in front of the flashlight's beam. "Do you see what I have here?"

"Don't you know what he does to children? I can tell you what he did to *me* when I was a child."

Mary is biting her lower lip. "Either you come down with me right now or I'll go back outside and lead Dr. Quinndell in here and I'll help him climb up into this attic and then *he* can deal with you."

Claire hesitates only a moment before starting to make her way across the floor joists, telling Mary, "You must be so ashamed of yourself."

Lyon doesn't exactly remember being transferred from Quinndell's car to the backseat of his own rental car, sitting there now with his hands tied in front of him as he runs through a casual inventory of his pain. His front teeth hurt in a vaguely fuzzy way, as if from a morning visit to the dentist, the puncture wound in his calf and the wounds from the pipe blows to his left shin are old aches too, like football injuries that act up now and then, and his scalded thigh is last week's sunburn—with only his right shin, where the Gigli wire bit into bone, still hurting in the present tense.

He's drugged of course. Drugged and broken, bound and tired.

Quinndell is in the front seat humming some show tune.

Whoever re-dressed Lyon in his dirty and torn

clothing—he doesn't recall that part either—didn't put his shoes back on and it's only now that he notices his feet are bare, wiggling toes to make sure both feet are indeed attached. He does remember Quinndell saying something to Mary about using the rental car because it has to be found at Randolph's place, but Lyon doesn't know or care to know what this means.

He leans over to rest his cheek against the glass of the backdoor window just in time to watch Mary bringing Claire out of the cabin. Claire's hands are tied at the wrist too, and she's wearing a nurse's uniform. Lyon is so unmoved seeing her that he doesn't even raise his head away from the glass until Mary opens the door.

As soon as Claire is seated she loops her bound whands around Lyon's neck, pulling him close while he tries to remember . . . yes, something he wanted to tell her, whispering "I'm sorry" into Claire's ear.

Up in the front seat, Quinndell is whispering too. "Let's go, Mary."

After they've driven a mile into the woods, Quinndell turns around and tells Claire, "It's been awhile, hasn't it?"

Lyon watches her expression, trying to figure out if it is frightened or defiant.

"I take something of a proprietary interest in you," Quinndell is whispering, "seeing as how I had the honor of deflowering you."

No doubt about her expression now, furious. She asks Quinndell, "Did you get the coffin I sent?"

Momentarily nonplussed, Quinndell eventually manages a yellow smile. "It's because I respect your powers that I have gone to such extraordinary lengths to acquire you this evening."

"I'm wearing my grandmother's uniform."

Quinndell turns his blind eyes to Mary. "Is she?"

"Yes. Wearing it inside out."

"Claire is still protecting me," Claire says.

He spits out his whispered reply, "We'll see."

"Still out to get you!"

"We'll see about that too."

Lyon watches both of them, but inside he feels dead.

Claire raises her hands to touch his face. "What's he done to you? He's got you on drugs, doesn't he? John, what happened?"

"Oh yes, tell her, John."

Claire asks Quinndell, "Why are you whispering? Is it supposed to be scaring me?"

Lyon blinks several times. "Whispering because I almost choked him to death."

"Good for you!" Claire exclaims and then, to avoid his injured mouth, she carefully kisses him on both cheeks.

From the front seat, Quinndell laughs. "Before you anoint him the hero," he says, "you should perhaps hear the entire story. After his futile effort to attack me and once I had him subdued, your precious John *begged* me to exchange his life for yours. 'I know where she's hiding, take her, not me!' Ask him, go ahead. Lover boy is no hero, my dear—he betrayed you most eagerly."

Although horrified to hear this, Lyon makes no effort to correct Quinndell's version. What's the point? He *did* betray her eagerly.

They drive for another quarter of an hour before Claire breaks the silence by addressing Mary, "You could save us. Just stop the car. You can force him out, you're the one with the gun. No matter what he's paying you—"

Quinndell laughs and then chokes on that laughter, reaching quickly for his handkerchief and coughing into it.

Claire tells him, "I thought I would be terrified ever to see you again, to be in your presence, but now I realize you're nothing, you're pitiful. Banal. If you didn't have people like Mary working for you—"

"But she *does* work for me," Quinndell interrupts with a harsh whisper. "In fact, I could order her to stop the car right now and hold a gun on you so I could *sample* you again, for old time's sake, and you know what, Mary would do it—wouldn't you, Mary?"

She doesn't reply.

"Mary?"

"Yes."

"Yes what?"

"Yes, I would," she says, thinking if she can only make it through until dawn, this horror show will be over once and for all.

Quinndell turns to face Claire again. "See? And your boyfriend there, he wouldn't try to stop me either—would you, John?"

Lyon doesn't speak but he thinks Quinndell is probably right, Lyon would do nothing to protect Claire. He's all used up.

"John and I compared notes on you," Quinndell says.

Lyon doesn't have the energy to deny it.

"Men sometimes do that when they've shared an especially choice piece of ass, you'll excuse my French. Not very gentlemanly of us, I realize—"

"I'd die before I ever let you touch me again."

"That can be arranged too, my dear."

"Mary!" Claire shouts. "Stop the car! *Please!*"

"Oh, for godssake she's not going to stop the car. Mary and I have forged a very intricate arrangement. In exchange for one year's companionship and obedience—"

"Please don't," Mary begs.

"What's the harm? Either we listen to Claire continue bleating about how you should help her escape or we get her to shut up by explaining your devotion." Then he faces Claire and continues on in that strained whisper. "Mary has already received a bank transfer and tomorrow morning she'll use it to withdraw a quarter of a million dollars from one of my accounts. But neither Mary nor I would want you to think she's so avaricious as to sell her soul exclusively for money. No. Mary is motivated by a mother's love." He's grinning. "She had a daughter out of wedlock twelve years ago and gave the precious child up for adoption."

Mary is crying, Quinndell pointedly ignoring her.

"I used my connections in the field to find out who adopted the girl and where the family is living. I also acquired twelve photographs of the little darling— one taken on each of her birthdays. A really beautiful child. And when Mary has fulfilled her obligations to me I will turn over an envelope I keep in my safe, an envelope containing those twelve pictures *and* the little girl's address. I believe Mary will be able to meet her daughter because it's quite fashionable these days for adoptive parents to introduce children to their biological parents. The idea is to demystify them. And God knows that's going to be the case when Mary's daughter meets the whore who happens to be *her* mother."

Mary can barely keep the car on the road, hating Quinndell and herself, crying for this daughter she has never seen, a daughter who has become an icon of justification: I'm doing this for her, Mary chants in her mind—make things right with *her* and then all this is somehow worth it.

"Mary is not going to jeopardize a quarter of a million dollars and the chance to meet her daughter for the likes of you," Quinndell tells Claire.

And appreciating the truth of this, Claire sits back in her seat and takes Lyon's bound hands in her own.

"Another thing your boyfriend told me," Quinndell whispers. "Oh, John was quite talkative about you once I threatened him with a little pain. He said you made your appearance in a coffin. And Mary told me he had a severe bite wound on his stomach. If you two are into something really kinky, I'd love to hear about it."

Claire keeps her eyes on Lyon's.

"And why did you take John out to Barbara's house? Did you know that I lived with those two women for a while after I was blinded? Did you?" He hates not being answered. "I wanted to learn something about how they managed such independent lives—and what I learned was that blindness is a handicap only in relation to other people's sightedness. When the three of us were living there alone we weren't handicapped, any more than you're handicapped by not having a dog's sense of smell or a bat's radar. We became handicapped only when a sighted person was around. If I could blind the rest of the world I could reign again the way I did when I had my own eyes."

Claire and Lyon say nothing.

"Are the two of you stunned into silence? John, please describe Claire for me. Last I saw her she was a scrawny girl, all arms and legs. Has she . . . blossomed?"

Claire shakes her head but Lyon, after looking at her for a long time, says, *"Black."* His tongue is thick and disobedient. "Anthracite." Forcing him to speak slowly, carefully. "Shiny black glass. Ob . . . sidian."

"My," Quinndell whispers mockingly.

"I wish she were even blacker."

Claire continues shaking her head. "John, what did he do to you?"

At this Quinndell laughs aloud and turns around in the seat. Mary, still crying, is concentrating on driving as the doctor begins to hum "Some Enchanted Evening."

With her bound hands, Claire undoes several buttons from the front of the nurse's uniform. Because she's wearing the uniform inside out, Claire has to reach inside to get to a pocket—where she withdraws the wax figure she fashioned in the attic and then leans forward to slip it over Quinndell's shoulder, into his lap.

Startled by this, the doctor stiffens and shouts to Mary to tell him what it is, Mary looking back and forth from the road to Quinndell's lap, explaining that it's a wax doll similar to the one she found in that box on the doorstep.

Claire is chanting something as the doctor jerks around and screams obscenities at her, flinging the figure into the backseat, Claire and Quinndell livid with their mutual hatred, with the anger and the fear they possess for one another.

David Martin

It is then that Lyon turns to look out the window into the darkness sweeping by, feeling totally docile. None of this has anything to do with him, he's already completed his work for the night. Betrayal is exhausting, surely nothing more can be asked of him.

 **40**

DOGS!"

"What?"

Having stopped the car, Mary stares at the scene illuminated by the headlights.

"Damn you, answer me!" Quinndell demands impatiently, still angry from his exchange with Claire, forcing his voice painfully above a whisper.

"*Dogs.* I thought they were . . . bodies. But they're dogs, three of them, two lying on the ground by Carl's patrol car, one hanging out the window. Blood everywhere."

This description delights Quinndell, changing his mood instantly. "Goodness, I wonder what it looks like *inside.*"

Mary keeps both hands on the steering wheel, still staring out the windshield, waiting for orders.

Quinndell asks if she has the pistol.

"Yes."

"Prepared to use it?"

She mumbles another yes.

"Then let's escort our guests inside and find out what Carl's big surprise is."

Mary exits the car and opens a back door. Claire helps Lyon get out. The three of them stand there looking up at the lighted shack. It's dark here in the yard, no wind tonight, the air heavy and hot, suggestive of an approaching storm front.

Quinndell is waiting by the front of the car. He asks Mary the time and she tells him it's nearly four.

"Let's hurry then. Wouldn't want the sun to find us."

Holding lightly to Quinndell's elbow, Mary herds Lyon and Claire up the slope. Even under the influence of the painkillers Quinndell gave him, Lyon is unable to put his full weight on that left ankle. He has to lean heavily on Claire and is bewildered by being barefoot, trying to recall the last time he went barefoot outside. As a boy. Claire is staying very close to him, struggling to keep herself and Lyon upright.

A wild-eyed and red-faced Carl meets them on the porch. "I shot him, Doc! Nearly got killed by his dogs but I—" Then he looks at Claire, puzzled by the nurse's uniform.

"Mr. Welby is dead?" Quinndell asks in a whisper. "You shot him with one of his own guns as I instructed—and he's dead?"

Now it is Mary at whom Carl stares, as if she has the answer he needs.

"Carl?" Quinndell presses.

"The reason I called, Doc," he says, lowering his voice in deference to Quinndell's whispering, "is I ran into a little problem."

But before the flustered Carl can continue, Quinndell orders everyone inside.

Across the middle of the main room are four six-by-six supports that were added some years ago to keep the sagging ceiling from falling, and to one of those uprights Randolph Welby is tied: sitting on the floor, his left leg wrapped in a bloody sheet, a rope under his arms and knotted to the back of the post. He's still wearing the bandoliers and chaps, the cowboy hat jammed low on his head. Lyon recognizes him but says nothing; Mary and Claire can't stop staring.

But Randolph Welby has eyes only for Dr. Mason Quinndell, the most beautiful man Randolph Welby has ever seen, though the hermit would never say this of course and, in fact, wonders if his mother would consider it improper, Randolph thinking of a man as "beautiful." It should be "handsome." But as the hermit continues watching Quinndell, illuminated as the doctor is by the flattering light from the oil lamps Carl has kept burning all around the room, Randolph keeps coming back to *beautiful*.

The doctor showered and changed clothes after torturing Lyon. His pinstriped suit fits him perfectly, the lapels flat and no bulge in the material at the back of his neck either, his shirt so white that Randolph thinks there should be another name for it, something beyond regular white, the French cuffs *glowing* white at the doctor's wrists. He is trim and perfectly postured, a strong face, his hair as black as the shirt is white, thick hair combed straight back with no part showing, curling jauntily above his ears and collar. His nose is long but without bumps, skin smooth—really, Randolph thinks, here is a man who looks how the king of England should look when he's going around in regular clothes, that is, when he's not wearing robes and crown, a man you'd have to call beautiful, that's all there is to it.

"Now please tell me what happened, Carl," Quinndell requests in a softly encouraging whisper.

"Like I said, nearly got killed by them dogs, had to fight my way up to the porch, and he was standing there waiting to ambush me, *armed,* so I had no choice, Doc, had to shoot him."

"You mean you shot him with your own weapon?"

"Had to!" Carl is looking at Mary for support, for some sign of approval.

"Killed him?"

"Unh-uh."

"Carl, please, I'm tiring of this guessing game."

"He's right over there against one of the pillars, all tied up so he can't get away." Carl glances toward the door to the back room. "But here's the thing, Doc—"

"Introduce me to him."

"Huh?"

"If Mr. Welby is conscious, please introduce me."

The deputy takes Quinndell to the post. "He's down sitting on the floor. I shot him in the leg, bleeding a lot but he ain't dead, you can talk to him."

The other three—Lyon, Claire, and Mary—are fascinated by this, Quinndell kneeling to speak to a gnomish man dressed in an outrageous Western outfit, bandoliers crossing at his chest and an overly large cowboy hat sitting low on his ears.

"Mr. Welby, my name is Dr. Mason Quinndell."

Randolph has no idea how to address so regal a man.

"You got into that cave somehow, didn't you?"

"I bewieve so." Randolph is whispering too.

"And you found those children I left there for God, didn't you?"

"I bewieve—"

Randolph's eyes enlarge. He hadn't recognized the voice because of Quinndell's whispering but *now* Randolph knows who this is. The little man brings up his arm, extending his index finger, pointing it right into the doctor's beautiful face. *"Satan."*

Chuckling, Quinndell stands and brushes off his trousers. "Yes, well, better to rule in Hell, and so on and so forth."

Quinndell orders Carl to bind Claire and John so they can't get loose, where they won't be in the way, the deputy assuring him he knows just how to do it, untying Lyon's hands, making him face one of the uprights, putting his arms around it, then securing his wrists together on the far side of the post. He does the same to Claire at another of the supports.

"All done, Doc." Carl is again looking toward the back room, Mary and Claire both noticing this and wondering what's back there that's making the enormous deputy so nervous.

Lyon, meanwhile, is finally coming down from the effects of the drugs, aware of his pain and smelling his own rancid sweat.

"Here's the challenge, Carl," Quinndell whispers. "How can we still make it appear that John and Claire came out here to question Randolph about rumors they heard, Randolph stealing babies and all that, he kills them both, sets his own house on fire, and then commits suicide—how can we create that scenario when he's carrying in his leg a bullet from your weapon?"

Carl is alternately nodding and shaking his head, his uniform thoroughly sweated through, taking this opportunity to stuff his tiny mouth with chewing tobacco.

"Mary, get my black case."

"It's in my purse, out in the car."

"Fetch!"

When she's gone, Quinndell leans close to Carl. "You and the fair Mary will be together before the sun rises, that I promise you."

This embarrasses Carl—but arouses him too.

Mary reenters the shack carrying a black zippered case the size of a paperback. Knowing the routine, she opens the case and prepares a hypodermic.

The doctor takes off his suitcoat and hands it to Mary, rolling up a sleeve and then offering his forearm, Mary finding a vein and administering the drug.

Quinndell puts his head back and sucks in air with a long hiss as Mary hastily puts away the hypodermic, zippers the case shut, and steps back out of the way.

After a moment of rocking unsteadily on his feet, Quinndell slowly rolls his sleeve back down, slips in the cufflink, and turns for Mary to help him on with the suitcoat. The doctor carefully straightens the coat before turning around and whispering more to himself than to anyone else in the room. "Where to start, where to start."

Carl hasn't seen this before, startled by Quinndell as he twists back and forth on the balls of his feet, pounding the bottoms of his palms together in a kind of silent applause, becoming increasingly agitated, smoothing his hair with both hands, taking a step in

314

one direction and then the other. "What I need to know," he whispers, touching his bruised throat, smiling, turning, once again striking his palms together, "what I need to know . . . is it still *dark out*, children?"

"Here's how we involve you in the new scenario," Quinndell whispers to Carl, the doctor having fun with this, his graceful white hands on Carl's fat-humped shoulders, standing close enough to the deputy to kiss him. "You came out here to investigate Sheriff Stone's disappearance. I don't suppose you've run across the wayward sheriff, have you?"

Carl rolls the tobacco in his cheek and says no.

Quinndell puts his fine head way back and grins widely, so intoxicated by the contents of that hypodermic that he can barely contain himself, whispering in delight to the deputy, "You're out here looking for the sheriff, dogs attack you, you heroically fight them off, advance to the house here, confronted by the evil Mr. Welby, he attacks you. But what weapon does he use?"

The deputy doesn't know the answer.

"Get a knife from his kitchen."

Carl eagerly waddles out of the main room, Mary and Claire and Lyon and Randolph watching all of this as an audience would.

"Got a big one here, Doc!" Carl announces upon his return, handing the butcher knife to Quinndell.

"Excellent, excellent." Quinndell feels the blade. "You can tell a lot about a man by the way he keeps his knives. Sharp, this one. *Now Carl!*"

"Right here, Doc."

Holding the butcher knife in his right hand, Quinndell places his left on Carl's shoulder. "The evil hermit advances on you, you shoot him in the leg, but he makes one last desperate lunge, managing somehow . . ."

Quinndell pauses, Carl waits. Then the doctor instructs Carl to give his pistol to Mary. Carl does so without hesitation, returning to his former position facing Quinndell, who once again grasps Carl's right shoulder, the point of that butcher knife close now to the fat man's neck.

"Close your eyes, Carl."

He stops chewing the tobacco:

"You trust me, don't you?"

"Sure."

"Then close your eyes."

"Wait, I gotta spit."

"Not yet. I want you to close your eyes and *see* the scene I'm creating, do you have them closed?"

"Yeah."

"You've wounded Mr. Welby but he still has this knife, and with one last dying, desperate effort, he manages to strike a mortal blow."

Mortal? Carl thinks about this a moment before opening his eyes.

Quinndell finds those eyes with his fingers and closes them gently. "Can you *see* that mortal blow being struck?"

"Well—"

"Like this," the doctor whispers, plunging the butcher knife into the left side of Carl's corpulent neck, maintaining his grip on the knife handle and working it violently back and forth as both of Carl's hands shoot up to grab the knife, fighting Quinndell for the handle, Carl's eyes opened wide now, the crude features of the deputy's face contorted more with utter astonishment than pain, staring into Quinndell's glass eyes. The deputy moves back and tries to speak, making a whooping sound as if beginning a war chant. "The trick," Quinndell whispers, following Carl, "is to catch the common carotid artery *and* the jugular vein, get you coming and going, so to speak." Quinndell's one hand holds tightly to Carl's shoulder, the other hand again manipulating the knife as the two men continue stepping across the room, Carl stumbling backward and Quinndell following in some kind of awful dance. "Not an easy procedure on a neck as fat as yours, Carl." Until an arterial stream arcs from the wound and Quinndell finally releases Carl, the doctor taking out a handkerchief and wiping his hands. "But I could do it blindfolded."

Carl bumps against the post where Claire is tied, Carl with both hands clamped to his neck, holding them tightly around the blade but not trying to pull it out, unable to speak, pivoting on one foot as blood and tobacco juice vomit from his mouth.

When he drops hard to his knees the entire floor shakes, his bloody hands still trying to stem the flow from his throat, that arterial stream occasionally finding a space between fingers, Carl's tremendous blood pressure shooting the stream in a ten-foot arc.

He's gagging and when he opens his mouth what emerges looks like a roiling mass of black and bloody maggots—the plug of chewing tobacco—Carl taking a long time to die, again shaking the floor when he falls treelike on his side, choking and occasionally kicking out with one leg, neither hand having left his throat, the knife still embedded there, the deputy mounting a final pitiful attempt to get to his feet, but he slips in the mess he's made on the floor and falls forward, right on his face, dying finally with the sound of gargling his own blood.

Although Lyon and Mary and Claire keep watching, transfixed, Randolph has long ago averted his eyes.

41

MARY QUIETLY SIDESTEPS TOWARD THE DOOR.

"Mary?" But because she has moved, Quinndell is whispering her name to an empty space. He does a slow swivel, searching for her, Mary motionless now, having stopped just a few feet from the shack's open door. "Mary?"

Lyon wonders why she doesn't simply run away. He and Claire are tied to the posts but Mary is free to go and she's holding all that firepower—Carl's heavy pistol in one hand, the little silver thirty-eight in her other—and even if she wasn't concerned about saving anyone else's life, she could easily save her own. Claire, however, understands Mary's hesitancy: to leave now would mean running out on her daughter.

"Oh, *Mary*," the doctor sings.

Although she hasn't pointed either pistol at Quinndell, Mary has her index fingers curled around the triggers.

"I know you're still here, why are you acting so

silly?" Quinndell asks pleasantly, turning slowly until he finally faces Mary, as if some internal guidance system has located her position. "I'm not going to hurt *you* for goodness sakes. Carl was a cretin. Didn't follow orders. And eventually he would've talked about this, you know he would have. But I *trust* you."

Mary makes a small contemptuous sound.

Having at last heard her, the doctor noticeably relaxes. "I *do* trust you, implicitly. We have a deal, remember?"

Mary is listening.

"I trust you because I know that once you leave here and have invested in a nice little restaurant, have arranged to meet your daughter, become friends with the adoptive parents, take an active role in your daughter's life—"

"Stop it!"

Quinndell smiles only enough to show the tips of his teeth. "I know that once you start your new life, Mary, you won't be any threat to me, I'll never need to contact you in the future. And if I were to hurt you *now,* how could I possibly get back into town? Carl *soiled* me, didn't he?" Quinndell asks, touching the wet bloodstains on his suitcoat. "I have to go home and change. How am I going to do that without you? How would I get to the airport?"

"Let's go then."

"Fine. But first we must make it appear that Mr. Welby killed Claire and John too, otherwise the authorities will be looking for us. Give me Carl's pistol."

"No."

"No? Do you see an alternative to what I've just outlined? Are you suggesting we leave these people here to talk with the police?"

"I don't know!"

"Give me the gun. I'll do it."

But when the doctor steps toward her, Mary raises the pistols and cocks both hammers.

Quinndell stops.

"Shoot him!" Lyon yells.

"You're not going to shoot me, are you, Mary?"

"I'll drive you into town and you can give me the envelope."

"Ah, the envelope." He smooths back his hair with both hands, straightens the suitcoat, and lightly touches the bruises on his throat. "I know how much you want the envelope, Mary, but you're not thinking clearly. We leave these people here and the police will be picking up both of us within twenty-four hours. I disposed of four babies before you came to live with me and this past March you drove me to the cave so I could dispose of the fifth one, you and I are in this very deeply and very much together. Now give me Carl's pistol."

"No!"

"Then tell me what *your* plan is."

"I don't have a plan!" Mary just doesn't want to see anyone else killed. Nor does she want to shoot anyone herself, not even the doctor. Mary just wants to leave.

Quinndell is exasperated. He clears his throat and winces, telling Mary in a raspy whisper, "Is this how you want your daughter to find out who her real mother is, reading about you in some tabloid, *baby-killer?*"

She lowers the pistols.

Claire warns, "You can't trust him."

With an anguished expression, Mary looks from Claire to Lyon and then down at Randolph, who tells her in a quiet voice, "Do what's wight."

"Yes, Mary," Quinndell says, "do what's right, what's right for you and . . ." Here he reaches into the suit jacket's inside pocket, bringing out an envelope. "And do what's right for your daughter." Quinndell opens the envelope's flap and pulls out some photographs, just enough that Mary can see their edges. "I am told that she is a very beautiful young girl, and my contacts also tell me that although she is only an average student, *B*s and *C*s, she has an artistic flair. Plays in the school band. Clarinet, I believe. Sews some of her own dresses. Absolutely devoted to animals."

Mary is weeping and Claire screams at Quinndell, calling him despicable names as Lyon tells Mary, for godssake just shoot Quinndell and then take the envelope for herself. But Mary has never killed anyone and for the moment she is transfixed by the envelope full of photographs of her daughter. What does she look like?

Quinndell whispers on relentlessly. "Knowing that you would in all likelihood be meeting her before the summer was over, I made some inquiries last month. Saving the information as a surprise for you when I turned over this envelope. Apparently your daughter's little cocker spaniel was run over in the spring and her adoptive parents haven't bought her a new dog yet, waiting I suppose until they think she's emotionally ready to accept one. I was just thinking—okay, call me a sentimental old fool—but can you imagine meeting your daughter for the first time and there you are, holding a brand-new little puppy. You could be carrying it in a wicker basket, a ribbon around its neck and—"

"Mary!" Lyon shouts.

But Mary falls for it, body and soul, stepping close to Quinndell, putting one of the pistols under her arm, grasping the envelope.

He won't release it. "The weapons, please."

In a daze, Mary hands him the thirty-eight first, which Quinndell puts in his suitcoat pocket, then he takes Carl's pistol in his right hand, still holding the envelope in his left.

"Give it to me," she begs.

"Of course. That was our deal and I always keep my word." When he releases the envelope he tells Mary that her daughter's name is Penelope.

Trembling, Mary folds back the flap and takes out the twelve photographs. The first one is of Quinndell sticking his tongue out.

"Or maybe it's Heather."

Not listening to him, Mary turns quickly to the next photograph, showing Quinndell smiling broadly, his blue eyes opened comically wide.

"One of the advantages of never intending to keep your word," he whispers, taking a step back, "is that you can promise anything."

In the third photograph Quinndell is holding his rolled hands in front of his eyes like a pair of binoculars. Mary madly flips through the rest of the photographs, all of Quinndell—no little girl, no address, nothing but pictures of Quinndell mugging for the camera.

Still not getting it, not wanting to *believe* it, she demands, "Where are *my* pictures?"

"Oh, Mary, I have absolutely no idea what became of the little bastard you spawned."

And with that he pulls the trigger, a bullet opening a hole precisely between her breasts, Mary lifted slightly off her feet and then dropped to a sitting position on the floor, surrounded by photographs of Mason Quinndell, Mary's arms forward, hands resting on her legs, palms turned up as if she is meditating briefly before toppling over like a top-heavy toy.

And from the back room of Randolph's shack, a child cries.

42

QUINNDELL IS AT A LOSS FOR WORDS.

With the baby girl wailing at full volume, Randolph tries to raise up and is just about to say something when Claire slides her arms down along the post, kneeling so she can catch Randolph's eye, shaking her head and mouthing *no*. She looks over at Lyon and gives him the same message.

Quinndell's face is going through a remarkable series of changes, from surprise to confusion to fear and then finally there is an effort, not entirely successful, to appear casual. "Mr. Welby?"

Randolph has slumped against the rope around his chest, his eyes barely visible under the brim of his cowboy hat.

"Mr. Welby, please answer me. What are you doing with a child here? This is what Carl was trying to tell me, isn't it? Welby!"

Nothing.

Quinndell eases toward the center post where Randolph is tied, the doctor finding the little man's leg with the toe of his shoe, nudging him as the baby continues screaming in the back room. "What's that child doing here?"

Nothing.

Quinndell motions with the gun and kicks harder. "You rescued one of *mine,* didn't you?"

Nothing.

"Answer me, goddamn you!" Quinndell shouts as he repeatedly kicks Randolph's leg.

"Why are you doing that?" Claire asks. "He's dead."

"What did you say? I can't hear you with that fucking crying."

Claire waits a beat and then asks, "What crying?"

Quinndell brings the pistol up and points it in her direction, Claire quickly moving around to the far side of the post she's tied to. Lyon does the same.

"If either of you know anything about that baby," Quinndell demands, still shouting to be heard above the crying, hurting his injured throat, "you'd better tell me right now!"

Lyon calls to him. *"Quinndell,* you murder two people in cold blood and now you hear babies crying, what the hell was in that injection Mary gave you?"

"What? *What did you say?"* He fires in Lyon's direction, the bullet hitting a side wall as Lyon crouches to the floor, this second shot causing the child to scream all the louder. "I'll kill you, then I'll strangle the little bastard with my own hands."

"Killing us," Claire says calmly, "won't stop you from hearing crying babies, you'll hear them crying for the rest of your life."

"What?" Quinndell takes a moment to think this

through. "What, you're trying to make me think I'm insane, that's awfully feeble, my dear, that's—" But he can't talk with that goddamn crying going on, Quinndell again losing his composure and shouting toward the back room. "Shut up!"

The baby continues shrieking.

Quinndell's scalp suddenly itches and he begins scratching it, causing his hair to stick out all over his head. "I know what happened, nothing very mysterious about this, Welby found one of the babies before it rolled off that rock, he brought it back here—"

The crying has stopped.

Quinndell pauses, cocking his head one way and then the other.

"What's wrong now?" Claire asks.

"It stopped."

"What stopped?"

"The—" But then he catches himself. "Nice try, folks." Quinndell moves carefully toward a small table where two oil lamps are burning. "I smell kerosene so I know he has lanterns in here somewhere," the doctor says, moving his hands until they find the table. "I gave directions to the men who are picking me up, but I also told them that a fire would light their way." He has found one of the glass lamps and is grasping it by the base. "The scenario is perfectly clear. Welby killed Carl and Mary and then set the cabin on fire, burning himself to death along with you, Claire, and with your famous boyfriend too."

Claire asks him if he still hears babies crying.

Quinndell's face is set hard as he heads for the post where she is tied. "If you think *this* blind man is afraid of fire, you're sadly mistaken, dearie. I'll break this lamp at your feet, burn you at the stake for the witch you are, I'll dance to your screams. The baby will burn too, unless of course I was just *imagining*—"

"Hey, Doc," Lyon says, "if you're setting this up to make it look like Welby killed us all, how do you explain the fact that he's tied to a post?"

Quinndell stops. He doesn't want to give Lyon the satisfaction of being right but it's true of course, he can't leave the hermit tied up. Still holding the kerosene lamp, Quinndell slides his feet along the floor until he comes to Randolph's legs, which he kicks several times. "Dead," he says, kneeling on the floor, putting the lamp down, slipping the pistol into his pocket, reaching for the rope tied around Randolph's chest.

"I tink not."

Quinndell jerks back just as Randolph kicks out with his uninjured leg, knocking over the lamp, which breaks, spilling kerosene that ignites with blue and yellow flames spreading across the floor.

Making whimpering sounds, Quinndell leaps to his feet and takes rapid steps backward as he pats his legs with both hands, checking to see if the fire has ignited his clothing, carelessly backing up until he is within Lyon's reach.

Pressing his torso against the post, Lyon has stretched his arms out as far as he can, waiting for the doctor's arrival. Although his wrists are tied together, Lyon can still use his hands, grabbing Quinndell by the hair and pulling him close, the two of them struggling now, the post between them, Lyon determined not to let him go, not this time, no matter what.

Lyon slides his arms down the post, pulling Quinndell to the floor, one of Lyon's hands gripping the doctor's hair while the other is trying to reach his throat.

The kerosene fire has spread to a bookcase, igniting a row of westerns, filling the room with smoke as the baby begins crying again from the back room.

Now Lyon is trying to slip his tied wrists over Quinndell's head, wanting to use the rope as a garrote, but his position is made awkward by the post, and the doctor, flat on his back, manages to escape that intended choke-hold, trying to scoot out from under Lyon's hands, both of those hands ending up on Quinndell's face, Lyon's thumbs on those beautiful blue eyes.

"Bwind him, Mistah Wyon!" Randolph shouts as the infant cries all the more loudly.

Blind him? Lyon presses on the glass eyes but lacks the will to press harder, trying desperately to keep Quinndell's head from slipping away.

Now it is Claire who is screaming it. *"Blind him!"*

Quinndell eases his hold on Lyon's wrists, enabling Lyon to half stand, maneuvering to put his weight behind his arms, both fascinated and repulsed by the feel of those glass eyes under his thumbs.

"Please, John," Quinndell says as he sneaks a hand down to his coat pocket, reaching in for the pistol.

"What?" Lyon demands.

Quinndell has the gun out. "Please don't hurt me."

Claire shrieks a warning but Lyon pays it no attention, the doctor's plea having already enraged him, Lyon instantly dropping his weight onto his thumbs, driving them into the doctor's eyes.

Lyon watches as those blue and white eyes twist crazily in their sockets, briefly making Quinndell appear cross-eyed before the glass orbs are forced up out of the sockets, Lyon's thumbs replacing them as he pushes down harder, Quinndell struggling beneath this piercing like an animal being ritually tortured, the doctor losing the pistol as his body arches, as Lyon growls deep in his throat, gritting his teeth, spittle forming at the sides of his mouth, *bouncing* his weight onto his thumbs to drive them deeper into what feels like wet gristle, some kind of tough tissue that Lyon can't break through, Quinndell *howling,* Lyon increasing the torture by moving his thumbs around within those eye sockets, feeling a shelf of bone on the interior roof of the sockets, pressing hard against that flat bone, Lyon's fingers clawlike over Quinndell's forehead, getting a firm grip and pushing upward with his thumbs, using all his strength, that shelf of bone cracking and then breaking, cutting Lyon's thumbs as they push up into Quinndell's brain, the doctor's howling and the infant's crying competing in some kind of crazed bidding, each raise in volume matched and raised again until the howling and crying achieve merger, one voice now, inharmonious but joined, one single, final crescendo terrible enough for God to hear.

EPILOGUE

LYON STRAIGHTENS HIS SUITCOAT AND FIXES HIS EYES ON camera one, anticipating the red light.

"Good evening. At the top of our report tonight, an announcement of a new twist on an old peace proposal that has some United Nations negotiators cautiously optimistic for a settlement to the latest round of hostilities in the Middle East. Here's Michael Barnes reporting from Jerusalem. Michael."

When Lyon first resumed newscasting, the ratings set records for all the wrong reasons: people wondered if he would cry again and there was also a morbid curiosity about watching someone who had killed a man with his bare hands. But Lyon's former coldbloodedness was warmed now by a certain vulnerability and as he continued on-air over the fall of that year, viewers stayed with him.

The special, called "Bring Me Children," aired in mid-September and earned a decent thirteen rating points and twenty-three share. Everyone at the network was saying Emmy, and in the spring of the following year it proved true: Lyon became one of very few journalists ever to have won both a Pulitzer and an Emmy.

Killing Quinndell didn't save their lives. Claire, Randolph, and Lyon were still tied to the posts, the fire was spreading throughout Randolph's shack, the smoke became blinding and then made breathing dangerous, the baby still crying in the back room.

It was Claire who got them loose. She managed to reach Carl, pull the knife from his neck, and use it to cut the ropes from her wrists. Then she freed Lyon and he pulled Randolph from the shack while Claire ran into the back room and saved the infant girl.

The men Quinndell had hired showed up just before dawn. They watched the fire, honked the car's horn, called for the doctor, talked between themselves, watched the fire some more, and then left.

While Claire, Lyon, Randolph, and the baby were off in the woods, hiding and waiting for the men to depart, Lyon whispered an explanation of everything that Quinndell had told him.

"I don't know if Quinndell was ever a good doctor. When he did that awful thing to you, Claire, when you were fourteen, he was already falsifying the deaths of those babies, arranging for their adoptions to wealthy couples, already thinking of himself as God. But it wasn't until he lost his sight that he went truly insane. He believed his blindness was God's punishment, and he reacted by trying to punish God. Leaving those babies to die in a cave, killing others who were powerless. There's no way to explain it except for what your grandmother said. He's a monster. And what you said. Evil exists."

Randolph kept nodding. *See,* he thought—this is *exactly* what I wanted someone to do, explain everything.

As the sun finally began to backlight the eastern ridges and with only a stone chimney remaining of Randolph's shack, Claire carried the baby to the rental car and then half carried, half dragged the hermit there. When she came back for Lyon she told him he couldn't report what Quinndell had done with those twenty babies, faking their deaths and then arranging their adoptions.

Leaning on her and limping his way to the car, Lyon was incredulous.

"What's it going to accomplish?" she asked. "The twenty women who were told their babies died all those years ago will be devastated. How does a mother even begin to *think* about something like that? The adoptive parents will be horrified that now someone is going to take their children away from them. And the only innocent parties in this whole mess, the kids, they're going to be pulled apart. It'll be a circus, no one'll come out of it with any dignity."

Lyon said he had no choice: he was a reporter.

"Of course you have a choice. Report Quinndell's murders, just leave out the part—"

Lyon insisted that you can't leave out parts. And even if he didn't report it, someone else would. "People are going to be all over this story."

"Doing something because if you don't someone else will," Claire told him, "is an immoral argument."

But it was an argument they continued to have even after Lyon told the police the entire story, even after they returned to New York and Claire moved into Lyon's apartment, even after the Quinndell horrors were written about in newspapers—even after Claire's prediction turned out to be true: a troupe, a circus troupe, of lawyers and reporters converging on the twenty children whose deaths had been faked by Quinndell, some of the biological mothers suing for the return of their now teenage children, some of the adoptive parents fleeing the country with those children, no one coming out of it with any dignity.

She was never angry with Lyon for betraying her hiding place to Quinndell; in fact, the only time Claire ever mentioned it was to tell Lyon that betrayal under torture is not betrayal. But her opinion on the reporting of what happened to those twenty children was absolute. *"You* don't have to be a part of it," Claire kept insisting.

So when Lyon began working on the special that August, she moved out of his apartment.

"I'm John Lyon and that's our report for this Sunday evening. Thank you and goodnight." He keeps smiling until the red light goes off.

After the newscast he attends a meeting to discuss future assignments, deciding not to participate in another special the network is planning, this one on the adoption of foreign-born children. The producer says she's disappointed but understands Lyon's position.

After that meeting he has a drink with his director, who points out that it was exactly one year ago today that Lyon broke down and cried while reading that story about murdered children. "And now you're back on top, got an Emmy and all—who would've thought, huh?"

"Certainly not me."

He takes a cab home.

When the doorman, Jonathan, sees who it is limping up to the doors, he rushes to open them.

"Good evening, Mr. Lyon. Scorcher, huh?"

"That it is, Jonathan, that it is."

The doorman walks with him through the lobby, always unsure whether he should take Lyon's arm or not. "You need some help, Mr. Lyon?" Jonathan asks, wincing a little with each pained step Lyon takes.

"No, no, I'm fine, thank you. Some days it hurts worse than others, I don't know why."

The doorman stands there until the elevator arrives. As Lyon steps on, Jonathan tells him, "You're a hero, Mr. Lyon." He's said this maybe twenty times since Lyon's return.

And Lyon never knows how to reply to it. On this occasion he nods and smiles, pressing the button for his floor and waiting for the doors to close.

I don't feel like a hero, Lyon thinks on the way up. Claire's grandmother was a hero. And Randolph Welby too. Lyon paid to have a new cabin built for Randolph, who was pestered by reporters for a mercifully short time primarily because interviews with him consisted exclusively of Randolph replying either "I bewieve so" or "I tink not."

To Lyon's credit, in the "Bring Me Children" special, he tried his best to make sure people knew who the real heroes were.

He limps off the elevator, opens the door to his apartment, switches on the lights, and lowers the air-conditioning's thermostat. After listening to the messages on the answering machine, Lyon makes a sandwich and opens a bottle of beer. He eats, reads awhile, then goes to the bedroom and undresses, throwing his shirt over a thirty-five-pound concrete frog. Lyon's in bed by eleven.

The last thought he has before falling asleep is that his shin hurts worse than ever. Primarily psychosomatic, the doctors keep telling him. Yeah, Lyon thinks, that's what they said in retrospect about my emotional breakdown too—but just because it's all in your head doesn't mean it hurts any less.

He sleeps until a few minutes past midnight when he is awakened by a baby crying, Lyon bolting upright in bed, instantly awake.

He grabs his robe and limps into the living room.

His wife is on the couch with their two children. Lyon's treatment of her grandmother in the news special is the reason Claire began speaking to him again. She moved back into the apartment a week after that program aired; they were married at the beginning of October and because of the extraordinary circumstances involved were able to adopt the baby girl, the one who had been crying in Randolph's back room, by Thanksgiving. But it's not the little girl who is crying now; she is, in fact, fast asleep.

"You're late."

"You know how my sisters are when they get their hands on these children," Claire says. "I told you not to wait up."

"I didn't." Lyon takes the girl from Claire. "The crying woke me. How can this one," he says, patting the girl's back, "sleep through all that noise?"

"She can sleep through anything," Claire replies, laughing as she rearranges the howling baby boy on her knee. He was born in April, three months ago.

Lyon sits on the couch next to Claire and pulls the edge of a tiny hat away from the infant's face. The baby considers Lyon only briefly before scowling all the harder and then squalling all the louder. "I keep telling you, Claire, every day he looks more and more like a *café au lait* Winston Churchill."

"And I keep telling *you,* John, that every day he looks more and more like his father."

Recognizing the truth when he hears it, John Lyon doesn't know whether to laugh or cry.

About the Author

David Martin is the author of *The Crying Heart Tattoo, Final Harbor, Tethered, The Beginning of Sorrows,* and *Lie to Me*. A former Bread Loaf fellow, he lives with his wife, Arabel, on a farm in West Virginia.

"Stan Washburn brings wit and humanity to this taut narrative of the police pursuit of a serial rapist. Washburn shows assurance and a maturity unusual in first novels and admirable in any book."
—Richard North Patterson, author of <u>Degree of Guilt</u>

Blending unrelenting psychological suspense and a compasssionate, hauntingly realistic portrait of police investigation, *INTENT TO HARM* moves as swiftly and strikes as unpredicably as the terrifying assailant at its dark and mesmerizing heart—a savage serial rapist. What the novels of Thomas Harris have done for the inner workings of the FBI and the war of wits with the criminal mind, Stan Washburn now does with a police procedural that transcends the ordinary and transfixes its readers.

INTENT TO HARM

A NOVEL BY
STAN WASHBURN

Available in hardcover
from Pocket Books

POCKET
<u>BOOKS</u>

966-01